# Evil Little Fucks

# EVIL LITTLE FUCKS

## EDITED BY R.E. SARGENT
## AND STEVEN PAJAK

# EVIL LITTLE FUCKS

Edited by R.E. Sargent & Steven Pajak

P.O. Box 637, Newberg, OR 97132

Trade Hardcover ISBN – 978-1-953112-73-6

www.sinistersmilepress.com

# Contents

*"Maybe there is a beast...maybe it's only us."*

*William Golding*
*The Lord of the Flies*

# Pick Up Every Stitch
### Rebecca Rowland

Molly was too busy poking at the fuzzy red monster doll to notice the man in the white tank top sliding a slim jim into the window well of the driver's side door. The toy was one of those secondhand deals, a hand-me-down. Her mother, Rachel, scored it from a neighbor in the building after Molly was born, and it became painfully obvious that Mr. Rachel had skedaddled sometime between forgetting to bring a condom and forgetting Rachel's phone number once that third trimester rolled around.

The red monster was supposed to make a giggling sound, to say something about being tickled in a tone mildly reminiscent of a jubilant pedophile, but Rachel, unable to listen to its metallic whining any longer, had removed the batteries weeks ago. Molly was too young to know this and, despite its recent vow of silence, continued to prod the doll in tireless anticipation of eliciting a response.

The door's lock clicked, and in one fluid movement, Tank Top climbed inside and began to work on the ignition. The engine started in under sixty seconds, the late '90s Honda roaring to life as he cranked the gear shift into drive and cruised unnoticed out of the grocery store parking lot. He was halfway across the city before noticing the mop of strawberry-blond hair in the rearview mirror.

He screamed a few obscenities at the steering wheel, then pulled out a cell phone with a cracked screen. It was too late to drive back. The chop shop was expecting a drop-off by noon.

As he eased the car into the mechanic's bay, Tank Top spied the boss eating a sandwich: some kind of wrap that dripped yogurty dressing onto the cold concrete floor. Tank Top waved at him, then pushed the trunk release button on the console. There was a rickety stroller folded haphazardly atop piles of random garbage, personal effects that would be incinerator ash by dinnertime.

When he lifted Molly from the car seat, she dropped the monster doll. The toddler said nothing—not a peep—but wouldn't take her eyes from it, contorting her whole torso to watch as the crimson blob of synthetic fur grew smaller and smaller behind her.

You heard this story twice: once, while the two of you were holding sandwiches in the upstairs dining room. Tuna fish with relish, no celery. The second time, your hands were bound behind your back, zip-tied tightly to a fat metal pipe that elbowed down from the wall, disappearing into the basement's shabby floor covering. Your captor was kind enough to leave enough slack so you could lie down at night and sleep. She even provided a pillow, though you were suspicious about the last time its case had been washed. There was a faint brown stain on one of the corners.

"Did she ever get rescued?" you asked her. Both times.

Your captor shrugged noncommittally in response. Her eyes drifted down to your mouth. "You have nice teeth," she said and smiled warmly. Friendly-like. The way she did when she asked if you wanted to watch a movie at her house after school.

That was three days ago.

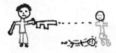

"DID YOU COLOR YOUR HAIR?" THE QUIET GIRL WITH THE thick braid in the seat in front of Molly asked, her eyes swiping back and forth along her classmate's forehead like windshield wipers.

"No," Molly said, "it's just dirty." The truth was she hadn't washed it in a week. Somehow, the smell of you, adolescent hormones smashed together with terrified sweat and confused desperation, leaped from your body and attached itself to hers. Molly's hair reeked of it, and if she turned sideways and buried her nose in the thatch beside her ear, she could breathe you in.

Thick Braid wrinkled her nose in response, then smiled hesitantly, her lips pressed tightly together. "You should color it darker," she said finally, her voice barely a whisper, before turning back around. "It looks good on you."

Molly wanted to return the compliment, to say something that would solidify a connection between her and the girl, but the moment had passed. She pulled on the cuff of her sleeve, then ran her index finger lightly along the inside of her own forearm. The skin hidden by the cotton fabric was hard and bumpy, sharp in places: a miniature cobblestone pathway, a Braille manuscript for the ages.

Molly closed her eyes and thought of you sitting alone in the basement room, the makeshift deejay booth Robert constructed four years ago when Molly started high school. He abandoned the hobby quickly, as he did most of his spontaneous pursuits, but kept the soundproof nook intact. He thought maybe Molly could use it to record podcasts or make reels or whatever kids these days did to be social.

"You got a pencil?" The new girl was leaning toward Molly, her eyes round.

Molly shook her head. "No." She did have pencils: five or six to spare, shoved at the bottom of her school bag, right next to the rape whistle Robert gave her a decade ago and the scalpel he did not.

Without skipping a beat, New Girl leaned toward the desk on the other side of her and asked another student. Molly watched her with curiosity. New Girl had taken it upon herself to commandeer the seat once occupied by the blue-haired girl, the student who had sat next to Molly since September but rarely attended morning classes. Since late March, she hadn't attended the class at all, but that wasn't unusual for Molly's school. It was a big city, and kids were always moving around. Blue Hair had begun the year with pink curls but soon dyed them a bright hue that reminded Molly of those photographs of beachfront vacations in the Mediterranean.

4

Molly had never been to the Mediterranean. She had never been to the ocean. She'd never been anywhere, really: not by herself and not with Robert. They stuck pretty close to home, kept the window blinds drawn tight twenty-four seven, and pretended to be absent when a neighbor or solicitor rang their doorbell unexpectedly.

Molly ran her finger along the inside of her arm again and glanced at the clock. There were two classes left in the day.

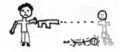

IT WAS JUST AFTER CHRISTMAS, EARLIER THAT SCHOOL year, the ground outside still covered in a yellowing layer of holiday snow, when Molly found herself sitting on the floor of the basement sound booth across from the soccer team captain, a delicate-framed girl with soft, wavy hair the color of corn silk. The athlete's torso and left arm were secured tightly to the pipe that jutted oddly from the carpeted floor. Molly wished the girl a Happy New Year, but Soccer Star only shook her head. A fat tear welled in the inner corner of one of her gray eyes, swelling until it burst and spilled down the side of her nose. Soccer Star's mouth gummed the air, the red bandana pulled tight, forcing her tongue to fold backward and the crease where the edges of her lips met to chafe. A muffled cry sounding somewhere between an elephant's trumpet and a blue jay's screech gurgled in her throat.

"What's that?" Molly asked, holding her hand cupped in back of her ear mockingly. "You are sorry for how you treated me?" The hand dropped into her lap. "Gosh, that's nice of you to say. Seems a little late for that now, huh?" She picked at a loose thread on the edge of her sweatpants. "Calling me a witch," she continued. "Putting dead mice in my backpack. Telling everyone I tried to kiss you in the locker room."

Soccer Star blinked rapidly. More tears leaked, but the faint wailing ceased. Instead, the girl shook her head in a weak attempt at protest.

"The mice made my books reek for weeks. Sucked trying to air out the bag. I still get a whiff of those little guys if I forget and leave my stuff too close to the radiator or if the car's heater blows on it when my dad drives me to school. But...just so we're clear: you're not my type." Molly's eyes narrowed, and she stared into her prisoner's saucer-sized pupils. "Out of curiosity: if you're so consumed with gay panic, why did you come to my house when I invited you?" She leaned forward so the tip of her nose nearly touched the girl's. The athlete's rapid exhales seeping through the cotton gag smelled slightly of wet mothballs. "Thou doth protest too much, methinks."

Soccer Star tried desperately to curve her mouth into a pout, a facial expression Molly suspected was the default reaction when the girl was posed any question or comment that necessitated an unflattering response. "Oh, come on." Molly sighed. "You can't *still* be inhabiting that cartoon of a cool-girl persona after five days."

Soccer Star's eyes narrowed. She glared at her captor, then forced out two unintelligible words, her top and bottom lips curving slightly around the gag at the end of her declaration. *You.*

Molly cupped her ear again. "Pardon?"

The girl's eyes flared with anger. She repeated the words slowly but louder, accentuating the guttural *k* sound on the first word.

Molly pretended to be lost in thought. Then, "Fuck *me*?"

The girl glared back and enthusiastically nodded her head.

Molly stared at Soccer Star for a long moment, then snatched one of her arms and wrenched it downward so that the wrist touched the industrial carpet. Before the girl could react, she pulled the filled syringe from her sweatshirt pocket and jabbed the needle into the fattest blue line she could see under the skin of Soccer Star's inner arm. Instead of pushing the plunger all the way down, however, she paused midway. "You're going to feel a little woozy," she explained. "Like when you drink too fast at a kegger after a night game. Been there, done that, right? Try to ride it out."

Molly pulled the syringe out, reached up to place it on top of the nearby shelf, but let her hand rest for a moment next to it. Soccer Star's eyes drooped, her rigid jawline suddenly falling slack. "Normally, I wait until after my friends are fast asleep to do this part, but a Division One athlete like you? You're metal enough to take it." When Molly pulled her hand back down, it was holding a large object wrapped in a ratty hand towel. She opened the bundle and pulled out a pair of heavy pliers. "'Course, there will be no racing down the sidelines on a break-away this time."

Molly opened and closed the instrument a few times, stretching its muscles in preparation for a challenging workout. Soccer Star's drowsy head leaned backward against the foam

7

padding on the wall, her eyes languid slits of white sclera. Molly held the bottom of the girl's face tightly with one hand while she positioned the open jaws of the pliers around one of her front teeth with the other, resting the tips of the tool on her deep pink gums. In one fluid motion, Molly tightened her grip, jerked her wrist slightly to the right, and felt the tooth break and give way.

Soccer Star's eyes flew open in agony and the guttural scream resumed, though when she attempted to push Molly away, her one free appendage only flailed lethargically as if swimming through mud. Easily weaving around one of her prisoner's swipes, Molly clenched the other front tooth within the mouth of the pliers and repeated her action. This time, when she removed the tool from the girl's mouth, both the tooth and a small chunk of jawbone followed behind it, as well as a gush of copper-smelling blood, soaking Soccer Star's T-shirt in a cherry-red stain. The terrible, smothered cry was extinguished quickly by a wet gurgling sound as the girl's head dropped forward, her body slipping into the gray haze of unconsciousness from shock.

Molly placed the pliers gently on the towel and rewrapped them. She would wash them thoroughly when she cleaned her trophies later that evening. In the meantime, she had to finish up her task. Changing up the routine was no excuse for sloppiness. She reached up to the nearby shelf and retrieved the syringe, slid the needle effortlessly into the still body of her classmate, and delivered the rest of the dose.

MOLLY WAS NINE WHEN ROBERT BEGAN WORKING FOR the veterinary clinic. He had been a medic in the Army, a damn fine one too. So good, in fact, that he'd enrolled in nursing school when he finished his second tour. When it came time to start his practicum, however, and the hospital ran his social security number through the criminal database, they declined to take him as an intern. Schoolboy hijinks were one thing, but a two-year stint in a minimum-security detention center for possession of opiates with intent to distribute was quite another. He could never hold a nursing license in the state. Ironically, he'd only enlisted in the military to avoid a confrontation with his old crew, and by the time he returned to the neighborhood almost a decade later, most of those boys were doing hard time, doped up, or dead.

You nodded your head as Molly told you these things, pretending to find the story fascinating when all you really wanted to do was pee in a real toilet again instead of the awkward bedpan she shoved into the space above the underwear and jeans she wrestled down.

He named her Molly because of her red hair, she explained. It reminded him of an actress who had appeared in all of the popular movies when he was a teenager. Molly never knew her mother; at least, she couldn't remember her. It was never clear to Molly what had happened to the woman, and every now and then, she paused to stare at strangers a beat too long, willing one of them to drop her groceries or garden hose and embrace her, to tell the seventeen-year-old that she was hers, that Molly *belonged* with her.

That's how she felt sometimes: like a broken item in the lost-

and-found bin, the growing pile of jackets, backpacks, and mismatched shoes in the janitor's closet at school. There was no identification on her person, the only proof of ownership an assertion by someone claiming dibs.

Robert worked the overnight shift, but his combat training wasn't used to treat injured and ailing pets. The animal clinic's chief benefactor was a high-ranking member of the local mob, and most of Robert's work involved human body work—repair or disposal—as well as procurement of the occasional antibiotic for a gangster whose moll was less than tidy in the nether region.

One evening years ago, Robert brought Molly along with him to work because the furnace was broken and he couldn't damn well leave the oven going and its door open for a twelve-year-old alone in the house.

"Bert," the doctor said, wiping one sweaty hand on his faded scrubs, "check the closet for Betadine. Gunshot coming in." He glanced at Molly sitting atop the stainless steel exam table, swinging her legs and chewing on a hangnail. When the girl did not acknowledge him, he turned to rummage through a nearby storage drawer for a long pair of forceps and handful of gauze pads.

Robert returned from the hallway carrying a gallon container of antiseptic in one hand and escorting an ashen-faced, poorly-shaven man with the other. The disheveled visitor held his arm across his chest, pressing his right palm against the top of his left arm. When Robert disengaged from his side, the man removed his hand to reveal a sticky, dark splotch and winced.

The doctor exhaled audibly. "Have a seat," he said, motioning to a nearby plastic visitor's chair. The man did as he was told, his face growing even paler beneath the mangy shadow of black hair speckling his jawline.

Molly never took her eyes off the procedure, even when the wound shot a spray of blood onto the doctor's cheek and the patient yelped in muffled agony through the makeshift bite block of his own leather wallet. After the metal slug clinked in a nearby waste pan and the doctor washed up in a nearby sink, Robert slowly and methodically sewed the wound back up with bright purple thread. "It's magic," he told Molly, never looking away from his careful stitching. "After a few weeks, the thread disappears. Poof!"

Molly frowned. "Where does it go?" The pasty-complexioned man unscrewed the top of a flask with his teeth and drank a hearty swallow, doing his best to keep his arm steady.

Robert sniffed. "The body absorbs it," he said, then smiled. "I guess you could say the patient becomes part thread from that point on. Ninety-nine-point-nine percent human, teeny-tiny percent sheep."

"Sheep?" Molly repeated.

Robert paused to finish his last stitch. "Yep," he said, securing the end of the suture and holding up the remaining thread from the needle to show her. "We call this stuff *catgut*. It's made of sheep intestines. Not sure why it's not called sheep gut."

The patient swallowed another gulp of the flask's contents and groaned. Molly, however, jumped down from the table and walked closer to him. She squinted her eyes to examine the tiny violet dashes stippling the swollen patch of skin stained iodine's golden-brown.

"Maybe you'll become a doctor someday," you offered when

your captor's pause in her story extended longer than necessary for dramatic effect, but your shameless attempt at flattery fell flat. Your classmate ignored you, picked up the soiled bedpan, and carried it carefully out of the room without another word.

It was the Friday before Memorial Day when you visited her house. Surely, the school would call your parents and ask where you were when you didn't show up for classes on Tuesday. Surely, you would be missed at the senior awards banquet. Graduation. Prom.

But you wondered.

THE FIRST POP OF SPRING COLOR—BRIGHT PURPLE AND yellow crocuses—peeked from the ground on the day Molly overheard the kids in her study hall talking about a body the police discovered at the cemetery, sticking out of the compost pile. A lifeless hand reached out, ghoul-like, from beneath a pile of rotting geranium pots and Easter lilies. Initial findings were that blunt-force trauma was the cause of death. Much of the corpse's jawbone was crushed.

The girl with the blue hair sat on the floor of the basement sound booth, pleading with the wall for her life. Sometimes, when Molly stood at the door just outside of the small room, she closed her eyes and imagined that the house was under water: every reverberation was muted, stuffed tight with cotton batting and sealed with a roll of silvery duct tape. The thick foam covering the walls and ceiling swallowed most noises whole.

Molly knew, logically, that Blue Hair's sobs originated from the other side of the wall, but standing with her hand paused on the doorknob, Molly could have believed they were echoes from another location, another dimension.

With few exceptions, the final stage of the routine was always the easiest. By then, her classmates became docile as lambs, exhausted and pliable. Molly entered the booth, sat cross-legged on the floor in front of Blue Hair, and reached behind the girl. Even after the needle punctured her skin, even after the sensation of hot lava pooling where the syringe entered her body, then snaked down her vein, pulling her down into a warm bath, Blue Hair didn't struggle. She felt herself falling backward, then nothing, despite Molly pulling her limp body forward to lean against hers, resting the girl's flaccid cheek on her shoulder.

Molly placed her index finger under Blue Hair's neck, measuring the metronomic throbbing of the girl's pulse, felt it grow sleepy until it stopped altogether. Molly poked the girl's soft cheek, waiting for a reaction. She ran her hand over her soft blue curls; she felt them give, then spring back. She wondered, for a long minute, if that was how it felt to touch the ocean.

That evening, Molly sat cross-legged in front of the television, streaming episodes of a 1980s sitcom on Netflix while she pushed a skein of special purple thread through the head of a sewing needle. She used the scalpel to make the shallow incision in her skin with the expertise of a veteran surgeon: a cut deep enough to reach the bottom of the epidermis without disturbing the subcutaneous layer, rich with blood.

The blue-haired girl's incisors were straight and clean. They slid effortlessly under the pocket she opened in her forearm and sidled obediently next to all the ones from before. Another pair, two tiny speed bumps to add to her highway of harvests. A tidy array of perfectly matched shoes she could walk around in.

After she graduated, Molly would venture out into the world. She promised herself that. There were so many people to see, so many people to *be*. And she could be anyone.

When she told you this, when she told you about what she had done to the girl with the blue hair, the soccer player, all of them, you nodded and forced a smile. And your body did not wait for the bedpan.

THICK BRAID FOLLOWED MOLLY'S EYES TO THE CLOCK. "Did you finish Morgan's homework?"

Molly frowned. Miss Morgan was their senior English teacher, a curvy, middle-aged number who sometimes forgot that her piece of chalk wasn't a cigarette and tried to smoke it. Molly's copy of *Jane Eyre* sat untouched in the bottom of her book bag despite nearly constant warnings from Miss Morgan that there would be reading quizzes in the near future. "I read the SparkNotes," Molly said. "Rochester is a gaslighter. The wife is in the attic the whole time, right?"

Thick Braid rolled her eyes slightly, but not enough to appear snide, and it made Molly's stomach spill butterflies into her chest. The girl turned her back to Molly for a moment, then produced a spiral-bound notebook. "You can read my notes," she said. "I have to write stuff down as I read. Otherwise, I forget what happened." She pushed the book closer to Molly, skulking inside her halo of personal space.

Molly cleared her throat uncomfortably. "Thanks," she replied softly, accepting the gift and tucking it into her book bag. "I'll get this back to you next period."

Thick Braid waved her hand dismissively. "I don't need them," she said. "Once I write something down, I remember it. Keep the notebook, too, if you want. I have a couple of others, and the year's almost over anyway." With that, the girl shrugged slightly then turned back around, the thick brown plait of hair swaying heavily behind her like a gong mallet.

Molly pushed up the sleeve of her shirt to expose the underbelly of her forearm and ran her fingers softly along its rutted surface. The skin was mottled in places where her stitches pulled the incisions together haphazardly around her collection of victims' dental donations, the sewn edges petulant from their strangulation into obedience. The most recent thread would dissolve eventually, leaving only a faint ring of stretched skin encircling two nodules within the reddish row of ridges. Molly's arm resembled a pink, fleshy ear of corn, the souvenirs of her secret hobby pressed tightly together like the scutes of an alligator's back.

Molly turned her head to let her eyes drift along the faces of her classmates. She might never know who she had been, not the way they knew themselves. But she could absorb just a small part of them, reclaim the abandoned pieces in the lost-and-found bin, if only for a short while.

"What happened?!" Thick Braid was staring at Molly's

exposed skin, her body turned around again so Molly could see knobby knees poking out from beneath the girl's skirt.

Molly yanked her sleeve back down. "I have a skin condition," she mumbled, strangely faltering in the excuse she had practiced saying a thousand times but never needed to use. Robert hadn't asked, even when he saw the healing incisions, the puckered skin and bulbous tracks beginning at her inner elbow and winding toward her wrist in an angry snake.

Thick Braid smiled sympathetically. "Oh," she said, her voice quiet and soothing. "I understand." She smiled wider, then, and inside her mouth was a railroad yard of metal tracks, braces struggling to pull her lopsided grin into formation. Molly saw more silver than enamel.

*We can never be friends*, Molly thought sadly.

You, however, still tied up in the cold, soundproof booth in the basement, will soon become her forever companion.

# NEVER LEAVE
## JOHN DURGIN

Andy Lancaster pulled his comforter to his chin, staring out the window into the night. He watched for the older boy with the green hood, who promised he'd be back to save him. Every day of Andy's life was a struggle, living in fear of not only his dad's abusive ways but of his mom's *mental* abuse. She blamed him for the way his dad was. She told him he was an accident and that the only reason they didn't abort him was because they had no money to pay for it. Now, at the age of eleven, Andy's parents were getting worse as the drugs took hold of their already miserable lives. He didn't ask for much. Their tiny two-bedroom apartment, with its paper-thin walls and the constant scent of beer and stale cigarettes, was more than enough for him. As long as they left him alone.

A few nights ago, the kid named Pete came to his window, promising a better life. A place where he wouldn't be hurt. A place where he could play as much as he wanted and never grow up. He called it The Never. Pete offered to take him the first night he visited, but Andy was too scared. Pete said that was normal, that he often had to come back once the kids had a chance to think things over. Andy had waited one night too many, as his dad had given him a massive shiner on his right eye for talking back.

One of the reasons he was so scared to leave was he feared if he ran away and they found him, the punishment would be far worse than any beating he'd ever received. But Pete told him that wouldn't happen. If he agreed to come, Andy's parents would never be able to make him go home.

Andy was ready to leave his family behind for good. Even if the land Pete talked about didn't turn out to be real, it couldn't be any worse than what he dealt with at home.

He remained focused on the window, hoping if he pictured his savior, eventually he'd appear. His parents were arguing about something in the next room, their typical nightly routine before they eventually ended up having sex so loud that Andy almost preferred the fighting. He could envision his slob of a dad, with his greasy, receding hairline, screaming at his mother as spittle flew from his mouth.

He continued to visualize the scene in the next room when movement outside snapped him out of it. The silhouette of Pete stood perched in the window, the moon shining down to give him a magical glow. Pete's eyes radiated with a golden hue, accompanying a smile that somehow gave Andy chills.

"Hey, Andy. Told ya I'd be back. I hear things are going swell," he said, nodding toward the wall of screaming.

"This is nothing. Just wait a few minutes if you want the real show," Andy said.

"You ready? To go to a place where you never have to deal with this again?" Pete asked.

He entered through the window, now standing in front of Andy's bed. His green hood hid most of his features, but Andy saw enough to know Pete couldn't be much older than him. The golden hue didn't just illuminate his eyes; it was as if his entire body was surrounded by some magical forcefield.

"Yes. I'm ready."

"The scariest part is what's about to happen. You won't remember anything until you wake up. But I promise, once you do, your life will be changed forever."

Andy's chest tightened. The thought of being forced to sleep was terrifying. He began to doubt the whole plan. He needed more information first.

"What about my parents? You said they couldn't find me once I left. How do you know that?"

"You have to trust me if you're going to be part of this. Your parents will not be a problem, I promise."

Andy thought it sounded pretty damn good. He climbed out of bed, now face-to-face with Pete, who was a few inches taller than him. Whatever came next, he was prepared to accept it.

"Okay. What do I do?"

Pete pulled a pouch from his pocket—the worn-out fabric looked like it had been used for a hundred years. A frayed draw-string held it sealed shut.

"Next, it's the not-fun part I told you about. I need you to close your eyes and trust me. Can you do that, Andy?" Pete asked while untying the pouch.

*What's he doing?*

*It doesn't matter... I have to trust him*, Andy thought.

He nodded.

Pete approached him, opening the pouch, which now had a glow similar to Pete's hugging the inside of the fabric.

"Close your eyes," Pete said.

Andy complied, sending the room into darkness. But he could sense Pete standing inches from him, the warmth of his breath tickling Andy's face. His parents had stopped arguing, and the disgusting sounds of make-up sex replaced the shouting. Andy couldn't wait to be out of this house.

Suddenly, the darkness brightened around him as something was placed over his head. He instinctively opened his eyes and realized it was the glow of the pouch, now covering his face. A suffocating panic hit him at once as he attempted a deep breath only to have his mouth fill with the battered cloth. It tasted of soil.

He lifted his hands, pulling at the sack, which felt as if it was tightening around his face, forming to his features. He tried to scream, but his voice was muffled.

"It's okay, Andy. Don't fight it. That'll only make it worse," Pete said.

Something was pumping through Andy's body. With each attempted breath, his lungs filled with it, producing a sharp pain traveling to his stomach. His legs turned to jelly, and he fell to his knees, continuing to pull at the fabric. His heart rammed against his chest, fighting to pull in oxygen. Stars floated through the bright glow, but he realized they were from lack of air and that he was now getting lightheaded. Andy had one last thought before losing consciousness.

*I've made a terrible mistake.*

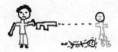

ANDY AWOKE TO A SEARING PAIN IN HIS LUNGS. THE sound of an ocean current filled his ears. He opened his eyes and was blasted with a radiant light. Blinking away the grogginess, he noticed he was no longer in his bedroom. He inhaled deeply to clear his lungs and took in the scenery. It looked like a screen-saver, with lush green mountains towering over a body of water as blue as the sky.

*The Never*, he thought.

He got to his feet, almost falling back to the ground.

"Easy does it, kid. It takes some getting used to," someone said from behind him.

He turned and saw not only Pete, but a group of seven or eight kids standing behind him. They all stared at Andy like he was an alien from a distant planet.

"Andy, meet the Lost Souls. All these kids went through the same thing you did, and they can vouch for the island and how we run things here," Pete said.

There were boys and girls of different races with a mash-up of different styles. Some dressed more modern like himself, and others wore clothes straight out of the '50s. But one thing they all had in common was their smile. They appeared genuinely happy. Andy didn't recall the last time he felt as happy as they looked.

"Nice to meet you, Andy," said a pretty girl with long blond hair braided to the side and resting on her left shoulder. "My name's Wendy. Like Pete said, you'll love it here. Some of us have been here over fifty years, if you can believe that."

"It's awesome," Andy said. He walked to the shoreline and kneeled to touch the ocean. It felt as warm as bathwater.

"I'd back away if I was you," Pete said.

Andy turned to him, unsure what the big deal was, but heeded the concerned stares of the other children. He walked back to them, taking in the wooded landscape as he did.

"Sorry, I didn't know."

"It's okay, my man. Just certain times you don't wanna go near the water. This happens to be one of them. We'll explain in a bit. But first, let's give you a tour of the island, shall we?"

Andy felt a tickle of anticipation in his stomach. The Never was real. Pete's story was *real*. The thought of never having to see his parents again was a huge relief. He'd heard that when kids ran away, they usually regretted it later and would come crawling back to their shitty homelife to have proper meals and a bed. He couldn't imagine a situation where he'd ever do that. Hell, he'd eat bugs and sleep on the dirt if it meant not going back home.

Andy approached Wendy as the crew Pete referred to as the Lost Souls entered a trail into the woods. Birds chirped overhead. He took a deep breath, inhaling the natural smell of the forest—a far cry from the nicotine-infused wallpaper back home. His eyes watered with happiness he never knew he could feel.

"So how long have you been here?" he asked Wendy.

"I'm one of the originals, back when Pete first started doing this. But age doesn't matter here, silly. You and I can come from two different worlds, and here, we're the same." She smiled at him, and his heart melted in his chest. She was the most beautiful girl he'd ever set eyes on.

"So how's it work? How do we get food? Where do we sleep? How do we...stay young?"

Wendy smiled again, then said, "Pete will tell you all about it at dinner. Whenever we bring a new Lost Soul to The Never, it's a cause for celebration. That's where we're heading now. Then, after we eat, we'll have the ceremony to initiate you as one of us."

That sounded odd, but Andy wasn't going to question it. They walked along the beaten path, a trail that was clearly man-made, heading deeper into the impenetrable forest. The kids walked ahead of him, joking and laughing. Any lingering doubts needed to get the hell out of his head—this was paradise. A soft breeze slid across his face, bringing with it Wendy's scent. It wasn't the smell of perfume, but her natural scent that brought a whole new obsession to him. He'd known the girl for maybe ten minutes, yet he thought he was in love.

Up ahead, the path descended a steady decline, the walkway narrowed, and the trees thickened. A few squirrels skittered up the side of a large tree, fighting over an acorn. Wildlife was abundant, unlike his decrepit-ass town, where the only animals he routinely saw were roaches and rats.

They entered beneath a large canopy of overhung branches, but instead of getting darker, it somehow got *brighter*. Once he spotted their destination, he realized why. An entire system of treehouses lined the woods with strings of lights traveling across the trees like telephone wires, illuminating everything below— an entire town hidden deep within the forest.

"Welcome to our humble abode, Andy. Why don't you get to know the crew while we get the ceremony ready?" Pete said. He slapped him on the shoulder and walked off with a few of the others, leaving Andy with Wendy and a group he didn't know yet.

Wendy noticed the amazement etched on Andy's face.

"It's incredible, isn't it? The more of us there are, the better it becomes too. Here, we all have each other."

"How does this all work? How do the grown-ups not find this place and bring all the kids home?" Andy asked.

"You'll see that tonight with your own eyes. The Never is magical. Nobody will be able to bring it down. *Ever*," she said.

Wendy made it sound like an armored fortress. How could she be so confident?

A tall, powerhouse of a boy with a red mohawk walked up to them. He was dressed in black leather pants and vest, reminding Andy of someone straight out of an '80s music video.

"Hey, dude. My name's Omos. Happy to have you here. Where you from?" he asked, shaking Andy's hand. Andy thought the grip was a bit too tight, but he shook it off.

"I'm from a town most people haven't heard of. Lempster, New Hampshire. It's really small."

"Wrong answer, my man."

"What?" Andy asked, confused.

"You're now a resident of Neverland. Forget everything you

left behind. Lumpster, or whatever the hell you called it, can kiss my leather-covered ass. You listen to Pete, and you'll be sitting pretty."

"Sounds good. So what does The Never or Neverland mean, anyway?"

Omos smiled, revealing sparkly white teeth.

"It means to never grow up. Where we can be kids forever. That's what Pete says."

"Cool."

The group went deeper into their world until they came to a clearing with a large table in the middle, lined with chairs carved from tree stumps. The table was set with dishes and silverware, with mounds of fruit and candy at its center. A few of the kids ran to the table cheering, then taking their seats. Andy followed Wendy and Omos, who sat near the head of the table, which Andy assumed was designated for Pete.

"Why don't you guys introduce yourselves to Andy?" Wendy said to the group.

"Name's Cricket," a short boy with a brown mullet said. His face was littered with freckles, and when he smiled, Andy saw that he had a huge gap between his front teeth. He also noticed that the tips of both front teeth were pointy, like fangs.

"Where the heck did you get a name like that?" Andy asked with a chuckle.

Cricket's eyes closed to tiny slits, and he hunched in his chair.

"Because you won't see me coming. You'll only hear my call. I can sneak up on anyone without them knowing."

They all laughed.

"Yeah, he's like a ninja in these woods," said Wendy.

"Let him hear your call," Omos urged.

Cricket pursed his lips, then inhaled. The noise that escaped sounded like an actual cricket. Had Andy not witnessed it, he wouldn't have known the difference.

"That's so cool!" Andy said.

A set of identical twin girls sat next to Cricket. They had a pale complexion that the overhanging lights amplified, giving them a ghostly moon glow. Both had short, spiky, jet-black hair. Their stares made Andy uncomfortable. Their pupils were smaller than two tiny black pebbles in the center of their almost entirely white eyes. Thankfully, they broke the awkward silence.

"I'm Regan, and this is my sister Rosemary. Happy to have you," Regan said. Although Andy had already forgotten which one was which.

"How the heck does anyone tell you two apart?"

"That's part of the fun now, isn't it?" Reg—no, Rosemary asked.

"Can you like...communicate to each other without talking?" Andy asked. "I heard twins can do that."

"We *can* do that. We can also feel what the other is feeling. Isn't that right, Regan?" Rosemary asked, then carved her sharp fingernail down the center of her forearm, drawing blood. Regan shouted, then looked down at her arm to see a trail of blood as well.

"That's insane! How can you do that?" Andy asked.

Rosemary smiled. "This island gives us all abilities that we wouldn't normally have elsewhere. You'll see when you get your power toni—"

"Please, dig in! The fruit here is the most delicious you'll ever eat," Wendy interrupted.

It seemed she didn't want any more talk on the subject. Or maybe he wasn't supposed to know everything yet. Either way, he'd wait and see.

"I'm not hungry. Whatever Pete did to me messed with my appetite," he lied, although it was somewhat true. The pain he'd felt in his stomach was mostly gone, but a dull sensation still sat in the pit of his belly.

Wendy raised her eyebrows in concern, then smiled. "It's okay. That'll go away soon."

They all continued to chat, and while Andy remained uncertain about the Lost Souls and their land, he had to admit it was much better than his homelife. But he continued to trust his gut, avoiding anything they offered him until he could get a better read on the place. Eventually, Pete and the kids who'd gone with him entered the dining area. He sat at the head of the table, just as Andy expected. Pete presented his trademark smile.

"Everyone, the time's come! Let's make this a night Andy'll never forget. Whaddya say?"

They all cheered in unison, and Andy's cheeks burned with embarrassment.

"First, let's eat! We feast on the finest foods the world can offer. Dig in," Pete said.

Andy watched as the Lost Souls all reached toward the center of the table, grabbing food aggressively, like the squirrels with the acorn earlier. They tore into the dishes like a horde of zombies ripping apart a human body. Andy grabbed a luscious apple, prepared to bite into it, but stopped himself when he saw all their eyes rolling back in their heads. The same golden aura clinging to the inside of Pete's hood now spread across the dishes of food like some enchanted virus. Pete noticed Andy hesitating and walked to him.

"Nothing to be scared of, my friend. Bite down and prepare to have your mind blown!" he shouted, slapping Andy on the shoulder hard enough to leave a dull throb that lingered well after contact.

Andy shrugged off the pain and bit into the apple. Pete smiled and walked back to his seat. As soon as he turned his back, Andy made sure nobody was looking and spit the apple into his hand, then dropped it beneath the table, sliding it farther away with his foot. The little flavor he did taste was absolutely as good as advertised, but he knew he'd made the right choice. He couldn't put a finger on it yet, but he sensed Pete was somehow controlling all the kids with whatever magic he possessed. Andy's hands trembled, and in an attempt to hide his nerves, he set them in his lap. He turned toward Wendy to find her staring at him. She looked like a worried mother—or at least what Andy pictured a worried mother looking like.

*Did she see me spit the apple out?*

She mouthed, "It's okay," then turned back to the festivities.

The Lost Souls ate the rest of their dinner in record time, no longer focusing on Andy and his food intake, much to his relief. When they were done, Pete stood and jumped up on the table, lifting his hands high above his head.

"And now...we head to the water for our boy Andy's initiation into the Lost Souls!"

The whole thing felt overly theatric to Andy, which creeped

him out even more. Instead of the kids laughing at how over-the-top Pete was, he had them in the palm of his hand. They all followed Pete single file through the woods, the sound of the ocean waves getting closer and closer as Andy wondered what the hell he'd got himself into.

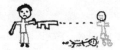

WITH NIGHTFALL NOW OWNING THE SKY, THE WATER NO longer appeared as beautiful to Andy as it had before. It looked like a massive black hole waiting to swallow anything that dared to get too close. It brought him back to when Pete warned him earlier not to go near the water.

They reached the sandy beach, where the first thing Andy noticed was a line of chairs parallel with the shoreline, facing the water, like some strange movie theater. The seats were far enough back from the water that the tide wouldn't reach them but close enough to be planted into the wet sand. Pete motioned for Andy to come front and center, then pushed him down into the middle chair.

"A front-row seat for our newest brother. You're going to want to be up close for this, Andy."

Wendy sat next to him, followed by Omos, Cricket, and the twins. The remaining seats were filled by kids Andy hadn't met yet. Pete approached the water and then turned back toward his audience. With the background now completely dark, the glow inside his hood radiated, revealing every feature of his face in high-definition detail.

"You're probably asking yourself, 'What in the world is crazy Pete up to?' Maybe even thinking you shouldn't have come here. But I'm a man of my word, Andy. I promised you a world where you'd never grow up. Where you'd never have to live with your parents again. A place where every day is a holiday, full of fun and games. That's what The Never is. But all good things come at a cost."

Andy's stomach tightened into a knot.

"Permanent youth isn't free. The good news is I've found a way to kill two birds with one stone. Or I should say two *parents*. Bring 'em out, guys!" Pete nodded toward an area of the woods that Andy had yet to explore.

Branches stirred as footsteps approached from the darkness. Leaves spread apart, revealing a few more kids, but they weren't alone. They were dragging two adult bodies with sacks over their heads, similar to what Andy wore when Pete brought him to The Never. Both grown-ups had their hands tied behind their backs.

Omos stood and helped his friends, kicking the male in the back and forcing him toward the shoreline.

"Move it, Pops," he said with a smirk.

Andy had no idea what was happening, but he knew it wasn't good. He turned to Wendy, who had a smile on her face.

"What's happening? Who are these people?"

"You'll see in a second. Your problems are about to be erased forever."

*Oh God. What are they going to do?*

Pete and Omos forced the adults to their knees, facing the chairs. Andy saw the sacks frantically moving on their faces as they attempted to take panicked breaths.

"If I asked you all why we're here, what would you say?" Pete asked.

Cricket raised his hand.

"This isn't school, Crick. Speak your mind."

"We make our own rules. The Never's not a place for parents...except when we feed the beast."

*Beast? What is he talking about?*

"Exactly! So, Andy. Tonight, you get the magic of lifetime childhood, all for the measly cost of these two useless living corpses. You see, to get the magic this land offers, we need to give it something in return. We need to feed the beast, as Cricket said. Or if we're being proper, it's *Vodyanoy* we're feeding. The god of the water. Vodyanoy is all over the world, shapeshifting into any form he chooses and living in different bodies of water that offer him what he needs... Sacrifices. And why sacrifice one of us when we have unlimited access to abusers and deadbeats?"

"I... What are you going to do with them?" Andy asked, dumbfounded at the revelation.

"First, let's introduce them, shall we?"

Pete walked up to the male, who continued to fight at the ropes to no avail. He slapped the man on the back of the head and laughed. Then he grabbed the sack, preparing to pull it off, and locked eyes with Andy.

"Sacrifice number one. Coming in from the scum-bucket town of Lempster, the man who made our new brother's life a living hell, Daddy Lancaster!" Pete ripped the sack off, revealing the disheveled face of Andy's dad.

"Dad?"

"Andy, you little shit! What is this? Who are these kids?"

"See, Daddy, that's not part of this game. In The Never, you don't get to ask the questions." Pete smirked.

"I swear to God, I'll tear your arm off and beat you to death with it, you little fuck!"

Andy flinched. Hearing the threats he grew up with spoken to another kid somehow felt far worse than when it was directed at him. Pete, however, didn't flinch. He laughed.

"If only, tough guy. Before we move on to your demise, let's introduce sacrifice number two!"

Omos yanked the sack off the woman, but Andy didn't need to see her face. He knew it was his mom. As the bag was ripped from her head, Omos caught some of her hair in his grip, tearing it from her scalp. She screamed and looked first to her husband, then Andy.

"Please...Andy, we'll be better. Don't do—"

Omos struck her in the temple with his fist, sending her face-first onto the sand.

"I didn't ask for this," Andy mumbled. He didn't think anyone heard him until Pete sprung over his mom like she was a hopscotch square. He kneeled, getting face-to-face with Andy.

"You don't have to ask for this, bud. We take care of our own here. Believe me, you'll get used to it."

The smile following that statement sent a chill down Andy's spine. He looked at all the other kids sitting next to him, hoping to see some of them as disturbed as he was. Instead, they all smiled, eyeing Pete like he was their hero. Even Wendy appeared to be enamored by him, which, despite the terrible moment, still gave Andy a tinge of jealousy.

"What are you going to do to them?" Andy asked.

"That's the best part, my friend! Watch this."

The kids all stood from their chairs and approached Andy's parents. Wendy remained seated next to Andy, holding his hand, watching the rest of the kids move with purpose. They surrounded his parents, getting closer and closer until Andy couldn't see them anymore because they were blocked behind a wall of crazed kids lifting his parents to their feet. His mom had succumbed to whatever was about to happen, staring at the ground, dead to the world. But his dad tried to break free, only to get a fist to the back of the head from Omos.

In the distance, a ripple traveled across the water. At first, it was barely noticeable, but as it moved along, the surface parted, creating powerful waves that crashed against the shoreline. Pete's golden smile widened.

"And now, Andy boy, here's the star of the show. The one who gives us this wonderful power. I introduce you to... VODYANOY!"

Andy wished he was back in his bedroom, listening to his parents grunt on the other side of the wall. He wished he was hiding in the closet, hoping his dad would forget about him long enough to allow the pain from the last beating to fade before striking again. He turned to Wendy, panic-stricken.

"We have to stop this. *Please!*"

She took her attention off the ceremony and looked at him. He saw the guilt in her eyes. As much as she praised Pete, there was still a good person inside her. He could see it.

The disturbance in the water increased as violent waves slammed against the island.

"Andy, it has to be this way. They deserve this, and so do you.

You *deserve* all the good that comes from their sacrifice," Wendy said, then put her hand over his and squeezed.

He pulled away, staring at her like she was the monster. He had to do something.

"How are you guys okay with this? You're no better than the grown-ups who hurt us. You want to kill them? Did you do this to all the parents of the kids here?" He was crying now.

Pete heard the question intended for Wendy and hurdled the group of kids with one swift leap, landing at Andy's feet. His body emitted a golden hue, as if the chaos made him stronger.

"Yes, Andy. We sacrifice all the parents. And the world is a better place for it. Do you realize that we've been doing this for almost a hundred years now? And we don't look a day older. In all that time, only one of the adults fled, but the island took care of that scum anyway. We haven't seen him for years. This is what must be done. And *you* must be the one to sacrifice your parents to Vodyanoy to get the magic. Can you do that, Andy?"

Andy hesitated, and Pete stepped closer, now only inches from his face. The nice boy who came to his window to save him was a thing of the past. What stood before him was a power-hungry sociopath. Andy knew he needed to get off the island. To get far, far away and never look back. But he knew he couldn't do that yet. He needed to play along.

"Yes... What do I need to do?" He hoped Pete couldn't see his hands trembling.

"You need to walk to the water. When Vodyanoy gets close, push your parents in. Do *not* hesitate, Andy. If Vodyanoy doesn't get what he needs, we'll all pay. Got it?"

Andy nodded but remained frozen in place. Pete shoved him

from behind toward the water. He approached, walking around the mass of kids blocking his parents. It wasn't until he got to the other side of them that he saw what they were doing. The kids were *torturing* his mom and dad. One at a time, they were taking turns getting their blows in. Cricket jumped on Andy's mom, biting into her cheek with his sharp front teeth. Andy screamed, not prepared for such brutality. His mom squealed in pain as the fangs tore down her face, then neck, leaving a rigid trail of skin and muscle in their wake. Meanwhile, Omos continued to strike Andy's dad, punching him in the face until it was unrecognizable.

"Why are you doing this to them? This isn't a sacrifice."

Pete shot a glance at him, his eyes crazed. "No. No, it's not part of it. But you know what? Our parents made us suffer our entire lives, so why should they get off easy before they die? They deserve to suffer first."

Suddenly, the kids stopped their beatings. Andy looked at the water and realized why. Whatever was causing the disturbance was getting closer, now only about thirty feet away. As it approached, Andy noticed a massive figure beneath the surface. Even in the moonlight, he could see that it had to be at least twenty feet long.

"You're up, Andy boy. Get movin'," Pete demanded.

Andy walked closer to his parents, although it was all a blur. He felt his body going through the motions, unable to take his eyes off the beast's colossal size. His dad stopped fighting, but Andy didn't know whether it was because he saw the beast or he was too beaten to defend himself.

The creature stopped its approach, but its large frame floated in place, awaiting whatever came next. Andy wasn't sure he could handle seeing it rise from the water—its enormous back was bad enough, lined with jagged green spikes that poked above the surface. It reminded Andy of an alligator the size of a blue whale.

"Which one first, Andy?" Pete asked. "It's your ceremony."

"I—I can't. This isn't what I pictured, Pete. Please let them go." Andy thought he could go along with it, pretending to approve of the nightmare. But now that he stood within feet of it, his plan was falling apart.

"Do it, Andy. Or I'll have no choice but to do it myself, and then it's not a true sacrifice. Which means Vodyanoy won't be happy. And I'll have to give one of our own to *make* him happy. I'm not about to off one of the Lost Souls who've put their full faith in me and this island. That leaves only one kid."

Andy's heart pumped so rapidly it hurt his ears. He couldn't do it. No matter what threats Pete made, he couldn't push his parents into the water. Instead, he cried. He knew what Pete meant. If he didn't sacrifice his own parents, Pete was going to sacrifice him.

*So why can't I just do what needs to be done? Because that would make me just like them.*

The kids all waited in anticipation to see what he was going to do. They were also awaiting instruction on what they should do, prepared to grab Andy if needed. Andy kept his eyes on the beast, but he could feel the Lost Souls' eyes burrowing into him. He had to come up with a distraction and get out of the situation before it was too late. And then, it was as if Wendy read his mind.

"Pete, we can find another way. He's not ready for this, but give me time with him and I can change his ways," she proffered from her chair.

All the kids turned to look at her, completely silent at the questioning of Pete's authority. Andy didn't waste the opportunity. He bolted for the woods, seeking the closest entry point into the forest. The branches clawed at his exposed skin as he pushed through the shrubbery. He heard Pete yelling from the beach and risked a glance back to see if he was being followed. The first thing he saw was a few kids heading his way. Then he shifted his attention to the water and saw the beast slowly emerging from the ocean's depths. The moonlight gave its green skin an unnatural brightness as it continued to rise. Andy froze in place, unable to take his eyes off it. The figure had to be twenty feet tall. Its head was shaped like an alligator, with a long, narrow maw full of razor-sharp teeth. Its eyes glowed white like the moon hovering over its massive shoulders. It had human-shaped arms, but the leathery skin covering its forearms transitioned to huge paws with curved claws.

The beast opened its mouth, strings of saliva stretching from top to bottom teeth, then roared, creating a gust of warm wind that blew through the forest. Pete shouted from the beach, but Andy couldn't hear what was said. He watched as Omos grabbed his dad and lifted him off the ground, throwing him into the water without hesitation. Pete said something to Omos, who turned and ran toward the woods.

Vodyanoy's paw swooped across the surface, wrapping limb-sized digits around the waist of his first victim and lifting him from the water. Andy's dad screamed—a sound Andy had never heard from the evil bastard. He always thought he'd enjoy hearing his dad suffer, but instead, he leaned over and vomited on the forest floor.

When he lifted his head, the kids were almost in the woods. The beast opened its mouth again, exposing deadly teeth. It squeezed, piercing its claws into his dad's abdomen. Even from the distance between them, Andy heard his dad's innards popping beneath the pressure. And then Vodyanoy chomped down on his head, silencing the screams. Tore the head clean off, leaving a geyser of blood in its place, pumping crimson into the ocean as the body twitched in Vodyanoy's grip.

The beast lifted the rest of his dad's lifeless body toward its mouth, but Andy had seen enough. He turned and took off running. He pushed forward, narrowly avoiding a collision with multiple trees along the way. The Lost Souls echoed in the background, yelling out demands to one another. The deeper he went, the darker it got, allowing only a few feet of visibility in front of him. His chest burned, but he forced himself to continue. Out here, there were no trails. No landmarks to help him find his way. It was just endless trees packed as tight as a can of sardines.

He needed to stop and rest but knew that would be a death sentence. There had to be a place to hide and catch his breath, maybe even lose the kids chasing him. Just when he thought there was nowhere to go, he spotted a fallen tree with a hollowed-out center thanks to years of rot. Andy crouched to check it out, relieved to see the opening appeared big enough to hide in. He dropped to his stomach and army crawled into the dark space, an instant feeling of claustrophobia taking over. But he had to continue if he wanted to live. His nostrils filled with the scent of water-logged mildew, the earthy aroma almost too much to handle.

Andy hoped there was a way out on the other end because the space was too narrow to turn around or crawl backward. The deeper he got, the less he could see, until he reached the center of the tree where a small section had caved in, creating a narrow opening. He used it as a makeshift "viewport," staring out for any sign of the kids.

He held his breath and listened. A small bug skittered past his face, forcing him to jump back and smack his head on the caved-in area. He could only imagine what else was crawling around in the darkness with him. In the distance, he spotted movement through the branches. Then he heard a familiar sound in the darkness—the sound of a cricket chirping. His chest tightened as he realized it wasn't an insect singing their nightly song, but more likely, the small boy with razor-sharp teeth signaling to the others that he was on Andy's trail.

"Andy, Andy. Would you like some *candy*?" the twins spoke in unison.

He watched, choking down fear as they closed in. Their foot-steps echoed through the silent forest, getting louder as their silhouettes grew. They stopped in a small clearing twenty feet from the fallen tree.

"Did you see which way he went?" Omos asked.

"We know he came this way, so he can't be far. Let's make this quick. Pete doesn't like the ceremony getting interrupted," said Cricket. "This kid sure made a dumb mistake, eh?"

"Rosemary and I will split up since we can communicate

with each other. You two spread out in the middle of us. Let's keep going before he gets too far," Regan said.

Andy's heart jumped in his throat as they got closer to his hiding spot. Omos' enormous figure stood just outside the hole. Andy wanted to move and distance himself from the opening above, but he was afraid any movement would create noise, which he couldn't risk right now. So he waited. It felt like an eternity, but eventually, the kids walked deeper into the woods out of sight.

No matter how long he waited, it didn't feel long enough. With the area returned to silence, the faint sounds of his mom screaming from the beach became audible. He closed his eyes and cried, realizing it was all his fault. Even if he did make it off the island, then what? Where would he go? Who would he live with?

None of that mattered at the moment. There was a pack of crazed kids hunting him, ready to feed him to the monster the first chance they got.

Slowly, he crawled the rest of the way, poking his head out of the other end of his refuge and breathing in the fresh air. He shimmied his way out with sweat leaking into his eyes. He needed something that would help him escape. But he had no idea how things worked here. Even if he found the answer, he wouldn't know the first thing about getting off the island. Pete had put the magic sack over his head, and then he woke up on the beach.

Andy sat up and leaned against the fallen tree. He closed his eyes to think. As he did, he sensed motion to his left. One of the kids must have hung back, tricking him into leaving his hiding spot. He opened his eyes, looking around frantically for the source of the movement. From the darkness, something glistened.

And then it moved.

A crouched figure snuck out of the foliage and entered the clearing. It was a grown man with long black hair and a scraggly beard. He looked as if he hadn't showered or shaved in months, maybe longer. Andy realized the thing he saw glistening was a piece of metal the man was holding. He moved in, and Andy prepared to get to his feet and run again.

"Stop," the man whispered.

Andy stood but didn't run. The man came closer. His shoes were beaten and worn, tearing at the toes. He wore a red tunic resembling an old captain's uniform, like something someone on a ship a hundred years ago might wear.

"Who...who are you?" Andy asked.

"Kid, we don't have much time. If you insist on introductions, my name's James Barrie. If you want to get off this island, I can help."

Everything clicked. This was the grown-up who'd escaped the beast.

"Are you the dad of one of the kids?"

"No, no. I was captain of a fishing ship. Years ago, we came across this island after a storm blew us off course. That boy, Pete. He's an evil sonofabitch. I'm sure he's filled your head with how awful adults are. How he sacrifices the bad people of the world. I never abused a single person in my life, son. Hell, I don't even have kids. He's willing to feed anyone to this monster if it benefits him. He tried it with me after we were shipwrecked, but I got away. My crew, they weren't so lucky."

He held up his arm, revealing a metal hook where his hand should've been.

"It got my hand before I escaped. But what those little shits didn't know was that I was a soldier before a captain. I was trained to take care of myself in the wild. I used the supplies I could find to stay alive, even made this nice little weapon for if they ever found me."

"This place was supposed to be a happy place," Andy muttered.

"They don't want people to find out about this place. Pete says it's called The Never because you never have to grow up. What he really means, boy, is you can *never* leave. But I know the source of his magic, and it's not the beast. That thing just keeps them young because of its agreement with Pete." His eyes narrowed. "And what's more...I know a way off the island."

JAMES TOLD ANDY HIS PLAN QUIETLY AS THEY TRAVELED through the forest, careful to avoid detection by the Lost Souls. He said Pete imprisoned a magical fairy, whom he forced to give him the powers she possessed or he'd kill her. And that Pete kept her locked in his treehouse, which was heavily guarded by kids. It sounded far-fetched, but after everything he'd seen on the island, he'd believe anything. James also told Andy he'd been able to survive so many years by sneaking the Lost Souls' food whenever he could. The food was enchanted by Vodyanoy and kept James and the kids at their current ages. Andy asked him why he hadn't tried to escape the island. His answer was simple. He wanted to take down Pete and the Lost Souls and wouldn't escape until that happened. For years, he'd been looking for the source of the power and had just recently discovered the fairy locked in Pete's treehouse. Until today, he hadn't come up with a plan to try and get in.

But now that there were two of them, one could distract the kids while the other snuck in to rescue the fairy. Once free, Pete's power would be nonexistent and the monster wouldn't have its source of food, which it required to provide youth. Without power, Pete and his followers would have no way to obtain sacrifices or bring new kids to the island. The plan was risky, but it was their only shot.

Andy and James reached the home base of the children and crouched in the dark underbrush, watching the Lost Souls go about their business around their living quarters. The kids moved urgently, and Andy heard his name mentioned multiple times. They were all upset with Wendy, who, in their eyes, had defied Pete and prioritized Andy over the group. James tapped Andy on the shoulder to get his attention.

"That treehouse there is Pete's. Always a few kids at the bottom keeping watch. I'm too big to fit in there since they built the damn thing for kids, so I'll distract them, make them follow me into the woods. As soon as I'm out of sight, you need to climb up and grab her."

Andy furrowed his brow. "How will I even know what the heck to look for?"

"Believe me, kid, you'll know. You ever seen a dog locked in a cage without being fed for a few days? When she sees you, she'll make sure you notice her. You need to take the cage he keeps her in and get it away from their home base before trying to open it. If you get in and out quickly, there's a chance we'll get off this island without confrontation."

"Okay. I can do it."

James stood from his crouch, ready to move. Andy didn't think he meant to do it now, but he looked down at Andy, nodded, and beelined toward the Lost Souls.

James snuck behind a kid Andy didn't know the name of, who had dragged his parents from the woods. He silently grabbed the boy's hair, and in one quick motion, he slid the hook across the kid's jugular, dropping the boy to the ground. Andy heard the choking sound of the boy trying to breathe, and for a second, he felt bad for him. He remained frozen in shock. James ran at a second unsuspecting follower, swinging his hook and forcing the bladed tip into the girl's temple with a sickening pop that reminded Andy of when his mother cut a watermelon in half. The girl let out the start of a scream before her brain shut down and body went limp. Her last plea to live alerted the other Lost Souls nearby, who turned to see what created the commotion. Four members closed in on James. Andy recognized the twins, but the other two kids were nameless to him. He wondered where the rest of the crew was.

"Well, well. If it isn't Mr. Barrie. We thought you were long dead. That the island ate you up and spit you out. But we'll finish the job," one of the twins said with a sadistic smile.

"Come get me, you little shits!" James led them away from the treehouse.

Andy knew he had to act. The hanging lights illuminated the forest, making him feel completely vulnerable. But James had the kids following him, exactly as planned. Andy made his move, approaching the man-made ladder built into the side of the large tree. He took two steps at a time, reaching a door resembling an attic entry. He pushed up, slamming the door on the treehouse floor, and climbed inside.

The walls were cluttered with items and papers surrounding a large map in the center of the back wall. A map of the island. He looked it over, realizing how big The Never was. As his eyes traveled the terrain, he spotted the beach area, and through the woods his parents had been dragged from, he noticed a large red X. He leaned in closer to read the small font below it: *portal*. That had to be his way back to the real world.

Remembering why he was in the treehouse, Andy looked around for any sign of the fairy. Pete's bed sat in the corner of the room next to a stack of books piled like a Jenga tower. No sign of a fairy.

*THUMP!*

The sound startled Andy. He wasn't sure where it came from, then it happened again, coming from a drawer of the desk against the back wall. He ran and opened the drawer, stifling a scream. Inside a small iron cage, a tiny figure lay curled up in a ball, breathing heavily. The cage—roughly a foot in length and height—took up the majority of the deep drawer. The fairy was at most six inches tall and looked sickly, her tattered clothes clinging to her ribs. Her hair was falling out in patches, leaving half her scalp exposed and covered in sores. She turned to face him, revealing two tiny golden dots for eyes. She opened her mouth and screamed, sounding like a squealing piglet.

"*Shhh.* Stop yelling. I'm here to help!"

"Who...are you? Get me out of here. *Please!*" Her voice came out angelic, unbefitting her pathetic appearance.

"I will. I need you to stay quiet. We're going to stop Pete. Make it so he can't do this to people anymore. Can you help?"

She cowered in the corner of her cage and frantically shook her head.

"He's pure evil. He tortures me...does things to me," she said.

Andy had no idea what she meant, but the possibilities made him sick to his stomach.

"We don't have much time. I have to get you out of here before they're back," he said, looking at the map again. "Is this *X* the way back home?"

"Yes. But he will find you. He *always* does."

Voices muffled by the forest were getting closer; the Lost Souls were coming home. Andy grabbed the cage and quickly headed for the door. He looped his arm through the iron bar of the cage, freeing up both hands to climb down. When he reached the bottom, he noticed the voices were gone. They must've taken another path in the woods. The only sounds remaining were his own heartbeat thumping against his chest and the crickets chirping in the forest.

*Crickets!*

Andy turned around just in time to see Cricket lunging, fangs bared. Andy fell on his backside, holding up the cage to shield his face. Cricket's teeth clanged off the metal bars, shattering into tiny fragments. The crazed kid rolled to his side, groaning in pain. Andy got to his feet and kicked Cricket in the face, flipping him onto his back.

"Let me out! I can help!" the fairy yelled.

Andy studied the cage, unsure how to open it. He saw no visible latch or lock. His delay gave Cricket enough time to stand and come in low, tackling Andy. The cage flew from his hands and bounced off the ground a few feet away. Cricket locked eyes with Andy, blood dripping from his mouth.

"You fool! We're going to kill you for this." Cricket wrapped his hands around Andy's throat, squeezing tightly. Bloody spittle flew as he hyperventilated, straining to end Andy's life.

Andy pried at his hands, but Cricket was crazed, his fingers viselike. Suddenly, a faint glow shone from behind Cricket's head, lighting up Andy's face. Cricket was confused at the sudden brightness and released his grip, turning to see the source. Cricket started to yell but was cut short when a flash zipped through his open mouth with the speed of a bullet and exited through the back of his head. Bloody brain matter splashed Andy's face as Cricket's body wobbled, then fell limp to the ground. Andy had no idea what just happened. He stood, looking for the cage.

He spotted it on the ground, but it was *empty*.

"We need to go. Now," the fairy said from the darkness.

Andy spun around, seeing a faint light in the bushes. When the cage fell to the ground, it must have somehow opened and freed her. Had it not been for her glow, he would've thought she was dead. She lay still, struggling to move.

"That took most of my power. I can't use any more until I've fully recovered."

He lifted her in his hand, reminded of his days catching toads and how he'd hold them gently so he wasn't squishing their small bodies in his grip. Together, they headed for the beach.

WHEN THEY ARRIVED, THE AREA WAS DESERTED. HIS parents were gone and the remaining Lost Souls were hunting James.

*But where's Pete?*

Andy felt guilty leaving without James, who'd spent an untold number of years trapped on the island. Had it not been for him, Andy would've had no idea how to leave.

"What about the man?" Andy asked.

"It's too late for him. This could be your only chance. We must go to the portal now."

He didn't like it, but she was right. They walked along the beach, keeping ample distance from the water as they approached the path. Behind them, a man yelling in agony stopped Andy in his tracks. He turned to see Omos and the twins dragging a bloody and beaten James to the beach. The fairy jumped from his hands into his pocket, hiding from her tormentors.

"Hey there, Andy, glad you could join us. Vodyanoy will be happy with a two-for-one meal tonight," Omos said.

From the other side of the forest, Pete exited, holding Wendy by the hair, ignoring her cries.

"Everyone's right on time," Pete said with his sadistic smile.

He dragged Wendy, who fought for her footing. Would he actually hurt her—or worse—for merely proposing an alternative?

Behind Andy, the water began to move, and he knew what he'd see when he turned around. The beast was back, ready for more.

"We have a buffet for ya, Vodyanoy! Three more useless pieces of meat for your taking."

Andy felt the fairy tense up in his pocket, but he didn't dare take his eyes off the Lost Souls closing in. He was tempted to run for the path, but he knew he wouldn't stand a chance against their powers. His only hope was the fairy helping him escape. James lifted his head and looked at Andy, who gave him a slight nod. A smile spread across James's face at the realization Andy had lived up to his part of the plan.

The beast approached the shallow water and rose above the surface, towering over everyone as water poured down its body like a mutated waterfall.

"So...who wants to go first? Wendy? How about the one-handed man? I think the best option is you, Andy boy. It's your fault this is happening tonight. It's *your* fault some of my followers are dead and Vodyanoy is pissed off." He turned to Rosemary and Regan. "Twins, you know what to do."

They ran toward Andy, their tiny pupils somehow shrinking even more as they zoned in on their target.

James noticed Omos was distracted watching the twins'

pursuit of Andy and that Pete was busy with Wendy. He drove his hook into Omos' calf muscle, tearing across the back of the leg until the hook broke free on the other side. Omos dropped to his knees and yelled. James swung again, and this time, the hook penetrated Omos' left eye. He pulled the hook with a quick, twisting motion, removing it from the socket. Omos fell face-first onto the sand, going still.

"NO!" Pete screamed, throwing Wendy to the ground.

He dashed toward James and struck him before the former captain knew what hit him. Pete's body was surrounded by the golden hue. He lifted James by his shirt, punching him in the face repeatedly. The blows were so powerful that James's face caved in, cracking the skull. His eyes rolled back in his head, and Andy knew nothing could be done to help his savior.

The twins were now stalking Andy, splitting up and forcing him to back up toward the water. The tide splashed against his feet, letting him know there was nowhere else to go. Vodyanoy's massive foot slammed down a few yards away, sending a blast of ocean water over the three of them as he prepared to grab his next meal.

*Please, no. It can't end like this.*

Pete threw the captain to the ground and leaped across the beach in one jump, landing behind the twins.

"It's over, Andy. Girls, he's *my* sacrifice."

They stepped aside, allowing their leader to come face-to-face with Andy. Pete smiled, then grabbed Andy by the throat, lifting him off the ground with ease. He walked into the water, holding Andy aloft the entire way. When Pete was waist-deep, he looked up at Vodyanoy.

"It didn't have to be this way, Andy boy. I liked you."

Andy felt a tickle traveling up his back. He realized it was the fairy crawling beneath his shirt. She came out of the collar and whispered in his ear, "The power is in his hood."

Pete was distracted by her appearance because until now, he had no idea she had escaped. Andy reached down and tore off the hood, revealing Pete's entire face for the first time. The golden hue vanished from his skin and with it his abnormal strength. Andy fell from his grasp as Pete reached for the hood, but Andy tossed it as far as he could into the water, watching it land between Vodyanoy's feet.

"No. NO, NO, NO!"

Pete dove into the water, swimming for the hood, and Andy ran for the shore. He turned to see Pete reaching for the cloth, but the beast scooped him from the water with its massive claws. Pete no longer had control without his magic. The leader of the Lost Souls screamed as his insides were squeezed like a lemon. His eyes bulged under the intense pain. He tried to plead, to smooth talk his way out of it, but Vodyanoy chomped down, severing his body in half. Pete's entrails emptied into the water like a bucket of chum.

Andy turned back to the land where the twins were still blocking his exit. Suddenly, their bodies started to transform. They hunched over, their skin wrinkling and hair turning white. They dropped to their knees and bellowed as their bodies aged a full lifetime in seconds. Liver-spotted skin clung to osteoporotic bones while their insides quickly disintegrated, then their bodies collapsed into two dusty corpses.

Wendy screamed next, and Andy saw her crawling across the

beach, now an old lady who could hardly move. She looked up at him, a final tear sliding down her weathered cheek.

"Thank you."

She dropped face-first onto the sand, her breathing slowed, and then Wendy was gone.

Vodyanoy dropped beneath the water and swam away, his gargantuan size shrinking in the distance. The agreement between Vodyanoy and Pete was ended.

Andy stood in place, unsure what to do next. Once he entered the portal and went back to the real world, he had no family, nowhere to go. Near the wall of trees heading into the forest, he noticed a faint glow emitting from within. He realized the fairy wasn't nearby and that she must be using her last bit of magic to open the portal for him.

He cut through the trees, spotting her near an open hole that lit the forest. She heard him coming and turned to smile.

"Thank you. You saved me and all the children from spending eternity in purgatory. The island is my home, and you gave it back to me. I wish you the best, young man."

Andy noticed that she now looked completely different from before, as if Pete's demise had healed her. In too much shock to say anything, he nodded his head. With one last look at The Never, Andy walked through the portal, back to the real world.

# THE BUTTERFLY BOY

## JEREMY MEGARGEE

The infant with the emerald eyes sits mooning on the fissured tar of the rooftop, just a few months fresh from the womb and drinking in those early experiences in life. This is the prime development stage when external stimuli matters the most, and the child is nothing but a blank canvas to be imprinted upon.

The baby's name is Dallas, and the sun boils down across his unblemished skin, threatening to burn if he doesn't find shade in the next hour or so. He is not being tended to. His caregivers are currently engaged in a pocket of chaos on the rooftop a few feet from him. There is a smashed light bulb pipe near them, the meth they had been smoking a few hours previous all played out, and the lack of a fix has driven them to a familiar frenzy of violence.

Dallas's mother is perched atop the prone body of her

boyfriend of the month, the flesh of her face dotted with sores from frequent picking, and her mouth is pulled into a rictus of rotting tombstone teeth. She's been digging her nicotine-stained claws into the man's moaning cheeks, and there are deep lacerations there, the flesh shredded to flapping ribbons. There is nothing in her now but rage and want, and Dallas has been entirely forgotten.

She is raining down blows on the man, and he's so high and ruined that he's completely incapable of defending himself. One eye has swollen up to grotesque proportions, and if the woman continues her onslaught, it threatens to pop free from the socket and roll over to Dallas. The innocent child would likely be tempted to pick it up and put it into his mouth, thinking it something soft and edible.

Dallas is watching his mother slowly but surely beat this man to death. He is a constant observer, and his environment is teaching him exactly how the world is. He should be shocked or afraid, blubbering, but he doesn't yet understand that what is happening in front of him is horribly traumatic. This is his normal. This is his familiar.

The man is howling now, this sickly sound forcing its way out his throat, blood bubbles forming and popping in the corners of his mouth. His eyes are flitting from side to side, glazed like a calf awaiting slaughter, and he murmurs curses at Dallas's mother even as he's in the process of being brutalized.

The infant's attention drifts to the opposite side of the roof, emerald gaze locked on a magical orange-winged thing that is fluttering from treetop to treetop. The monarch captivates

Dallas, a brand new life form to him, and he wants nothing more than to reach out that chubby little hand and graze the softness of the creature. It has the gift of flight, and Dallas wonders if he crawls to the edge of the roof and flops downward, will he sprout wings and fly too?

Dallas's mother has pulled a pair of heavy nail clippers from her ratty pocket, and she is using them to carve at her boyfriend like he's a jack-o'-lantern. She splits his lips, she rips at his nostrils, and she jams the sharp end into his brow over and over again, peppering the skin and relishing that puckered pop as the metal slides in and out.

The blood is pooling outward, creating a slick crimson ocean, and Dallas plays in it, his little feet bouncing up and down, soles coated in dripping red. The butterfly is pirouetting through the sky near him, lazy aerial acrobatics, and Dallas reaches questing fingertips up toward it, mouth agape in near toothless awe. He becomes excitable, drooling a bit, and the baby is barely aware of the murderous banshee that is still engaged in her tunnel vision butchery next to him.

The monarch gets closer and closer, riding the warmth of the summer breeze, and soon it's so near to Dallas's chocolate-smudged cheeks that he's able to hop upward and reach toward it with both hands, making come-hither gestures like he wants a hug so desperately that he'll do anything to get it.

There is new savagery afoot close at hand. Dallas's mother has dragged the man's shorts down to his ankles, exposing the sweat-soaked jungle of his scrotum, and the madwoman is gnawing at his genitals now, biting and blinded by unreasonable fury. There's a mushy hollow pop sound as one of the man's testicles deflates between her incisors, and he beats his hands and feet against the rooftop, made temporarily silent by world-shattering pain.

The butterfly lands on Dallas's sticky fingers, and it begins to suckle at the sugary stains on his skin. The baby marvels at the vibrant patterns on the wings and how delicate the legs are. He is as gentle as possible because he doesn't want to accidentally harm the critter.

Meanwhile, the mother has reached down with hands extended into animal claws, and she is pulling the skin taut around the man's mutilated loins, doing her best to tear at it like paper. She is succeeding, albeit slowly, the pressure required to rip the flesh causing beads of perspiration to dot both temples.

Dallas has started to watch her again. He doesn't understand what she is doing, but he learns. He observes. He drinks in what he sees, and he decides to emulate it to the best of his abilities. The baby takes hold of that delicate butterfly that has landed on him, and he does what his mother is doing. He rips. He tears. He carefully and gently mutilates. When it is finished, there is nothing left in his hands but ruined orange fluff, wings torn asunder, and twitching dismembered insect legs. His mother is finished too.

There is nothing left of the boyfriend but blood, gristle, and her shrieking hysteria as she digs her fingers into her own hair and tears at the roots.

This is one of Dallas's first memories.

This is how origin takes shape.

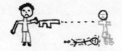

THE TODDLER WITH THE EMERALD EYES HAS LIVED A less-than-charmed life since his mother brutally murdered a man in a meth-fueled frenzy. She went into the prison system, and Dallas went into that bleak land of orphanages and foster homes. He has floated around like a ghost, no great emotional attachments, and his personality has bloomed pessimistic over the years. He expects disappointment, and he always steels himself for the worst.

He's no fan of his new foster home. It is one of the many child mills he has had the misfortune of existing within: a family interested only in receiving government benefits and housing children with minimal effort put into their actual care and welfare. At best, Dallas is neglected, and at worst, he is abused. The closed fists are hard to endure, but he hates the verbal stuff more. It seems to repeat in his brain, unwanted mantras, and it causes his budding self-esteem to tank each day.

The one bright spot in his life in the system is the pet turtle he was able to rescue from a highway a few months back. It had a little crack in its shell, but he mended that with superglue, and the turtle has been doing great since then. He named it Hope. He feeds it, he cleans its terrarium, and deep in his flawed heart, Dallas knows that he loves the small reptile.

The other boys in the home hate his turtle. They snicker and plot and feel repelled by the happiness the pet brings Dallas. This is a place where happiness is not meant to grow, for the soil is barren, the souls are dead, and it breeds endless envy when one child finds even a semblance of solace in something, be it object, person, or pet. The natural drive of the children in the home is to destroy, to make the playing field even again, and to ensure that misery is commonplace and everyone living there gets to experience it equally.

Dallas makes the mistake of leaving the terrarium unattended one day when he is taking care of daily chores. When he returns to his room later to feed his turtle, he is immediately concerned to see that there's no sign of Hope.

But there is jagged, nasty boy laughter coming from the kitchen, and Dallas reluctantly follows it. There is a little crowd formed there on the floor, hunched child figures like primitive villagers engaged in some nameless ritual. They are pouring various household chemicals and cleaning products into Hope's shell. Lye, bleach, and other noxious mixtures. The turtle's rough skin is bubbling and burning. It kicks its stumpy legs in an effort to escape, but it is held high, a sacrifice beneath flickering fluorescents. The beaked mouth opens and closes desperately, gasping for air, gasping for a reprieve from torment, but mercy does not come. Bleach comes, splattering blinking reptile eyes, burning reptile flesh, and making of the shell a hellish box that is corroding more and more with each passing minute.

Dallas wants to step in and put a stop to this, but he knows the outcome. The boys will beat him to a pulp and smear his blood and tears together on the tiles. It has happened before, and he knows it will happen again. They will torture him just as they are torturing his turtle. That is life in this place. That is the deeper meaning of existence, and Dallas has become accustomed to it in his boyhood.

So he stands there, forlorn and sagging into himself, and he watches his pet drown in caustic chemicals. He cries, but the tears are silent. He knows if he voices his weakness, they'll turn on him next, and the boys in the home are as relentless as starved hyenas. Dallas inhales the snot back up into his nostrils and wipes at his mouth.

He forces himself to keep watching despite the fact that everything within him wants to turn away. This is a lesson. This is another memory that is branding itself into his brain during his formative years. He watches even as the turtle defecates all over the floor out of sheer shock and trauma, its body voiding all contents as the pain worsens.

They've found dusty wrenches under the sink, and the boys are using them to crank at the shell, wanting to see the fragility of the body that hides within. There are dull cracking sounds that make Dallas want to crawl into a lightless hole for all eternity. He doesn't want to see the delicate internal structure of the turtle. Nature gave it a shell for a reason. Protection. Safety. A nice home.

But the boys are breaking it, and they will not stop. They're pulling and laughing and flinging bleach droplets from their dirty fingertips. They make sure to smile back at Dallas, leering demons in shadow, and he looks to the floor instead of meeting the emptiness in their shining eyes.

The shell clatters across the floor, popped clean open, and Dallas doesn't even need to look. He can smell the burned skin and sizzling tissue. The sounds, the aroma, all just a confirmation.

Hope has died in front of him. Hope was pulled apart. Hope no longer exists, and the little boy was a fool to ever think it did.

Dallas endures so many blackened experiences during his teenage years. He flees the foster homes and rides the lonely rails into big hive cities where he knows no one. These cities have names that he doesn't bother to learn most of the time because they're all the same meat grinder. He becomes a street kid, and his trials are numerous.

He begs and humiliates himself in order to eat, and too often even that isn't enough to scrape together a meal. So it's moldy bread from dumpsters, or a skirmish with the brazen rats to see who gets to gobble down that half-eaten dish of ravioli in the gutter behind the Italian restaurant.

Dallas becomes a fan of the needle, and heroin is his freedom from the grim reality of day-to-day life. He rides that rabid white horse and allows it to consume him. His pricked veins become more prominent and his weight drops until he's nearly cadaverous. He deals with persistent infections, and some nights he curls up on the sidewalk, weeping pus from what feels like a thousand wounds. He is still a kid, but he feels somehow hollowed out. There is nothing in him. No love and no light. It was never taught, and it was never given.

He offers up his emaciated body for those willing to use it in exchange for cash. He is treated like a filthy rag, rubbed to rawness and thrown away when the pleasure has dripped out of the rancid ghouls that rent him for a night.

He catches multiple STDs while engaged in this behavior, and each one makes him feel more tainted, more unwanted, more stained and smeared and coated in defects that will never go away. He is just another rat scurrying along underfoot, and he is invisible to the normal members of society going about their lives.

Dallas meets the addiction counselor at a point in his life when he's at rock bottom and aching to make some semblance of a change. The man is morbidly obese, middle-aged with graying scruff on his cheeks and thick glasses that magnify his eyes, but he seems to show a genuine interest in helping Dallas get clean. He promises to get him into a program and potentially even help him find housing if all goes well.

Hope starts to burst into Dallas's heart, but he has seen Hope die once, and it happens again with the addiction counselor. The man has a price, and his assistance isn't free. He has fetishes, and when he admits these to Dallas, the boy struggles not to let his nausea show on his face.

That's how Dallas finds himself in the counselor's grubby apartment, his stained underpants down around his ankles, mountains of fat pulsating, and long, thin needles pierced into the fat man's groin for sexual satisfaction. The man has a micropenis that is so small he's not able to achieve an erection or engage in intercourse. He shows and tells Dallas in agonizing detail while stroking at the impaled nub of his own sex. Due to this unfortunate impairment, he gains pleasure from more taboo pursuits. He got the idea for the impalement of needles from an old newspaper article about child killer, Albert Fish.

He delights in sadomasochism, and Dallas is on the receiving end of his perversity at this particular dark moment in time. The addiction counselor is using a relic of a WWII pistol to probe Dallas's bruised lips, making him perform fellatio on the barrel, mashing it up against his teeth and forcing it deeper and deeper into his throat. Dallas is gagging horribly, his eyes oozing with tears, and he feels his throat take on little abrasions as the hard steel jostles around within. The worst part is that the old gun is loaded, and although Dallas has no idea if it still functions properly, the threat alone is terrifying.

This is how the man gets off, and this is yet another layer of abuse for Dallas to compartmentalize deep inside. It has been building and building throughout his young life. The despair, the hopelessness, and the rising wave of contempt for himself and all others in this world.

The teen sucks at the gun barrel, tongue lashing and covered in sores, and the whale of a man watches with big, greedy eyes. He's rocking back and forth, loving the visual feast, and the putrid scent of his body odor almost makes Dallas vomit and clog up the barrel of the pistol.

There is a particular moment where the boy feels his soul being stripped of goodness. After being dehumanized consistently over a period of years, the light starts to fade out deeper within. Something else awakens in place of that lost light and tainted innocence. It is black, formless, and it slithers through Dallas's mind, permeating all that he is. He sees the world not as a safe place full of potential, but as a vindictive carnival that sends him twirling deeper and deeper into a bottomless abyss.

The metallic taste of the gun barrel lingers in Dallas's mouth long after the fat man removes it, a little milky puddle of sperm pooled in the chair around the mutilated mound of his groin. The boy takes the meager wad of bills that is offered to him, and he leaves the addiction counselor there in his own post-orgasmic bliss.

The wind is harsh outside on the sidewalk, and the cigarette Dallas places between his lips does nothing to eradicate how worthless he feels. He inhales deeply, letting the smoke just sit in him, and when he walks off into the gaping maw of the city nightscape, he isn't feeling much of anything anymore.

Numb and thinking of a butterfly from long ago. The sensation of something beautiful dead and scrubbed out in his palms. That colorful and delicate creature made just ugly guts and gristle, not worth looking at anymore, not even worth giving a single guilty thought to.

There are days when Dallas feels exactly like that butterfly. Worthless and wingless, and robbed of the ability to ever learn to fly.

DALLAS HAS REACHED THE GRAND OLD AGE OF EIGHTEEN, and his eyes don't look like emeralds anymore. They are tarnished jade set back into deeply dark sockets, resembling bloodshot orbs that are dried out like his insides. He is a juvenile, and his body should be in its prime, but it is not. There are pains in his abdomen with no definitive origin, and he often has to walk with a palm splayed against the throbbing flesh, almost like he's trying his best to keep corruption from oozing out.

His hair is thin and wispy, slicked back against his scalp, and his posture has degenerated over the years. He's comparable to a human weasel, always skulking, shoulders slumped and distrustful. Dallas no longer likes for people to see him. He is a vessel for shame, and it eats him up to be seen in such a loathsome state. He has taken to sleeping in the daylight and waking at night to avoid withering eyes that spill over with judgment.

But there is one who he welcomes being seen by. She is small and unblemished in this discordant universe. He sees the child not as the gullible rosebud that she is, but as a big, fleshy bag of potential that hasn't been sliced or diced by life. Dallas resents that. When he looks into her bright, curious eyes from afar, he is mocked by everything that he could have been. He circles the drain while this girl circles the sun, and where is the fairness in that?

Dallas approaches her as she rides on her tricycle in an empty section of the park's tennis courts. He has made a solid effort to shake some of the dirt from his clothes, and he has a little box in his hands. Splintered and worn, covered in the remnants of ornate carvings.

"Hello!"

The girl lifts her eyebrows and gives a little half-hearted wave in response.

"Ever seen a box of butterflies before?"

Dallas smiles, and one of the cold sores on the far corner of his mouth splits open. He wipes the fluid away and lifts the box up to his ear, cocking his head and listening. His eyes become large and comical, and the little girl scoots a bit closer to see what he's doing.

"You can hear them inside. Fluttering and trying to get out. I want to let them out, but I also want to share it with someone. Will you help me free them?"

She stares up at the strange man, not quite sure what to make of him. He looks like a dog that's been beaten so many times that it automatically whines when you approach it. But he seems enthusiastic about the butterflies, and the child loves butterflies.

"What colors are their wings?"

"All the colors in the rainbow. And who is asking?"

"Aubrey. My name is Aubrey."

Dallas actually offers up a theatrical bow, sweeping his tattered duster back in dramatic fashion. Those tarnished jade eyes are taking on a new shine, almost like the more ground he crosses with Aubrey, the more his confidence is growing.

"Come with me, Aubrey. There's a special place where we open the box."

Dallas is almost in shock after he starts walking and he hears the creak of her wheels following a short distance behind him. They leave the tennis courts and the playground area and venture to where the park enters a section of deep wilderness crisscrossed with trails for hikers to explore. After nearly a mile of walking, Dallas leaves the established trail and goes stalking off into the woods. Aubrey reluctantly abandons her trike, and she follows on foot, the snap of branches telling him she's not too far behind.

They stop at the bottom of a ravine, and it's a dead end with a large culvert blocking any forward motion. Dallas spins around to face the child, and he swallows deeply while looking down at his own shoes. For some unspeakable reason, he cannot meet her eyes.

"This is a good place to let things out."

"Okay. Lemme look, mister."

Dallas steps forward and opens the box. It is filled with mutilated monarchs, their wings torn, their legs curled up, and not a spark of life in those black gemstone eyes.

Aubrey's nose scrunches up.

"But these ones are dead. Broken."

Dallas looks down into the box, almost like he's seeing it for the first time. There is a look of profound apathy painted across his features.

"Did you break them apart like that?"

"I wanted them to feel like me, Aubrey."

His fingers loosen on the box and he lets it drop, and while it is still falling, iridescent wings twirling in distraction, Dallas removes the sickle from its hiding place tucked into the back of his belt. He stole the farm tool from an antique shop earlier in the day, and now he uses it. He brings it up in a slow arc and allows the tip of that rusted blade to puncture Aubrey's abdomen.

There is a little hissing sound as the gritty metal slides into untouched flesh, and the child looks down in surprise, not understanding what has happened. Dallas gently pushes her across the face, and her body tumbles down into a soft carpet of dead leaves. He crouches over top of her, and he begins to hack that sickle into her stomach over and over again. There is absolutely no rage or aggression behind the act. It is almost mechanical, and when the blood soaks her so bad that it looks like she's been drowned in red wine, Dallas pauses to wipe his fingertips off on the front of his shirt.

She is trying to form words, but her mouth is full of blood, and it is smeared all over her little rosebud chin like dark chocolate. There are brittle butterfly wing fragments tangled up in the girl's hair. She is trying to breathe, but there's an unnatural rattling sound emerging from her chest. It reminds Dallas of the sound of insects.

He looks down at the girl. He doesn't know why he stabbed her. He has been hurting, so he wanted something to hurt. It is done now. She is clutching at his sleeve and trying to close up the jagged knife splits in her body with small fingers. Her tiny fist balls up and pulls at his shirt, but he removes her fingers and lets the limb flop down bonelessly.

Dallas sighs and leans down, scooping up her body into his own arms. He rocks her back and forth, those dead leaves crunching under both of them. His eyes catch the sunlight. Before this, his irises were broken, lost, and eternally abused. Dallas feels the last of that vulnerability leaking out of him. His gaze darkens. His soul deadens.

Evil is born within him.

Evil seeded, sculpted, and nourished over the period of a lifetime. He embraces the cold dark flood of these feelings, and compassion wilts like a garden that never sees the sun. Dallas drops the girl and stands over top of her, lording there in shadow, simply passing the time and observing her death.

There is a monarch circling overhead, but it does not fly down to visit Dallas. It senses no innocence left there. Nothing sweet or good. It senses change, and not for the better.

Dallas walks off slowly into the woods, bootheels crunching to signal his departure.

He leaves what remains of his childhood bleeding on a deathbed of moss and branches.

# The Drop-off

## Megan Stockton

Jillian ran her bleeding fingertip beneath the cool stream of water, head hanging so far down that she could feel the droplets from the spray's pressure on her frizzy hair. Abby rubbed the back of her neck with a damp rag, then laid a half-opened Band-Aid on the countertop beside her. A pink cartoon dog peeked out from beneath the sterile white wrap.

"Feeling okay now?" Abby asked quietly, using the same voice she often used for the children when they were apprehensive. When Jillian first opened the daycare, she thought that finding good help would be the hardest part of her journey. Within the first week, Abby had applied: a teenager who had just gotten her driver's license and wanted to work every single weekend. She was a natural with children and one of the most trustworthy and responsible people that Jillian had ever met.

Jillian raised her head slowly, taking deep breaths between her lips as she shut off the water and quickly covered her wound with the Band-Aid. She couldn't respond at first, afraid that saying even a single word would bring back the uncontrollable nausea, and instead just nodded. She looked over at Abby in appreciation, and the younger girl smiled, hair bobbing around her shoulders.

"I'm... Whew. I'm good," Jillian finally said. "It's just...the sight of my own blood. I don't know, it gets me every time. I was rushing through cutting up the fruit for lunch and the knife just slipped. I better go finish up."

"No, no. I got it, Jill. I'll finish up the lunches. The littles are in the craft room with Mrs. Brenda. Everyone is here except the new boy. Already done a head count."

"He may be a no-show. On the phone his mother seemed really...nervous. You know, first-time jitters. It wouldn't surprise me if they didn't come at all."

As though the universe wanted to prove her wrong, the driveway alert beeped over the intercom. Jillian walked over to the desktop computer in the adjacent office and checked the security camera feed. Sure enough, a woman appeared to have parked just across the street and was already walking down the driveway to the front door. She wondered why the woman hadn't pulled her car in and instead risked the trek across the highway. The location of the daycare wasn't ideal: right on a busy road where everyone went ten miles minimum over the speed limit. There had been a reason the property was so cheap. The first big investment Jillian had made was plenty of security parameters and a massive eight-foot privacy fence on the half-acre plot. No one came, went, or opened any doors or windows without Jillian being notified immediately.

"Well, speak of the devil." Jillian laughed. "I'll go get her to sign the paperwork. You finish up that bloodthirsty fruit."

Abby grinned. "On it!"

Jillian smoothed down the front of her T-shirt, which had a smiling sun with the words WE KEEP ON THE SUNNY SIDE across the top in bold, bubbly letters. A splash of her blood stained the corner of the sun's grinning mouth, and she tried to wipe it away, effectively creating a purple smudge instead. She tsked at it but decided no one would ever know it was a bodily fluid. She came around the corner, face-to-face with a young woman and a little boy.

The woman was probably in her late twenties. Her face looked like it had once been very plump, and the way her skin now sagged against her bones did not look natural. She was pale, with dark circles beneath her eyes, and speaking of eyes... Jillian caught herself staring at the vessels that covered the woman's eyes: beyond bloodshot, with burst capillaries and rimmed in pink, with yellow-crusted lashes. This woman looked ill. Jillian quickly smiled and averted her gaze, looking at the blond boy who stood before her. He was clean, well cared for, and looked healthy. He didn't smile up at her but simply observed. Hesitant, which was typical for new children.

"You must be Mrs. Werner," Jillian said, clearing her throat. "And this is Seth?"

She just nodded in response.

"Well, I just have a few papers for you to fill out."

"I did those," she croaked. "I did those online."

"Oh? I thought our form was still down."

"No, it went through. Name, address, allergies...all of that."

Jillian shrugged and smiled. "Perfect. Will you wait here while I confirm, please? I'll go ahead and let Seth go with the other kids."

The woman nodded and muttered, "Thank you."

"Well, that's why we're here, isn't it?" Jillian said, crinkling her nose and puckering her lips in an affectionate smile.

"Thank you," she repeated.

Jillian reached her hand out to Seth, and he took it eagerly, following quietly along behind her as she unlocked the door to the craft room. Mrs. Brenda, a portly elderly woman, answered the door and beamed at Seth.

"Going to talk with Mom just a bit," Jillian said quietly. "I have to check a few things on her waivers and forms. This is Seth."

"Oh, Seth, you're just in time to join the fun! We're making art with different shaped pasta." She guided him inside, and Jillian heard her lock the door. Every door was equipped with double cylinder deadbolts, so they could be unlocked from either side. Safety, safety, safety. This was Jillian's top priority.

Her phone buzzed in her pocket, and she retrieved it, noting the alerts that read: FRONT DOOR AJAR, DRIVEWAY CAMERA MOTION DETECTED. Jillian didn't check the camera but instead continued the short trek to the front door. She could see Mrs. Werner standing at the end of the driveway, waiting to cross the road as cars whizzed by in chrome blurs. *Where the hell is she going?*

"Mrs. Werner!" Jillian called, hands cupped around her mouth for volume. "Please hang on, just a second. I really need to go over this paperwork with you before you leave Seth."

Mrs. Werner turned slowly to face her. She looked even more gaunt and pallid from a distance.

"Thank you," she repeated. The first time she said it, Jillian only saw her lips form to move the word. Her voice was lost in the whir of traffic. Then she said it again in a louder voice, and again in an even louder voice, and again... Until she was screaming it, tears running down her face and leaving black trails of mascara. She laughed, the most joyous and happy sound.

But there was also madness and desperation.

"Mrs. Werner?" Jillian asked quietly, now nearly at the end of the driveway. A few more steps and she could grab her by the elbows. She imagined she'd force her to sit on the painted concrete wall that bordered the property. The one with dozens of children's handprints on it and little plastic flowers "planted" above that twirled in the wind. She would ask her if she needed help, and she'd recommend a good therapist. She'd tell her that she had to get her head right for her son, for Seth.

But all of those comforting thoughts were cut short.

Mrs. Werner stepped backward, and for the first time, Jillian noticed her bare feet. She had no shoes on, but her feet were wrapped in white cloth, bloodied through. Her heel crossed over the white line in slow motion, and then it was like she disappeared into thin air. Jillian gasped, hands clamped over her mouth as she stared at the spot where Mrs. Werner had stood. A truck's brakes squealed as it spun to a stop a few yards away, having spun around to face the opposite direction. The driver was a teenage boy, and he got out of the driver's seat and started screaming.

Jillian still hadn't looked over at the truck or its driver yet, but she knew she had to. She heard Abby behind her, keys jingling on her pink lanyard as she jogged down the gravel drive.

"Oh... Oh, Jesus Christ. I'll call 911!" she squealed, running back into the daycare.

Thunder rolled overhead, and the trees were bending to a strong wind. There was a tornado watch in effect for today. Bad weather was moving in, and they had made the parents aware that they had a basement and generator in case the power went out. She had been prepared. Jillian was always prepared.

Not for this.

She finally turned to look at the truck, steam roiling from beneath its hood. The aftermarket grill was dented in, and Mrs. Werner's body was embedded in the metal there. Her arms were spread across the width of the truck like she had been crucified, feet hanging onto the pavement in worn-off nubs—jagged bones sticking out and barely pressed to the pavement like the toes of a ballerina.

Jillian had started walking toward the highway, noticing that traffic had stopped in a line both ways, hazard lights flashing for as far as she could see. In the distance, sirens wailed like hell-hounds, and the teenage boy was still screaming an incoherent language.

There on the bare stretch of pavement between the waiting cars and where she stood, Jillian saw the decapitated head of Mrs. Werner, face still twisted into an exalted smile.

JILLIAN FELT LIKE SHE WAS SEEING HERSELF IN THE
third person, positioned just behind where her body stood as the
police officer took her statement. Abby was wringing her hands
beside them, face completely devoid of color. It looked as though
even her lipstick had melted away to reveal the colorless lips
beneath. The young cop's own hands were shaking as he wrote
down every word that Jillian managed to utter. She'd watched
him, just moments earlier, turn an evidence bag inside out
around his hand to grab Mrs. Werner's decapitated head like it
was a pile of dog shit. She could tell he'd never seen anything
like this. None of them had.

"We are going to have to close the road down both ways for
about fifteen minutes...maybe a half hour tops. Clean up and
photography."

"But the children," Abby pipped. "Their parents will want to
come get them. I don't think we can keep working today. Not
after what Jill had to witness."

"I'm fine," Jillian croaked, surprising herself. "It'll be fine. A
half hour...but oh God. Seth. The little boy."

Abby put her hand to her mouth as she, too, realized.

The officer looked between them, a green tinge of sickness
returning around his eyes. "Who's Seth?"

"The woman..." Jillian waved her hand toward the highway,
unable to speak of the event that had just occurred. "She had
just dropped off her son for his first day with us. Can you take
him?"

"We'll have to get somebody down here from CPS. Right
now, you don't want him outside, and I think it's best if you
don't tell him what's happened just yet. We'll get a caseworker

down here to handle that situation. Just keep...keep on with your regularly scheduled programming, all right? Just for fifteen, twenty minutes...ish."

He added the "ish" quickly, shrugging his shoulders as he stuffed the notebook into his armpit and clicked the pen closed. "Plus the storm coming in... We're under a severe weather advisory too. It's probably best to just hunker down and hold tight. Does the kid have any family you can call?"

Abby responded, "No. Jillian was just about to have the mom sign paperwork. She claimed she filled out everything online, but our forms have been down. So we have *no* information on her other than her name and phone number."

The officer nodded. "Okay, we'll see what we can figure out. She didn't have a wallet or purse on her or in her car... Well, not that we've found. It looked like she had been living in her car for a while, though, so we have a lot of trash to sift through. If you need anything, here's my direct line."

He smoothly flipped a card out of his breast pocket and put it into Jillian's numb fingers before he headed out the door. A strong, warm breeze blew moisture inside, whipping the man's baggy pants around his ankles as he closed the door behind him.

"Jill, what are we going to do?"

"We're just going to act like nothing has happened until they get the roads cleared. Will you go down into the office and start contacting the parents? Let them know there's been an accident on the highway and we will call them as soon as the roads are clear to pick the kids up."

Abby nodded slowly. "Yeah, sure. I can do that."

"Take a flashlight in case the power goes out. There are a bunch under the sink in the kitchen."

Jillian watched as Abby left down the hall before she started her own journey to the craft room. She stood outside the door, fumbling slowly through the keys around her neck.

She was intentionally delaying. All she needed right now was some quiet, some time to herself where she could try to relax and decompress. She didn't want to walk in and be overwhelmed by the children rushing to climb up her legs and pull at her blouse, wanting her attention all to themselves. Normally she loved this, she loved the way they *loved* her...but now she was overstimulated before she had even stepped inside.

As she put the correct key into the lock, she heard something inside that made her hesitate, fingers pinching the cold key as she leaned forward. She could hear the children whispering...in a rhythmic sort of way like they were reciting a poem or a song... but their voices ebbed and flowed like the buzzing of insects. Then she heard the raspy groan of something else, a moan so akin to sexual that her hair stood on end. She jolted upward, straight-spined, as she struggled to get the key to turn.

It wouldn't open. She could turn the knob, but the door wouldn't swing open. The hum of the voices on the other side intensified, and Jillian desperately put her shoulder against the door, finding that with some pressure, it gave an inch...and another...and another...

And then it popped open.

The children were sitting in a semicircle, mouths moving in unison. They had tears streaking their cheeks, every single one of them. The sound she had heard didn't match the way their lips moved, and the smell of sulfur flooded her nostrils. It smelled like natural gas or maybe something awry with a septic system. She covered her mouth, fingers against her nose, and made a small noise in her throat.

With that small sound, it was as though all of the children suddenly realized she was there. Their voices stopped, jaws dropped slack to reveal uneven and missing baby teeth and silver caps. Then their mouths snapped closed, and they all began sobbing loudly. One little girl screamed, the ear-splitting squeal causing her neighbors to cover their ears. One sobbed for his mommy, and some of them reached for her to comfort them.

"What in the world..." Jillian breathed, reaching down to pull every child into her body. "What—"

Then she heard the moaning again. She had nearly forgotten the eerie sound that had caused her to burst through the door in the first place. Jillian glanced over her shoulder and saw Mrs. Brenda slumped against the door, body now crumpled where Jillian had shoved it open. Her chest was slowly rising and falling, and with every slow exhale, she let out a long groan. Her eyes were wide and fixed, unblinking and wholly black: pupils blown out and unresponsive. She had blood staining the front of her kitten-patterned blouse and covering her nostrils and mouth. Clutched in her hands was a bloody pair of scissors.

"Oh my god. Oh Jesus," Jillian cried. "Come on, children. Hurry now, hurry. Let's get into the movie room, okay? Let's go on in there..."

A loud roll of thunder shook the building, and the children screamed. Jillian was shaking but tried to pull herself together.

"Single file, like good little ducks. Come on. I'll be right behind you. Go to your mats."

The children hurried out the door, their bare feet making little quiet smacks against the short carpet. None of the children seemed to be injured. Not physically. Mrs. Brenda was quiet and still now. Jillian knew she needed to go over and check her pulse, just to be sure she wasn't lying there comatose and suffering. She couldn't bring herself to do it. She sidestepped across the room and out the door, keeping her eyes on Mrs. Brenda's body as though it may spring to life and come after her.

She rushed into the movie room where the children were obediently sitting on their mats, still sniffling and whining in their throats. Several of them snuggled against stuffed animals or blankets. At the sight of her, they relaxed.

"Counting heads, everyone, stay on your mats, please," she whispered, tapping her finger through the air as she took mental note of every child. It was then, through all of the anxiety and trauma, that she realized Seth was gone.

"Seth? Seth Werner?" Jillian said, looking through the familiar eyes.

"Who?" a little girl, freckled and dark-haired, managed to squeak.

"Seth is new. He was just here today."

Two boys screeched in unison, and Jillian put her hands together. "*Shhh...* Let's use our words. Please, let's use our words. I can't help you if you don't use your words with me. Melly? Can you tell me?"

Jillian turned back to the freckled girl, knowing that Melly was by far the most mature and willing to please. Melly took a deep breath, lower lip puckering.

"Mrs. Brenda tried to hurt Seth," she said, voice shaking. "She was helping him cut his paper. His colored paper. He said something to her, and she tried to hurt him bad."

Jillian covered her mouth. "Where is Seth now? Where is he, Melly?"

"He walked out the door when you came in...when we all wanted hugs."

"Okay, Melly... Listen to me, you're in charge for a few minutes, okay? Does everyone hear that? Melly gets to be the leader. I'm going to put on a fun movie, and you all stay bundled up. I'm going to go find Ms. Abby. I'll lock this door behind me. I can see you. Remember that Ms. Jill has eyes everywhere."

The kids smiled a little, pointing at their eyes and glancing at the cameras in the corner.

"What if he comes back, though? Before you do?" Melly asked.

"Who?"

"Seth."

"Just have him sit with everyone else. I'll be right back."

Melly shook her head. "Seth is a really bad boy, Ms. Jill."

ABBY LEANED OVER THE DESK, PRESSING THE PHONE receiver to her ear as she struggled to hear through the static. There wasn't the dull dial tone or the repetitive beep that let you know that a phone was out of service. Just the sound of the ocean in a shell, the mind-numbing *scchhhhhhhhh*. She fingered the hook once, twice, three times. But the static whoosh continued. She hung the phone up and stared at it. When she first started working here, she didn't even know how to use the corded phone. Jillian insisted that it was one less thing the kids could get ahold of and lose.

Thunder rolled, and Abby jumped in surprise. It seemed to rattle the whole building, and she thought she could hear the children upstairs squeal in fear. She probably needed to head back upstairs and let Jillian know the phone seemed to be down. She reached into her pocket to retrieve her cell phone, unlocking the screen and noticing the exclamation point beside her service bars. Cell signal was shitty, but that could've just been because she was in the basement. She could try upstairs and let Jillian know she didn't mind using her personal phone to contact the parents.

Abby heard a strange wet splat, and then a few seconds later, she heard an identical sound. She recognized the moist noise somehow, although she could not put her finger on what it was exactly. She furrowed her brow, pushing herself away from the computer desk. The chair made a rattling sound like dancing cartoon skeletons as it rolled across the uneven laminate floor. She slowly stood, walking the short distance down the hallway to the spare room where they kept the chick incubator for the kids. Every year they incubated chicken and quail eggs and let the kids watch the miracle of hatching, then Jillian took the baby birds to her brother's farm on the other end of town. It was a win-win for everyone involved, and it had always been one of

Abby's favorite projects to do with the kids. They would guess the color of the babies, how many would hatch, when they would hatch... Abby joked she was running a child gambling ring, taking bets on the little birds in the currency of juice pouches and cookies.

As she approached the open doorway, the incubator fan made a loud whir, and she realized very quickly that something was...wrong.

The lid to the incubator lay to the side, fan trying desperately to blow warm air as the thermometer detected the cool ambient air. In the corner, she saw a little boy standing with the base of the incubator in his arms, dropping one egg at a time onto the tile floor. The damp squelch of the shell separating was what Abby had been hearing. The congealed, partially developed remains of chicken fetuses were a ring of bloody roses around his feet.

"Oh my God." Abby choked in surprise, putting her hand to her mouth. "Seth? What are you doing?"

At first, she didn't even know if it *was* Seth. All she knew was that she didn't recognize the child's hair and build. She could recognize the ten regulars from behind at four or five yards away easily. She knew her kids.

The little boy turned to look at her, dropping another egg as he made eye contact. She watched as his bare feet shuffled toward her just a few steps, crushing a small, feathered body underfoot. Yolk and venous jelly squished between his little toes, bubbling and frothing.

"Stop," she whispered.

"If I can't have a family...they don't deserve one either," Seth said through gritted teeth. His voice easily belonged to a child, but what he said, and the way he said it, was not that of youth. He sounded old, bitter, jealous. There was no remorse, and there was a deep understanding of what he had done.

"Seth, sweetheart..." Abby said, reaching out a shaking hand. "Let's just...let's go upstairs and find Ms. Jill, okay?"

Seth dropped all of the eggs from his arms, and Abby winced at the sound of the incubator's base clattering to the floor. She forced herself not to look, hoping somehow some eggs could be salvaged.

There was something wrong with Seth. She could only imagine what had been going on at home in the days preceding this one. His mother was obviously troubled. Was it an abusive father? Mental illness?

The boy took her hand, and she noted how cold and dry his was. She started walking toward the stairs, slowly ascending with him in tow.

"You don't have a family, either, do you, Abigail?"

Abby paused, looking down at the wide, green eyes. They were wholly fixated on her, purposefully locked on like a predator onto something vulnerable. His pupils had constricted to a pinprick, so small they were barely visible—just a pool of viridian beneath his dark brows.

"What did you say to me?" She didn't recognize her own voice, so small and meek and without joy. Every question that surfaced raised with it more and more panic. How did he know her full name? An intelligent child could assume, maybe. What else could Abby possibly be short for? How did he know she had no family? He didn't. He couldn't have; he must have just guessed. He's scared, insecure, looking for some sort of support and understanding.

She released his hand, taking a deep breath.

"It's okay, Seth. We're all family here. Lots of people don't have mommies and daddies. But we can sometimes create our own families. Getting to pick who we want to be our aunts and uncles and brothers and sisters. Isn't that fun?"

"You could have had a family," Seth said, releasing her hand and moving up to share the step with her. His tiny body gave off no warmth.

Abby felt her blood run cold. Her lips quivered as she tried to find her voice, but nothing came.

"It's okay," Seth said, smiling like someone who had shared a dirty joke. "I don't blame you. We don't blame you."

"I don't... I don't know what you mean," she finally said.

"You could have had a family, Abigail. You had the chance."

"You don't understand..." She sobbed, voice cracking.

Seth went up another step, now almost eye level with her. "Do you hear it? Can you hear it?"

At first, all that she could hear was the ambient hum of the neglected incubator echoing in the spacious basement. Then she heard it...the faintest cry, a distant yowling. It started low and cooing, and then it escalated to a gargling wail. The staccato of a baby's frantic scream was soon bouncing from wall to wall, and Abby clasped her hands over her ears. It didn't help to muffle the sound, as though it was within her own skull.

Suddenly the sound stopped, and Seth leaned toward her, whispering, "Blessed shall be he who takes your infants and dashes them against the stones."

Then he raised his hands and shoved her. Abby reached forward to grapple for his shirt, fingertips grazing the fabric before she fell backward.

Abby didn't hit a single step on her descent into the dark basement. She sailed through the air in slow motion, watching as Seth's form became nothing more than a dark figure at the top of the stairs, and she thought she saw his eyes glisten with the reflective green quality of an animal. She didn't feel herself land on the floor, not immediately. It wasn't until she realized that she was no longer airborne that the pain flooded her body.

The back of her skull was so swollen, instantly, that it felt like she was lying on a waterbed. Her left arm was broken and probably both of her legs. Every inhale was spikes piercing her suffering lungs. She screamed, voice cracking from the force.

"Help me!"

Seth walked up to the top of the stairs and shut the door behind him, and the lights went off at the same time, encasing her in darkness. Abby couldn't move; she was immobilized either from her injuries or out of fear and shock. She continued to call for help, until she heard the sound of a baby again.

It cooed at first, just like it had before.

"Please, no. Please, please, please…"

The sound diminished, and then she heard a slow and repetitive clicking. The *clop, clop, clop, clop* that could have belonged to nothing other than…hooves. She looked down with her eyes as much as she could, unable to even lift her head to try and see what may have been making the sound. She saw something orange and illuminated at the end of the hall, and it was approaching her with a slow dedication.

"Hello? Jill, is that you? Please, God, is that you?"

It wasn't Jill, and it wasn't God.

The creature stood seven feet tall, was covered in grizzled black hair, and she thought it looked remarkably like a burly man except for the cloven hooves at the end of its muscular legs. It held a staff in its left hand and a blazing lantern in its right. She began wailing even before it came to stand over her.

It leaned over her, bringing the end of the staff toward her face. As it entered the gentle glow of the lamp, what little remained of Abby's awareness noted that on the end of the staff was an impaled fetus, limbs and chest bruised and bleeding. It didn't have eyes, just dark masses beneath thin flesh, and its mouth opened to shriek at her, chest fluttering with the effort of its screams.

Abby's entire body felt like it was engulfed in flames, and she suddenly found the ability to move, thrashing on the floor as she realized she *was* burning.

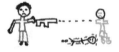

JILLIAN HAD LOCKED THE CHILDREN IN THE MOVIE ROOM, heading to retrieve a flashlight from beneath the sink before she went to find Abby. Another clap of thunder had the power out, but the generator immediately kicked on, and she sighed a breath of relief. She had been against the cost of the standby generator, but her brother insisted having one that would start up on its own would be a godsend in a bad storm. She was thankful for it now as she heard the movie start back up again in the locked room. Jillian made her way first over to the window at the front of the daycare, peering out into the darkness. It had gone pitch-black out; she couldn't even squint enough to make out the flower boxes beneath the window or the hedges just beyond. A flash of lightning illuminated the highway, and she thought she could see a figure standing there at the entrance to the pathway. Jillian leaned so close to the window that her nose smashed against it, holding her breath to prevent fogging the glass as she cupped her hands around her eyes to see better.

A useless flicker did little more than cause a twinge of pain behind her eyes, but it was followed by such a bright burst of light that the exterior of the building was day...for just a moment.

For just that moment, Jillian swore she saw someone standing with their arms straight out, head lolling against their chest. Not unlike the final resting pose of Mrs. Werner.

Jillian jumped away from the window, shaking hands digging through her pockets feverishly. She pulled out her phone followed by the cop's card. She dialed the number as quickly as she could, keeping her back to the window but leaning toward it so that she could gather as much service from the atmosphere as possible (if that's how that worked).

The phone rang against her ear, and she exhaled a sigh of relief.

"Hello?"

Jillian was caught off guard by the lack of professional intro-duction, wondering if she even had the right number. "Uhm... Yes, is this the officer from earlier? The accident at the daycare?"

"Oh, yeah. We've got everything cleaned up out there. You

can start letting the kids go home anytime now. I'm sorry, I knocked, but no one answered, and the door was locked. I assumed you all were just weathering the storm."

"Is CPS coming?"

"About that... It doesn't appear that the Werner woman had any children. None that we can find anyway. Did you say she dropped off a child this morning or was just inquiring about dropping off a child? It seems like she may have had some mental health issues. She was living out of her car, just a sad story there... But that's beside the point."

"I need someone back out here. There's been an accident...or something. Someone is—" Her voice caught.

"Ma'am? Is someone hurt?"

"I think one of my employees is dead, and there's something not right here. Something is wrong. I can feel it. Can you please send someone here?"

"We will head straight there. Just sit tight. I'll get an ambulance out there too. Please leave the front door unlocked for us."

"Yes, please hurry."

She hung up the phone, dropping it back into her pocket as she reached over and unlocked the door. She heard something behind her, like the shuffle of small feet against the carpet, and she spun around. She didn't see anything, but she also couldn't shake the feeling that something was there.

"Abby?"

In the silence, she headed toward the basement door, detecting another foul surge of sulfuric odor. What *was* that smell? She wondered if the storm had flooded the septic tank. She opened the door and was greeted by a different smell. The beam of her flashlight caught tendrils of smoke, something that Jillian first mistook for fog or steam. It billowed upward and curled its fingers against the ceiling, and she allowed the light to follow it down to the floor where she saw the charred corpse of a young woman.

Had it not been for the remaining fabric of the girl's top, Jillian would not have been able to recognize it as Abby. Embers still glowed inside the blackened flesh, white teeth forming a permanent grin on the melted face. Her gut had collapsed and was flat, the crest of both hips peeking through the destroyed flesh. Her hands were up, what remained of her fingers curled defensively.

Jillian's hands went numb, and the flashlight fell from her grip, bouncing against the steps before rolling across the floor at the bottom. She thought she could see something standing there in the dark, something black and imposing. Something eerily human.

She lunged for the door, slamming it between her and the... thing. She gasped against the door, tears streaming down her face.

"I know what you did too."

It was a little boy's voice that came from behind her, and Jillian found herself turning slowly to face Seth with the pair of bloody scissors in his hands.

"Seth." She breathed, exhaling all of her stress and trying to sound collected. Every flutter of her eyelids stung, and her chest ached. "We need to get you with the other children. There's help on the way, okay? Just put the scissors down for Ms. Jill."

"Do you really want to do that? Let me get to the children? That's what I want, you know."

"What do you mean, sweetheart?"

Seth leaned forward, eyes twinkling with too much animation, something more chaotic and alive than mankind ever had been. "I want to slit their throats and listen to them plead for what miserable lives they will someday lead. I want to bathe in their innocent blood and eat their untainted hearts."

"What..." Jillian backed away from him, sliding against the wall toward the movie room door. It was locked, but if she could get there fast enough, she might be able to get inside.

"I don't want *you*, Jillian. I know the filthy things you've done, the filthy things you think of at night." His voice was grating, too deep now for a child's. When had it changed? Jillian looked at him now, the way his shoulders seemed to roll, his entire presence dynamic in a way that she couldn't fathom.

"Put the scissors down, Seth," she said again, voice calm.

The boy threw the scissors to the ground at her feet, grinning with teeth that had been filed to points, too large for his small mouth.

"I don't need the scissors, Jillian. I will destroy everything you love with my bare hands."

"You don't know anything about me."

She didn't recognize her own voice at first. She would never have argued with a child, but this was no child. There was something unnatural here. She knew, she just *knew*, he had killed both Brenda and Abby. He wanted to kill the children; he wanted to kill her. Jillian didn't have it in her to hurt a child. She couldn't even pull their Band-Aids off, instead leaving it for their parents to suffer through at home later on, but she didn't recognize this as a child at all. It wasn't even human. It was something much, much more.

"I know just who to visit first. Can you guess who? Does the name Clarissa ring a bell? She has daddy issues, just like me. I think we'll get on *so well*."

Her heart lurched, and her hands balled into fists. "If you touch her..."

Seth snarked at her, nose scrunching so much that she thought she saw permanent ridges form along his cheeks and brow. He was morphing into some kind of monster. He turned away from her and began walking toward the front door.

"Stop it! You come back here right now," she yelled, putting on her most sincere and demanding authoritative tone. He didn't hesitate.

Jillian snatched up the scissors. Looking first at the object in her hand before looking back up as Seth continued his trek to the door, leaving filthy footprints on the carpet as he did so. He didn't turn to look at her, and he didn't say anything at all.

"You little son of a bitch!" She snarled, tackling him to the floor. Despite the fact that he was the size of any regular child, he felt like he weighed as much as an adult. She struggled to pin him to the floor, and he flailed his arms at her and growled, clawing at her forearms and tearing at her clothing.

She heard the front door open, but she didn't stop, clasping both hands around the scissors as she raised them above her head, preparing to plunge them into Seth's chest with all of her force.

"Please, Ms. Jill," Seth suddenly said, voice quiet and low.

"Why are you doing this?"

Jillian hesitated, heart twisting itself into knots as she looked down at the little boy. She realized they were both swathed in flashing red and blue lights.

"Drop the weapon!"

She looked at the open door to see police cruisers parked out front and an officer with a gun pointed at her.

"Put the weapon down, ma'am." Another cop entered behind him, the man from earlier. He scrunched his nose. "Do you smell that?"

"Yeah. Gas. Get the kids out of here. Ma'am. Please put the weapon down. Where are the children?"

The familiar cop's brow was furrowed, pleading, "You aren't thinking clearly. You're probably experiencing some toxicity from the gas. That's a little boy. Do you see him? He's just a little boy. Please put the scissors down."

Jillian's mind reeled. Was this all a hallucination? She turned her head slowly to look back down at Seth, and when she locked eyes with him those fearful orbs became glassy and cold. He smiled.

Jillian roared, rearing back again with the scissors.

She didn't feel the taser hit her, but as she fell convulsing to the floor she wished she had been shot instead. Froth poured from her mouth as she tried to tell them that was no little boy. Her face was hot, veins bulging in her temples and her eyes bursting with damaged capillaries as she watched the cop scoop Seth up into his arms and rush him outside.

Over the officer's shoulder, Seth smiled at her with his pointed teeth and waved with just his fingers.

# Three, Two, One...
## Bridgett Nelson

Porter

"Three, two, one. Three, two, one. Three, two, one," Porter recited as he set up his watercolor paints, lined up just as he liked them, in rows of three: ultramarine, cobalt, and cerulean blue; viridian, sap, and emerald green; burnt umber, raw umber, and mars black.

*Three, two, one.*

*Three, two, one.*

*Three, two, one.*

Once they were all in order, he pulled out his pad and a graphite pencil, looked at the blankness of the white page before him—eyes twitching, evaluating the potential of the empty space—and began drawing.

His body rocked back and forth as the pencil flew over the pad with deft strokes. Quiet hums and tiny giggles emanated from his throat. He periodically checked the watercolors to make sure they were still in the proper position.

*Three, two, one.*

*Three, two, one.*

*Three, two, one.*

Feeling at ease, he set the pad down and walked three laps—on his tiptoes—around the rooftop. It was his absolute favorite place. He came up here a lot. His family lived in the tall apartment building: him, his parents, and his little sister.

Oddy.

When he was younger, he'd had trouble saying Audrina's name. Sometimes, he still did. Pronunciation was hard for him, partially because of his tongue-tie and partially because of his neurodivergence.

At least that's what his doctor said, anyway. But Oddy said it didn't matter because he was the coolest guy she knew. She even let him call her Oddy at school, though he'd heard her tell Mom that the other kids made fun of her for it.

Porter excitedly flapped his hands thinking about his sister. He hadn't liked her much when she was born. She made a lot of noise, especially at night, and was pretty smelly. But that was before. Now he loved her. She was the only person who made him feel truly at ease. He hoped she knew how special she was to him, even if he couldn't hug her.

Hugs...hurt.

The doctor called it sensory processing dysfunction. Most things hurt when they touched his body. Sometimes they felt itchy, sometimes they felt like millions of little stabs, and sometimes it felt like his body was one big bruise—but it was always uncomfortable.

It had taken his parents a lot of research and a great deal of expense—Porter knew because he looked at the receipts and kept a running total in his head; someday he'd pay them back— to find clothes he could tolerate: athletic pants and shorts, tagless compression shirts, seam-free socks, and his beloved weighted vest, which was too bulky to wear to school. His class-mates had said some very unkind things the one time he did, but as soon as he got home each day, the first thing he did was put it on. It made him feel calmer. Better able to focus. Less anxious.

Today was Saturday, so he'd had it on since he'd climbed out of bed this morning at precisely six thirty a.m.

"Good morning, Porter-Peanut-Butter! How did you sleep?"

As usual, he'd slept snuggled with one of his stuffed toys—a Dr. Seuss character he'd dubbed "Yellow Guy."

"Good, Mom."

He'd suffered from years of insomnia, and it had affected his health, but the doctor said the melatonin seemed to be helping.

He'd had his usual breakfast—two fried eggs, two sausage patties, and applesauce—the same he'd had every day since he was old enough to eat solid food. Then he'd sat on the edge of the couch cushion and pulled out his handheld Nintendo Switch controller. *Super Mario Bros.* made everything better.

After carefully brushing his teeth, he'd watched *The Day After Tomorrow* for the forty-ninth time. It wasn't a joke; according to the calculations in his head, which were never wrong, he'd actually watched the movie exactly that many times. His second favorite, *Into the Storm*, he'd watched forty-two times.

Physically, he might have been almost fourteen years old, but the doctor said, mentally and emotionally, he hovered around seven or eight.

When the movie finished, he'd gathered his art supplies, as well as Yellow Guy, and headed to the roof.

"Two hours until lunch, Porter!" Mom had called after him. "Set your alarm so you don't forget!"

Porter hated the Apple Watch. It was very uncomfortable on his wrist. But his teachers would send him cues on it, like, "Ask a classmate how he or she is doing today," and Porter would oblige. He also lost track of time a lot, especially when he was painting, so it was useful that way too.

"Okay, I will," he'd yelled, shutting the door firmly behind him and then jiggling the handle to make sure it was locked.

Now, Porter paused his walk around the rooftop as he noticed the sun hiding behind a dark cloud. He frowned. *Is it supposed to rain?* He hoped not, but the day had taken on a decidedly ominous cast. He returned to his drawing and began expertly adding muted colors. Soon, he was totally involved in his art.

A sudden voice from behind him—a voice he'd grown to hate —made him jump.

"Hey, it's the 'tard!"

He whirled to see Roman, accompanied by two other class-mates, all of whom also lived in the building. They strolled confi-dently toward him, leering grins spread across their prepubescent faces.

Roman, whose voice was already undergoing the typical teenage changes, went on. "*'Tard* Boy! Good to see you. We never run into you at school since you're in all the 'tard classes. How ya doing?"

He slapped Porter on the back...hard. Porter fell, scattering his watercolors across the rooftop, as Sammy and Danielle laughed. Tears flooded his eyes.

*Three, two...no. No, no, no.*

Why were they on the rooftop? They never came up here. Nobody did. That's why he loved it so much. He could paint and flap and mutter and walk around with his odd gait and never feel self-conscious.

He bent to pick up his paints, but Roman grabbed a thick swatch of his hair, making him yelp.

"Wait, buddy, not so fast." Roman nodded to his friends, who gleefully stomped on the art supplies with their knockoff Doc Marten boots.

"Don't! Please, don't!" Porter's tongue felt too big for his mouth, and he knew his words came out heavy and slurred. As the paints he'd been using since Christmas—his favorites— became nothing more than smudges of colored dust on the concrete, he couldn't help it... He cried.

"Jesus, dude, what a crybaby," Danielle said, her voice a sneer.

Porter poked a finger at the chalky residue. "No more three, two, one?" he asked pitifully.

"What the hell does that mean?" Sammy asked. Without waiting for an answer, he brought his boot down on Porter's finger.

The bone snapped, pushing a shard through the skin with a spurt of blood. Porter screamed.

Danielle winced, but when she noticed Roman and Sammy laughing, she gave a nervous chuckle. "Damn, dudes, that's seriously fucked up."

"Aw, does da baby's finger have a boo-boo?" Roman pulled Porter to his feet.

Porter whimpered, cupping his injured hand against his chest. They surrounded him, sharks drawn to blood-filled water.

"Why ya gotta be such a doofus?" Roman shoved him against the metal railing.

Porter sobbed, wiping a wet trail of snot across his cheek. He tried to ask why they wanted to hurt him—he was a nice boy!—but he couldn't speak.

"Porter! Mom says it's time for lunch!" Oddy called as she emerged onto the rooftop. "Did you forget to set—?"

She stopped abruptly when she saw the tears and the blood. Completely ignoring the others, she ran to him.

"What happened? Are you okay?" Seeing the bone shard, she gasped and covered her mouth. "Oh my gosh, Porter, you need to go to the hospital! Come on!" She put an arm around him and led him toward the door.

"Uh, not so fast, *Oddball*." Roman stepped in front of them.

"Can't you see he's hurt? Get out of the way!" When she tried to move around Roman, Sammy and Danielle blocked the way. "What is *wrong* with all of you?"

"We know he's hurt," Sammy said. "We hurt him."

Danielle snickered. "You're not much smarter than your idiot brother, are you?"

"'Tard Boy and Oddball," jeered Roman.

"Move or I'll...I'll scream!"

"Oddy, stop," Porter said. It sounded like, *'Aw, op.'* "They'll hurt you." *'Dayurt oo.'*

Sammy towered over Oddy. "Go ahead and scream, little girl." Spittle flew from his lips. "You'll be dead before anyone hears you and decides to check it out." He looked far more menacing than he sounded.

"Oh, come on now, Sammy. You know macho man here won't let anything happen to his baby sis." Roman laughed so loudly, Porter was forced to cover his ears. Blood dripped down the side of his face from his injured hand.

"We could test that theory," Danielle said, eyeing Oddy. "Lift her up!"

At Dani's urging, Roman tucked his hands beneath Oddy's armpits while Sammy grabbed at her ankles.

"What are you doing? Let go of me!" She squirmed in their grip.

Porter squeezed his eyes shut, his hands still firmly blanketing his ears. His nervous system had taken all it could take... Overstimulation made him immobile.

"Get him to stop being a fuckin' idiot and look," Roman said.

Danielle gave Porter an aggressive smack on the back of the head. "Pay attention, dumbass," she said. "Your sister needs you."

His eyes flew open, and his hands dropped to his sides.

"Over here!" Roman called.

He and Sammy were at the edge of the rooftop, dangling Oddy's tiny, struggling body over the railing. Porter could see her panic-stricken eyes.

"Oddy!" *'Aw!'* "Pull her back!" *'Ool ur ack!'*

Porter made to rush to her, but before he could move, Danielle punched him in the gut. He doubled over.

"Say goodbye to your precious Oddball!" Roman taunted.

Sammy suddenly sounded alarmed. "She's wiggling too much, Ro! I'm losing my grip!"

"Shit, don't let her fall!" Danielle cried.

"Hold fucking still, Oddball!" Roman yelled. Droplets of sweat stood on his upper lip.

Porter, understanding they were about to drop her, snatched up Yellow Guy and bolted across the rooftop.

"Oddy, grab him!" *'Aw, bab um!'* he cried, thrusting the stuffed animal toward her.

Yellow Guy would never let anything bad happen!

Oddy frantically grasped the toy. Porter, desperate, helped Roman and Sammy pull her over the railing, back to safety. She sprawled on the rooftop, fighting for breath.

"I'm impressed." Roman looked from Porter to Oddy and back again. "You really showed us, didn't you? Guess your muscles are bigger than your brain."

Sammy snort-laughed but refused to look anyone in the eye.

Porter remained silent, his body still shaking with adrenaline.

"Come on, 'Tard Boy! Don't you have anything to say?"

He lifted his head and looked into Roman's eyes...something he never did with anyone because it was unbearably uncomfortable.

"I did show you, Roman." The words came out nearly perfect. "And it was easy. I may have autism, but at least I'm not a giant, brainless turd."

Roman smirked. "That the best you got?"

Porter paused, then added, "Danielle will never be your girlfriend. I heard she's been kissing Jake Harris behind the school at lunch every day."

Anger flared in Roman's eyes. With a roar, he rushed forward and gave Porter a hard push. Unprepared, Porter was driven backward. His bottom hit the railing as his upper body, unable to find its balance, flipped over, somersaulting into the humid, late spring air.

He fell twelve stories, Yellow Guy still clutched in his thin, reedy arms.

He never made a peep all the way down.

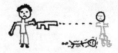

"What..." Audrina sat in stunned shock. "What did you buttholes *do?*"

Ignoring her, cursing at each other, Roman, Sammy, and Danielle ran through the rooftop door and disappeared.

Audrina crawled to the railing and pulled herself upright. As she peered over the edge, all she could do was scream.

And scream.

And scream.

## Life Sucks

*Movement. Lights. Voices. Pain. So much pain. Pain filled his body —pain defined all he was.*

*Liquid.*

*Burning warmth.*

*The pain began to fade. So did the lights...*

*Three...two...one...*

NONSTOP BEEPING MADE PORTER DESPERATELY WANT TO cover his ears, but he couldn't move.

Then he heard sniffles and somebody blowing their nose.

*Ew. Boogers.*

A voice he didn't recognize was speaking from far, far away.

"I won't make any guarantees, and given the severity of the situation, I couldn't even if I wanted to. We did the best we could. It's really as simple as that. The only thing that saved him was landing on the awning before falling to the sidewalk. But even with a softer surface like that, the sudden deceleration from such a height caused a great deal of damage. He has multiple broken bones, as well as a significant amount of internal bleeding. The next seventy-two hours are critical."

The voice continued, but Porter did his best to tune it out.

He was so tired. And the pain was all gone. He just wanted to sleep. That's all. Just sle...

"YOU PROBABLY DON'T HAVE MUCH MEMORY OF BEING IN traction, but when we did surgery, we used a variety of metal screws, wires, rods, and plates to repair the damage to your fractured neck. Now that the breathing tube is out, we can start working on rehabilitation. I'm going to be frank with you, son. It's going to take years and lots of hard work…"

"COME ON, PORTER! YOU CAN DO THIS! I KNOW IT HURTS. I know it's excruciating. But push through it so you can walk again! Three more!"

The physical therapist was really mean. But Porter did as he was told.

*Three, two, one…*

"INTERNALLY, THINGS ARE LOOKING GOOD. HOW THE aorta didn't rupture from the fall, I have no idea, but the heart is pumping beautifully, and the organs are adequately perfused. The internal lacerations and bruising have healed. I don't believe there will be any long-term issues…"

"I'M SORRY TO HAVE TO TELL YOU THIS, BUT THE swelling and pain is caused by a malunion of the fractured ends of your femur, and it's more severe than any I've seen. We need to go in and repair it, I'm afraid, and it's likely to be a painful recovery..."

"WHEN WE TAKE THE BANDAGES OFF, DON'T BE frightened. You're not going to look the same. We had to do extensive work on the skeletal structure of your face. But don't worry. You're going to be quite the handsome fellow..."

"YES, YOU'RE WALKING, PORTER, BUT WITH A WALKER. You're young! You're healthy! You don't need the damn thing. Ignore the aching and throbbing. Let's do this!"

He hated his physical therapist...

"HI, PORTER. MY NAME IS JASON, AND I'M A SPEECH pathologist. While you're healing from your most recent surgery, we're going to focus our attention on your words..."

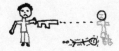

"YOU'VE GROWN A LOT IN THE PAST FEW YEARS, SO WE need to go back in and do some renovation on that spine of yours..."

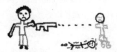

"HI, THERE. MY NAME IS ALI, AND I'M A SENSORY integrative therapist. Your mother hired me to help with your sensory issues..."

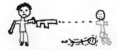

"TODAY IS THE BIG DAY! AS YOU KNOW, WE HAD TO PUT temporary growing rods into your spine, then mechanically lengthen and adjust them as your body became that of a young man. But it's time to take them out and perform a spinal fusion using permanent metal rods. If all goes well, this might very well be your final surgery..."

FIFTEEN YEARS AFTER THE FALL

"Hey, whazzzup, bro?" Sammy pulled Roman in for a hug, then followed up with the inevitable manly back pats.

"Sammy-Whammy! Hey, my man! Life is good... Life is good."

Roman couldn't help but notice Sammy looked pretty rough. His clothes were filthy and frayed, his hair was greasy and aromatic, and he couldn't stop sniffing and wiping his nose.

"Jeez, man. Couldn't even be bothered to put on a clean shirt?" Roman said good-naturedly, but Sammy just shrugged.

"A shirt's a shirt, dude. But hey, great to hear you're doin' well! Hard to believe it's been a decade since we ditched juvie once and for all, eh?" Sammy ran his fingers through his hair, then wiped the residual grease across his pant leg. "Whaddya doing these days?"

Roman straightened the suit jacket he'd found on clearance at Walmart and said, "I'm an entrepreneur. Started my own business." He didn't mention his business was selling drugs from his apartment in the projects. "And I see my daughter every weekend. She's a peach, man. You'd love her."

"Cool, cool," Sammy muttered.

"What about you? Did juvie make an honest man of you?"

"Having a little trouble findin' work, actually." He looked away, face flushed. "The economy, ya know?"

"Oh, sure. I get it. You married?"

"Nah. Never been that stupid." He laughed, and Roman noticed he was missing several teeth. "I'm living with my maw. 'Member her? But I pay rent and stuff. I ain't no freeloader."

"Hey, we all need a little help now and again," Roman replied courteously, with just an edge of haughtiness.

"Well, if it isn't two of the three amigos!" came a feminine voice, followed by a tinkling laugh.

"Dani!" Roman picked her up and spun her around.

He inhaled the familiar coconut scent of her brunette curls and was instantly transported back in time. Although he'd never admit it, he'd been in love with Danielle since elementary school. When he finally set her down, Sammy gave her a quick hug. Her nostrils flared, and a flash of disgust flickered across her face, but she recovered quickly.

"Why don't we find a table and catch up?" she suggested. "Isn't that what a class reunion is for?"

"Indeed," Roman said. "What's your poison? First round is on me." Once they were all seated, their drinks refreshed, he went on. "So, fill us in, Dani. What have we missed?"

"I'm the night shift manager at a local restaurant." The pride in her voice was obvious. "Recently divorced, with six kids...four girls and two boys."

Sammy choked on his whiskey. "You have *six* kids?"

"Yep. How many you got?"

"None."

"That you know of," Dani said.

They paused as a man cleared his throat and motioned to the last vacant chair at their table. "Do you mind if I join you?"

Dani, eyeing the tall, handsome stranger, said, "Not at all. Take a load off."

Roman's fists clenched in annoyance, while Sammy largely ignored the newcomer.

"Did you graduate from Avondale High too?" Dani asked.

"I did." He grinned. "You're Danielle, right?"

"Yep. And you are...?"

"Stellan." He shook Dani's hand. "Stellan Justice."

"I sure as hell don't remember anybody with that name," Roman said.

"I went by SJ back then."

Danielle studied him. "You do look vaguely familiar. Did you play football?"

"Yep. Wide receiver."

"Sure, sure. I remember you." She smiled.

"Great, now that we've all shared kisses and reminisced, why don't we discuss who gets the next round of drinks?" said Sammy.

"It'd be my pleasure," Stellan responded. He looked around. "Or we can ditch this lame excuse for a party and head back to my Airbnb. I've got lots of booze...and a few other choice treats."

Sammy perked up. "Oh, yeah? Like what?"

"What does it matter?" Roman interjected. "We don't even know this guy. Do we really want to go running off with him?"

"Sure we know him! He's SJ the football player!" Danielle lightly rubbed Stellan's arm.

"What treats do you have?" Sammy asked again.

"Blow and *X*."

"Oh, hell yeah. Let's do this!" Sammy was already halfway out of his chair.

"I'm down," Danielle said, winking at Stellan. "You comin', Roman? Or are you gonna be left all by your lonesome?"

Roman's jaw clenched. He looked around the venue and realized he recognized almost no one. The few he did know were stuck-up preps he wanted nothing to do with. "Yeah, I'm in."

"I'll drive," Stellan said. "I rented an SUV. Plenty of room."

"Damn, somebody must have a good job," Danielle said, tucking her arm into his.

"I do all right," he replied but didn't elaborate as he led them to the car.

Once they were all settled, Roman said, "So you must not live in Atlanta anymore."

"Nah. Not even in Georgia."

"How long 'til we get there?" Sammy's whole body was twitching with need.

"Fifteen, maybe twenty minutes."

"If your rental car is this nice, I can't wait to see your home away from home," Danielle said.

"I hope you'll like it." Stellan glanced at her and smiled.

She blushed and lit a cigarette.

"Something tells me this is going to be a night to remember!"

"I think," Stellan said, "that you are very right."


THREE

Sammy opened his eyes and yawned. The room was lit by only a faint red glow. His head was pounding, and his mouth tasted like the ass end of a rotting donkey carcass.

*Damn, that must've been one hell of a class reunion.*

He chuckled and tried to stretch.

Then he tried again.

"What the fuck?" He couldn't move. When he tried, he heard a metallic sound.

*Handcuffs?*

Why would he let somebody handcuff him? Some kinky sex thing? He closed his eyes and tried to recall what had happened.

*Oh yeah, that Stellan guy. Brought us to some gorgeous place in Buckhead. We had drinks, he passed around a bunch of pills, and then he cut lines of coke.*

Try as he might, Sammy couldn't remember anything more after that. He was so damn foggy, all he wanted was to go back to sleep.

He was almost there when he heard a door creak open, followed by quiet footsteps. An eerie blue light clicked on. Sammy saw it came from an X-ray screen mounted to the wall, a full-body X-ray clipped to its surface.

In the scan, he could see handcuffs on the skeleton's wrists and ankles.

*Is that* me*? Am I on an X-ray table?*

A robed figure moved toward him, wearing a weird mask... white, cracked paint with pink cheeks and bloodred lips. Blue tears dripped from haunting batwing-shaped eyes.

Across the chin were the words *to save your life.*

"Hello, Sammy." The voice was distorted. Unidentifiable.

"I ain't sure what the hell is gawn on here, but you needta let me go right fuckin' now."

Laughter.

Loud.

Unkind.

"Oh, Sammy. You always were the least intelligent of your trio."

"Hey, just 'cuz Roman was the leader don't mean—"

The masked figure cut him off. "Don't argue with me,

Sammy. We haven't the time." It moved to the X-ray board and tapped on the illuminated image. "Do you know who this is?"

"I reckon it's me."

"You would reckon correctly. That is your skeletal system all lit up and pretty, the bones perfectly aligned and intact." The mask turned toward him, those haunting pitch-black batwing eyes staring coldly.

Sammy shivered and realized for the first time that he was nude.

"Wouldn't it be terrible if we crushed those bones? Pulverized them, really. Maybe created some compound fractures, where the bones protrude through the skin. Wouldn't that be, like, so cool, Sammy?"

He shook his head frantically. "N-n-no. That don't sound cool at all."

"So it's okay for you to do it to someone else, but it's not cool when it's done to you. Is that what I'm hearing you say, *Sammy-Whammy*?"

"Wha da fuck you talkin' about?"

"Porter Noble."

Although his brain hurt like a motherfucker, he had no trouble remembering that name.

"Aw, c'mon. I was just a kid. And I paid for my crimes."

"Did you? Did you, really?" The masked figure clambered onto the table where Sammy lay sprawled, naked and vulnerable, and stood over him. The robe lifted just enough to showcase a brand-new pair of Doc Martens, heavy with tread.

The heel of one boot came down on his right hand.

Once.

Twice.

Crimson blood spurted.

Screaming, Sammy twisted his head to view the handcuffed, mangled ruin. All four of his fingers were bent the wrong way, and his thumb was hanging by nothing but a thread of skin. Bone protruded, and the intensity of the pain was unlike anything he'd felt before.

His tormentor jumped off the table and strode to another—this one covered in a yellow drape—which the masked figure removed with a flourish. Beneath the shroud was an array of bone-breaking instruments: baseball bat, tire iron, nunchucks, a length of chain, police baton, crowbar, hockey stick, golf club, a wicked-looking hammer, pipe wrench, brass knuckles, sledge-hammer...even a frying pan!

*Oh God. Not good. Not good at all.*

A gloved hand moved indecisively over the weapons, debating...debating. It stopped by the hammer, and Sammy began sobbing.

"Please don't do this to me. I'm poor. Got nuttin'. Can't get laid to save my life. I'm beggin' ya."

Just before the hammer came down on his knee, the distorted voice said, "It's all for Porter."

TWO

*Hush, little baby, don't say a word,*
*Momma's gonna buy you a mockingbird.*

.  .  .

DANIELLE AWOKE SLOWLY, THE STRAINS OF THE OLD lullaby playing softly in the background. *Where am I?* She couldn't really see anything, despite a scatter of little pink and blue nightlights.

She was sitting upright in a chair—a pretty comfy one, actually—and although her feet and hands seemed to be tightly bound to it, she was able to swivel it a full three hundred sixty degrees.

Eh. She wasn't worried. She'd been in much weirder situations before. Being a "paid companion" wasn't always easy, but it kept food in her kids' mouths. And hell...they didn't need to know they all had different fathers. No good could come from it.

*AND IF THAT MOCKINGBIRD WON'T SING,*
  *Momma's gonna buy you a diamond ring.*

A DOOR OPENED. DANIELLE TURNED HER CHAIR TOWARD the noise, her eyes squinting in the dim light.

"Hello, Danielle."

*Is that Stellan? It sure as hell doesn't sound like him—doesn't even sound human.*

"Uh, hello." She cleared her throat. "Who are you?"

"An old friend."

"Okay, old friend, how about you untie me? My hands and feet are numb."

"Hmm. Maybe later. For now, we play a game."

"A game? This headache roaring through my skull says, 'No, thanks.'"

"That headache roaring through your skull has no say in the matter." The speaker moved closer, and Danielle could see the faint outline of a robe and some sort of white mask.

"The fuck is this? We starrin' in *The Purge*?"

"Nope."

"Aw. Darn. That coulda been fun." Danielle kept rotating her chair to follow the figure. "You a man or woman?"

"Does it matter?"

"Gotcha. You're non-binary."

"Sure. That's what I am."

"Yeah, yeah. Whatever. Can we move this along? I'd like to find a bed somewhere and sleep this headache off."

*AND IF THAT DIAMOND RING TURNS TO BRASS,*
*Momma's gonna buy you a looking glass.*

"YOU'RE A HOOKER, IS THAT CORRECT, DANIELLE?"

"No, I work at a restaurant."

"Oh, come on. Are you really sticking with that story?"

Danielle's lower lip protruded. "Fine, but I prefer the term *escort*."

"And you have six children?"

"Yeah."

A long pause. "*These* six children?"

Large spotlighted art canvases lined the walls, displaying

pictures of each of her kids. Watercolor portraits. Her respirations increased, and her skin felt clammy. Actual paintings? Why the hell would someone commission paintings of her children? What kind of rich psychopath was she dealing with?

"Who the hell do you think you are? We don't bring my kids into whatever the fuck this is. Nuh-uh. No way. No how."

*AND IF THAT LOOKING GLASS GETS BROKE,*
*Momma's gonna buy you a billy goat.*

"WE DO WHAT I SAY, DANIELLE. YOU'RE NOT EXACTLY IN a position to be negotiating."

The figure moved closer. She could now see the mask in all its glory. It was white, with three large, black, vacant circles painted for both eyes and the mouth. A faint blue-gray sheen surrounded each circle, giving the mask an alienesque appearance. Written across the forehead were the words *too late.*

"Interesting look, weirdo."

"Thanks. I quite like it. Now let's get started. Here are the rules. We're going to see how good of a mother you are, Danielle. I'm going to ask you one simple question about each of your children. If you answer correctly, your child will be put back to bed, safe and warm and well cared-for. If you answer incorrectly, I will break one of your bones, and your child will be dangled off the roof of your eight-story building. Got it?"

"Sure, sure. I totally believe you. I have a babysitter and a shit-ton of locks. Try again, freak."

The figure pulled out a remote and pushed a button. A television screen pulsed to life, momentarily blinding Danielle with its sudden light. On it, she saw her six children huddled together on a rooftop, surrounded by men with guns.

"Jesus Christ, what is this? You can't hurt my kids! They haven't done anything!"

*AND IF THAT BILLY GOAT WON'T PULL,*
    *Momma's gonna buy you a cart and bull.*

IGNORING HER PROTESTS, THE FIGURE BEGAN. "ONE: Your oldest child, Miley, is nine years old. Nearly the same age as Audrina Noble when your friends dangled her over the side of the apartment building. Tell me Miley's favorite food and color."

"Audrina? Is *that* what this is about? That's bullshit, we didn't do anything wro—"

"You have five seconds to answer."

"Fine. Easy peasy. Her favorite food is pizza, and her favorite color is pink."

*AND IF THAT CART AND BULL TURN OVER,*
    *Momma's gonna buy you a dog named Rover.*

"EXCELLENT."

On the television, one of the men led Miley from the rooftop.

"Two: Your next child, Peter, is an eight-year-old boy. You named him that because you were high as a kite when he was born. When you saw his penis, you charmingly said, 'Might as well name him Peter... Isn't that what all boys think with?'"

Danielle stared at the floor.

"What does Peter pray for each night when he says his bedtime prayers?"

She said nothing.

"Five seconds, Danielle."

Just kept staring at the floor.

"Three. Two."

"He prays for a daddy, okay?" Danielle's voice broke.


*AND IF THAT DOG NAMED ROVER WON'T BARK,*
*Momma's gonna buy you a horse and cart.*


"THAT'S CORRECT! WOW, WELL DONE! I DIDN'T THINK there was a chance in hell you listened to your kids' prayers. What a pleasant surprise."

On the screen, Peter was led away.

"Let's keep trucking along. Three: Your third child is also a boy. Seven years old. Named Leo, after your favorite actor. Tell me, what will Leo be asking Santa for this year?"

Danielle's body tensed. "But it's only May! He hasn't even talked about it yet!"

"Answer the question."

"This isn't fair!

"Five seconds."

"How could I know that so early in the year?!"

"Three seconds."

"Shit. He wants...a Nintendo Switch!"

*AND IF THAT HORSE AND CART FALL DOWN,*
*You'll still be the sweetest little baby in town!*

"A reasonable guess. Let's see what Leo said."

The screen switched to a video clip showing Leo's tear-streaked face. In the background, a voice asked him what he wanted Santa to bring. His big, brown eyes brightened, and he said, "I'm asking Santa for a mommy who really loves me!"

The image changed again to a live shot of a muscular man holding Leo over the edge of the building. Danielle cursed and screamed, until she realized Leo was securely fastened and couldn't actually fall.

But poor little Leo didn't realize that. The raw terror on his face was heartbreaking, as were the tears pouring down his chubby cheeks. Danielle felt her snarky exterior crumble. She wept.

"Make it stop. Please. He doesn't deserve that. He's just a little boy."

After several unbearable seconds, Leo was finally pulled to safety and led away.

"I'm sorry, but you answered incorrectly." The masked figure moved toward Danielle, holding a tire iron. "I've wanted to do this for a long time, you evil bitch."

It happened so fast Danielle didn't have time to respond. The tire iron smashed into her shoulder, breaking and dislocating it, leaving her arm dangling uselessly in its socket, with part of her clavicle poking through her skin. A trail of gore trickled down her chest and into her substantial cleavage.

"Please, have mercy." Her breaths came in rapid gasps as her eyes rolled in pain.


*SO, HUSH, LITTLE BABY, DON'T YOU CRY, CUZ*
   *Daddy loves you and so do I.*


BEFORE SHE COULD PASS OUT, A HARSH WHIFF OF smelling salts brought her around, sputtering and coughing.

"Oh, not yet," said the voice. "There are still three more children awaiting their fates, after all. One, two, three...three, two, one."


ONE

*What is this, some sort of tube?*

Roman awoke lying flat on his back, encased in something tall and cylindrical and clear and filled with blindingly bright light. It rose above him to a height of at least two hundred feet. Everything outside the tube was cloaked in darkness.

His brain was having a hard time processing anything, and his pounding headache didn't help.

Somewhere beneath him, the low rumble of a motor kicked on. A mild breeze wafted up through a grate beneath him. It felt pleasant against his sweat-soaked skin. He lay there, eyes closed, unmoving, as the faint vibrations from the chugging motor massaged his aching body, and the quaint breeze cooled and relaxed him.

The next thing he knew, he was flipped upside down and spinning through the air. His body slammed into the side of the tube, his wrist shattering from the impact. He knew he was screaming, but giant gusts of wind had replaced the gentle breeze. The roar was deafening.

He kept his eyes closed and tried to relax into the buffeting air currents tossing him violently about. Unfortunately, that didn't work; his face met the tube next, busting his nose and fracturing his eye socket. Blood splashed the clear plexiglass.

*What the fuck is happening?*

Tears poured from his eyes but dried instantly in the relentless gale. He screamed again, screamed for help, but knew it was a lost cause. The forceful wind carried him higher and higher. Another crash into the wall shattered his knee.

Then he heard a voice, somehow louder than the wind and the motor creating it.

"Hello, Roman. Wave if you can hear me."

His body hurt so aggressively that it was hard to think, but he flapped the hand with the still-functioning wrist.

"Perfect!"

As he continued to be blown chaotically around the tube,

exterior lights came on, illuminating a chamber beyond and revealing he was several stories off the ground.

Terror seized him, and it took a moment for him to spot the mask-wearing figure below. He could only catch brief glimpses as his body twisted and turned, but the mask looked like the one from *V for Vendetta*—the cheekbones rouged red and squeezed high by an eerie, almost psychotic-looking grin, the infamous black mustache and goatee painted precisely.

Whatever it was, it didn't bode well.

He hit the wall feetfirst and felt several toes snap.

"Help me! Please! I'll do anything!" he howled, unable to bear the pain coursing through his body with every heartbeat.

"I don't think you're done quite yet, Roman. Let me just crank the air up a bit more. It's important you know what Porter Noble experienced when you shoved him off the roof."

*Porter? That's what this is about? The kid hadn't even died!*

The wind increased, the sound deafening. It was impossible to breathe. His body was hurled and tumbled more violently than ever. He felt more bones breaking—a shoulder blade, a humerus, his tailbone pulverized.

Roman was almost unconscious when the motor shut down, and his broken form plummeted two hundred feet.


## ALL'S RIGHT WITH THE WORLD

"Roman! Come on, wake up!" a voice whispered urgently into his ear. "We need to get out of here! Now!"

He opened his eyes and saw Dani—his angel—leaning over him.

Had he died?

Was this heaven?

He tried to smile, but the pain in his body decided to come alive at that very moment. Sizzling white bolts of heat tore through his core. He couldn't help it; embarrassing or not, he screamed.

"Jesus Christ, Dani, shut him up!" Sammy said. "We're still alive, somehow. Let's stay that way, yeah?"

"Come on, baby. Hush, hush." Dani ran her fingers through his hair. "That's right, Roman. I need you to roll over. Can you do that for me?"

He did, with no idea where they were, how he'd gotten out of the tube, or how he'd survived the fall. Dani next coaxed him as close to upright as he could manage. It was a slow, excruciating process, but bleeding and broken, they limped and hobbled across a shadowed room, arms supportively wrapped around each other as they headed for a door.

"Ah-ah-ah...and where do my little miscreants think they're going?"

They froze simultaneously. Not a word was spoken.

"I'll ask again. Where do you think you're going?" The masked figure stepped through the door.

Now close enough to see more clearly, Roman could read the word *Never* written in a flowing, carefree script above the mask's painted eyebrows.

"Where do you think?" he gasped. "The fuckin' hospital."

"Remember when Porter needed a hospital, and you wouldn't let him go?"

"Knock it off!" Dani spat. "You're obviously Porter. Who else would want this much revenge?"

"My nose was itching," came a cheerful voice from behind them. "Talking about me? Which one of you fine, upstanding human beings said my name?" Another figure, unmasked and familiar, strolled into view.

"Stellan?" Dani gasped. "*You're* Porter?"

He nodded.

"But...your face...?"

"I had *a lot* of reconstructive surgery," he said. "Sorry for fibbing at the class reunion."

"Wait, wait," Sammy said. "If'n you're Porter, then who the hell...?"

They all turned to look at the masked figure.

"Go ahead," Porter encouraged. "It's fine."

A gloved hand lifted off the *V for Vendetta* mask. Even tousle-haired and sweaty, everyone recognized the face beneath.

"Oddball?" Roman blurted, then caught himself. "I mean, Audrina? *You* did all this?"

"Well, I'm the one who funded it," said Porter. "I've done quite well for myself; that part wasn't a fib. But I don't have the taste for revenge that Oddy here does. At least, not the physical kind. She planned and implemented everything." He gazed fondly at her. "You three pissed off the *wrong* girl."

"He's right," said Audrina. "You did. And if you start thinking that maybe you'll go to the cops, remember this... I know *every* detail of your pasts. *Every sordid detail.* Criminal histories and all. Enough to put you away for the rest of this lifetime and the next." She stared coldly at their battered faces. "Get me?"

There were shaky nods from all three.

"Such smart friends we have, Porter. Don't you agree?"

"Oh, certainly. Smart, indeed." He pulled out a phone. "Now, if we're done here, I'll have the car brought around. Time to get back to work. That next *Super Mario* game isn't going to write itself."

Audrina laughed as they headed for the exit.

Then Porter stopped mid-stride and turned around.

"Want to know what *my* revenge is?" He smiled sweetly. "Living well. While you go back to your shitty lives, I'll be living my best one. I'm happy. Successful. Can you say the same thing?"

None of them met his eyes.

He smiled. "It's not too late, though. Not for any of you. Oh, before I forget, we left each of you a little something—a memento of your time here. You'll find them on the counter on your way out."

ON THE COUNTER BY THE EXIT SAT THREE PRETTILY wrapped gift boxes. Inside each was a yellow stuffed animal, brand new and identical to the one Porter had held on the rooftop so long ago. Notes reading *Pull the string!* were taped to their chests.

None of them wanted to, scared they might be booby-trapped, but Roman finally relented.

In Porter's recorded voice, the plush toy said, *"Never too late to save your life."*

## AUTHOR'S NOTE

As many of you probably know, my son, Parker, is on the autism spectrum. He was diagnosed in 2005, just shy of three years old. He'll be twenty-two on his next birthday. The teenage version of Porter is based almost entirely on my Parker, and I'll be frank... writing this story was damn hard. But an anthology titled *Evil Little Fucks* needs a ray of sunshine and hope...a sweet, lovable character to get behind. I hope you'll agree that's what Parker/Porter is—a happy, giggly, carefree ray of sunshine who loves *Super Mario Bros.* and his sister more than anything.

Be kind, and love each other.

Don't make Parker give you the loser sign.

# THE CRAB APPLE GAME

## CANDACE NOLA

T*HWACK!*

Ginny giggled as the crab apple splattered against the side of the old barn. Her brothers, Tommy and Jeff, guffawed as they slid more rotten apples onto their spiked branches and got ready to launch them.

"Nice one, Ginny!" Tommy said. "But watch this!"

Tommy took a couple of steps back, raised his branch like a baseball player getting ready to take aim, eyed the barn through narrowed eyes, and then whipped the apple-laden stick forward as hard as he could. The crab apple soared through the field and smashed to pieces against the weathered planks of the barn.

Jeff and Ginny cheered and then both stepped up to launch their apples, still giggling as bits of Tommy's apple slid down the side and fell into the cluster of dead weeds and wildflowers that grew along the base of the barn. The twins let their apples fly as Tommy watched, cheering them on.

Only Ginny's apple hit the faded red bullseye that Tommy had spray-painted on the old structure the previous fall. Jeff scowled at first, then laughed it off. His apple had come close to the target, thudding against the ancient wood just inches from the outer red ring. They turned to watch Tommy take aim with his next one. Ginny held her breath as Tommy lined up his shot.

A bunny poked its head up moments before Tommy sent his apple flying into the air. Jeff gasped. Tommy watched curiously. The apple went wild, knocking the bunny sideways into the tree, dazing it. Tommy let out a belly laugh as the stunned creature twitched for a moment before bounding away in a panic. Ginny stared after it, fascinated, then she shrugged and giggled.

"Man, did you guys see that?" Tommy crowed. "Got him right between the ears!"

"Bet you can't do that again," Ginny teased him. Her eyes glinted in the sun as she watched the bunny, still hopping in circles a few yards away. It looked like it was still dazed. She pointed when Tommy looked at her.

"It's still there. See?" she told her brother, pointing out the furry brown creature.

"I bet I can do it again," Tommy said. "Just watch."

He stepped away from his siblings, scrounging beneath the tree for another apple. He tested a few of them before he grinned, finding a perfect one. Not too rotten, solid enough to sting, ripe enough for his branch to impale it. He straightened and showed the twins.

"I bet I can knock it out with this one."

"Aww, man. Leave the bunny alone," Jeff said, his voice taking on a whiny quality that Ginny despised. He always sounded like he was one sneeze away from a head cold. When he whined, it only made it worse.

"It's just a dumb bunny," Tommy sneered. "What do you care?"

"I mean, I don't care, not really. Just don't think we should hurt it, that's all." Jeff shuffled away a few paces, drawing lines in the dirt with the scuffed toe of his sneaker. "It's just a little bunny."

"You're such a wuss," Ginny said. "It's a rotten apple. It won't kill it. Just knock it over like last time."

Tommy shook his head at Jeff and stuck the branch through the apple. It made a wet, crunching sound as the core was pierced. Juice ran down the branch, dribbling onto Tommy's already sticky fingers. Ginny sidled a bit closer to the bunny, careful not to spook it.

She wanted to see what would happen, if anything happened. Hitting the barn was fun for a bit, good target practice, but seeing the bunny go flying when Tommy's apple struck it had sparked something in her gut. Adrenaline rush, she guessed, musing it over in her head. That's what her dad had called it. Same feeling she got when she rode her bike down the hill to the dairy farm. Wind in her hair, her arms held out to the sides, letting the bike coast as it flew down the hill to certain death.

Of course, she always stopped right at the driveway at the base of the hill, standing hard on the brake, skidding into the turn and kicking up dust and gravel. There was nothing like that feeling, that heady rush of being out of control, leaving it all up to fate. Her twin thought she was crazy, but Tommy loved it as much as she did. The two of them often had to wait for Jeff to bike slowly down the hill, riding the brake while they jeered him on, laughing at his fear.

Ginny watched Tommy get ready to launch the apple. She crouched down, feeling the weeds brush the backs of her legs. She locked on to the rabbit, which was nibbling on fallen apples ten feet from her. Jeff inhaled behind her as the *THWAAPP* of Tommy's branch whipping forward broke the silence. Seconds later, the bunny fell over. Ginny cheered. Tommy snickered.

She rose and walked over to it, waiting for it to move or twitch. Ginny bent down, hearing her brothers approach like bulls in a china shop. As much noise as they made, it was surprising the rabbit had even come near them. The summer had been hot and dry. The field across from their house was a barren wasteland of cracked ground, dead grass, and prickly berry bushes with no fruit to show. The apples were probably the only source of food for the rodents around here.

Her brothers stood behind her, watching as she poked it with her stick. Her lips turned upward a bit as she did so, jabbing the animal a little harder. Nothing. No twitch. No movement. She tried again.

"Is it dead?" Jeff asked.

"Nah, can't be," Tommy said. "Probably just stunned like last time."

"I don't think so. It's not moving at all." Ginny jabbed it again. "Pretty sure it's dead."

"Come on, you guys. Let's go home. I'm bored," Jeff said, whining again. He didn't like the look on Ginny's face. Her eyes looked dark in the afternoon sun, and she was staring at the bunny with an odd expression. Tommy poked the animal with his stick, then shrugged, looking at the twins.

"Yeah. I think it's dead too. Oh well. Let's go down to the creek. We can catch crayfish there." Tommy dropped his stick and wiped his hands on his shorts. "Think we used all the apples we could anyway, at least until the rest drop."

The boys turned to leave as Ginny was still crouched over the bunny, staring at the dribble of blood oozing from one ear. Neither of them saw her stand up and quickly ram her sharpened branch into the bunny's neck. Blood spurted from the wound as she watched. She yanked the stick out and did it again, making a second hole. She waited for another minute, watching as the bright red mixed with the dirt, then she dropped the stick and followed her brothers, grinning to herself the entire time.

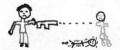

THEY SPENT THE AFTERNOON SLOSHING THROUGH THE shallow creek near the dairy, using discarded tin cans to scoop out crayfish. Jeff didn't like it much, afraid of the pincers. Tommy liked to catch several at once, then set them free to see which one was the fastest to disappear back into the muddy gunk beneath the slime-coated rocks. Ginny loved hunting for the tiny lobster-like creatures. She loved the feel of the cool mud on her hands. The sloshing of dank water in her shoes as she searched. It was sport to her, a hunter and its prey.

Ginny skipped the cans, preferring to snatch them from the water like a hawk snatches a mouse from the field. Then the real fun began. Ginny would go a few feet from her brothers, feigning a new search. When she was sure they weren't watching her, she would pull their claws from their bodies, loving how they would thrash and flail between her fingers. She would giggle at the sight.

When they had been declawed, she would set them down on a rock, find another rock that fit neatly into her palm, and then crush them like cockroaches. Their innards would squirt out between the rocks, making a rusty watery puddle of goo, nothing but bits of shell and vertebrae left. Ginny would crouch over the mess, grinding one rock against the other, until she could no longer hear the crunching sound of shell and thorax. Then she would wipe the whole mess into the stream and go in search of more crayfish to slaughter.

Tommy had caught her doing it once and just stared at her. She shrugged it off.

"It bit me," she said by way of explanation. Tommy had snorted.

"Guess you showed him, huh?" he said and walked away in search of more, shaking his head.

Unbeknownst to Ginny, Tommy was watching her right then from upstream. Jeff was perched on a big rock in the middle of the stream, just swinging his feet with his back turned to his siblings. He'd rather be home reading a book, but his twin was there, downstream, pulverizing crayfish. Tommy shrugged, knowing what she was doing but not caring. It wasn't the first time he had witnessed her murdering the tiny creatures. It was hot. They were bored. And he had been the one to show her how to do it in the first place. Who was he to judge her for doing it now?

Ginny was odd, but he loved it. She was as twisted as he was, maybe a bit more. She was certainly more fun than Jeff had ever been. Ginny would jump off bridges with him, race downhill on their Schwinns, and she was a better crab apple launcher than he had ever been. She had no fear, and a little pain never seemed to bother her either. He saw her wreck her bike more times than he could count and get right back on with a busted lip and bloody knees. It was like life itself had issued a silent challenge to her, and she was determined to win.

Jeff, on the other hand, was weak and often sickly. He was bullied a lot by kids at school and by him and Ginny, but they didn't stand for other kids picking on Jeff. He was their brother and theirs to bully, no one else's. Ginny and Tommy made sure that everyone knew it.

Ginny was popular, but she was also feared at school. Sixth grade had been interesting as Ginny and Jeff joined him in the middle school building, and by midyear, Ginny had quite the reputation of not being one to mess with. She was fiercely protective of her twin, and by the end of the first quarter, everyone knew Jeff was off-limits, teachers included. She had an angelic face and a sweet disposition that the teachers loved, but cross her and the devil himself made an appearance in those light hazel eyes. Tommy had found himself flinching from her wrath on more than occasion, albeit deservedly so, but still, Ginny was his favorite of the twins.

He left her to her hunting and went to bother Jeff, taking joy in getting his little brother soaking wet in the cold stream. They splashed and roughhoused while Ginny silently pulverized a dozen tiny creatures on the rocks. The trio didn't start for home until the fingers of the sun grew skeletal between the trees and the shrill whistle of their father reached their ears, letting them know they had fifteen minutes to reach the house.

THE FOLLOWING WEEKEND, GINNY WAS OFF ON HER OWN, wandering through the woods along their normal trail. They used it a lot to go on their adventures. When she came to the fork in it, she paused, lips pursed and eyebrows furrowed in thought. She tapped her branch on her shoulder and patted the crab apples in her pocket, then smiled. She chose her path and skipped on ahead, happy that she was alone for the day. It wasn't quite noon yet, but the sun was already high and bright over-head as she followed the path from the woods into the open fields.

Ginny squinted as her eyes adjusted to the brightness of the open landscape. She could see the tree line just over the rise on the other side, and beyond that, she knew the old train trestle still stood high over the roadway beneath. She reached for the rainbow-colored backpack on her shoulder and grabbed a water bottle from the side pocket. Ginny let the cool water slide down her throat, glad she thought to bring it. She trudged along, humming a random song she had stuck in her head.

She didn't mind Tommy coming along with her, but Jeff was a burden more often than not. Always whining, always afraid.

She was appalled that someone like him was her twin, albeit in looks only. Jeff was a timid little shit, scared of his own shadow. Ginny lived for the rush. She loved not knowing what might happen if she did something a little risky, a little bit frowned upon. Today, that was exactly what she had in mind.

She had gotten bored with the bullseye on the barn. She wanted a new target, and Ginny had an idea. She grinned as she disappeared into the trees, grateful for the shade once more. Ginny swung her branch around as she walked, smacking it off trees and bushes, pretending to beat off bad guys as she did.

"*THWACK!* Take that!" she yelled, hitting another sapling. "And that!" She thrashed another bush, and bright red berries scattered to the ground, bursting beneath her sneakers, splattering like bloodstains.

She laughed as she went along, content with life, warm under the sunshine-soaked trees, enjoying her new game and anxiously anticipating the one to come.

GINNY REACHED THE CLEARING AND TURNED RIGHT onto the old gravel road that would take her to the trestle. She grabbed her water bottle and took another drink, kicking rocks along as she went. Dust covered her faded tennis shoes, and thorns from bramble bushes stuck to her laces. Sweat plastered her hair to her forehead and droplets ran down her spine. Her yellow T-shirt was almost soaked under her arms from the heat, but she didn't care.

A little sweat didn't bother her. It meant her body was working properly, and she was exercising it. Exercise was good for the mind and body, as her father liked to say. That man was a health nut and ran five miles a day to prove it, not to mention the hour of weight training every morning. Her dad spent his life moving, it seemed to her. Always something to build or fix or do, some place to go, a new adventure waited. She supposed she got her love of excitement from him, not to mention her strength. She could bench press more weight than the guys in her class, and her arms and legs were lean and toned from running and lifting.

She grinned when a chipmunk darted into her path, and she launched a large chunk of gravel right for it, giggling as the sudden motion startled it away. It vanished into the brush, and Ginny kicked up another dust storm of dirt and rock in the direction it went. She chuckled and continued on her way, seeing the trestle just ahead. When she reached the tracks, she set her bag down against a tall oak and took the apples from the inside pocket, adding those to the ones already in her jacket pockets.

When she had them all, she grabbed her branch, checked the tip to make sure it was still sharp enough to impale the half-rotted fruit, then began to walk out onto the boards between the tracks. Sunlight glittered off the rusted steel beams that ran along the trestle. The boards were weathered and cracked, some missing chunks that had dropped to the road below. Ginny wasn't bothered by the gaps in the boards. They'd been here before, many times over the years. She could probably walk it blindfolded.

When she reached the halfway point, she stepped over the track, staring at the roadway below. It wasn't a busy road but still saw a few dozen cars a day. Seeing as it was near lunchtime now, she didn't expect to see many cars. She turned toward the other side, peering down the shimmering stretch of asphalt. Nothing appeared in the distance. She shrugged and grabbed an apple from her pocket, sliding it onto the branch. Juice dribbled from the puncture and ran down the wood onto her fingers.

Ginny adjusted her grip, stepped back over the track onto the middle board, and took her stance. A mix between a baseball player about to bat and a fisherman about to cast. She closed her eyes for a moment, listening for any sound of traffic below. No sound came. She exhaled, gripped the stick, and launched.

*THWACK!* The apple left the branch and soared into the air. A perfect arc flung it high over the railing of the bridge and dropped it neatly into a spiraling descent toward the road below. Ginny watched it go. Her eyes were locked on the descending fruit like a golfer might watch his ball soaring over the next green. Ginny grinned as the apple splattered onto the road below, just a few feet shy of the yellow line.

She shouted with glee as she threaded another apple and got ready to launch again.

*THWACK! THWACK!* Ginny let two more soar, whipping the branch as hard as she could, then leaning over the rail to watch them strike down and splat far below. A glint of chrome in the distance caught her eye, and she grinned. Quickly, she got an apple ready and got into position. She stepped back a few steps, placing her body slightly between the posts on the bridge. The vehicle drew closer to the bridge, an old pickup truck toddling along at a medium speed. She began counting, waiting for its approach.

"One. Two. Three. Four." She got ready, raising her arm, shifted her stance. "Five," she whispered and whipped the branch forward. She dropped to her knees and shimmied ahead, peering between the boards. As the vehicle passed beneath the bridge, she stuck her lip out in a pout. The apple splattered just behind it, right where it had been only seconds before.

"Damn it," she said. Ginny pushed herself up and brushed off her knees. She grabbed her branch and a fresh apple and got ready once more. This time, she waited and watched. If one vehicle came by, surely there would be another. She checked her watch, just a few minutes after noon. Ginny pursed her lips and began to whistle, trying to mimic the piercing sound her father was able to make. She shouldered the branch like a rifle and marched back and forth on the old boards, whistling and waiting.

On her tenth march across the boards, she saw another shimmer in the distance, approaching fast from the opposite side of the first. She smiled, trudged to her spot in the middle, and readied her apple. This time, she kept her eyes locked on the target. Seconds before it reached the sweet spot, she let it fly and ducked down.

A dull splat met her ears as the apple hit its mark, smack dab in the middle of the windshield. She watched wide-eyed as the van swerved to one side, then the other. The rear end fishtailed as the driver stomped on the brakes. Black marks appeared on the asphalt as the van skidded into the ditch. The horn blared. The lights flashed. Ginny cackled softly and kept watch. Minutes passed as smoke poured from under the hood of the van. Finally, the door opened, and a woman stumbled out, clutching her head.

Ginny gasped, a low giggle in her throat. Bright crimson poured from beneath the woman's hand and soaked her shirt. She watched her stagger to the hood to try to lift it, but it had buckled when it slammed into the ditch. Ginny snorted as the woman tried again with both hands. Blood ran freely down her face and into her eyes. She cussed and wiped at it, trying to clear her vision.

Ginny watched from her perch, keeping hidden on the boards. Her eyes shone with mirth and her whole body shook with laughter. She had nailed her good. The women below looked around, up and down the empty road, then overhead at the trestle. Ginny held her breath, knowing she couldn't be seen, but her stomach clenched anyway. She watched the woman stagger back to the open van door and reach inside.

When she stepped back, she had a massive shoulder bag that she began to rummage through. Ginny assumed she was searching for her phone. She sighed, bored now. The woman would call for help, and that would be that. Ginny knew she wouldn't get another chance until the road was clear once more.

She rose quietly and began to pad softly across the weathered wood. She was so high up that it seemed silly to be so cautious, but she was far from stupid. She knew the trouble she would get into and had no desire for her fun and games to stop so suddenly. She grinned as she picked up her bag and vanished into the trees, already planning the next weekend.

THE NEXT FOUR WEEKS PASSED IN A BLUR OF EXCITEMENT for Ginny. She had excelled at slipping away from home unnoticed after her chores were done. Tommy and Jeff had started asking questions, Jeff more so because he felt like Ginny belonged to him, was supposed to do everything with him. Being a twin was a pain in the ass. Ginny hated it more every day. Tommy asked a few times where she kept disappearing to, but she was able to throw him off track with stories about going to Lara's house or to the library. Neither were things Tommy nor Jeff wanted to do.

The trestle had become her secret spot. Ginny had amassed several dozen apples that were waiting for her in a rusty pail. A large pile of rocks sat beside it as she found that she was pretty good at dropping the stones from between the boards and watching the cars and trucks swerve and wreck trying to dodge whatever was being thrown at them. She had taken out three pickup trucks, two more vans, a big moving truck, and an empty school bus.

No dead bodies but plenty of dented hoods, flat tires, and hopping-mad drivers. Watching their reaction was the best part. They would stagger around, clutching heads, arms, or shoulders, bleeding from shallow injuries. Dazed expressions, angry curse words, the customary walk around their vehicle to see the damage and the cause. The bewildered ranting as they found nothing but splattered apples on the pavement or a random rock.

There was never anything more to find, and no one had ever spotted her.

Ginny was eager for blood, though. She wanted to see one really bad accident. She wanted to see a person come through the windshield or fall from the open door of their wrecked car, dead and bloody. She wanted to scramble down the embankment and get close enough to touch them. To stick her fingers in their blood, stare into empty eyes, poke and prod their dead flesh.

She wanted to experience that rush. That ultimate high of knowing you held their life in your hands, that you could call for help or put pressure on their wounds, knowing you could help, but would not. Ginny wanted to see the hope fade from their eyes as they realized that help was not coming. She wanted to smile at them as they finally understood that Ginny was not their savior, but their executioner. She wanted to watch as they breathed their last breath and died in a heap on the pavement. Killed by crab apples and a little girl.

She grinned as she imagined the scene playing out in her head. Giggled out loud as she loaded her pockets with apples and palm-sized rocks, then set out across the bridge. Ginny had discovered two weeks ago that Sunday was a much better day for the Crab Apple Game as the nearby folks would be traveling to and from the local churches. Traffic was never busy, and Ginny always had at least a half dozen cars to choose from before and after church hours.

She knelt down and made a pile of her projectiles against the steel beam of the old railroad track, then set her knife down alongside it. The knife had once been her father's, but he had given it to her last fall during a hunting trip. It was nicely balanced, fit her hand perfectly, and sported a razor-sharp blade. She loved the smoothness of the handle, the faded bloodstains that were sunk deep into the golden hue of the hilt. It made her feel like the blade had drunk the blood, taken it into itself as life left the eyes of the creature it penetrated. Ginny felt invincible with it, powerful even, and she was, after all, hunting, wasn't she?

With her armory settled within reach, she reached into her bag for one more thing: lunch. She had come prepared for the day. She sat cross-legged on the rough beams, settling back against the raised steel of the train track. Eagerly she dug into her bag and pulled out a wax paper–wrapped sandwich of turkey and Swiss. She reached back in and pulled more tasty treats from the bag, adding a bag of carrot sticks, two of her mother's home-made sugar cookies, and a juice box to the pile beside her. Her final item was a set of paper towels folded into squares.

She took half of these out, replaced the rest, then unfolded one towel to set her sandwich and carrot sticks on. She opened her juice and set that in its proper place, top left corner, and added the cookies to the top right corner. Her sandwich and carrot sticks were in the bottom left and right corners, respec-tively. She smiled, straightened the meal to its proper angles to each other, and began to eat. Ginny went through this ritual at every mealtime. Food could not touch each other, and each item had to be set in a square corner before she could begin.

Her brother teased her, and her parents patiently indulged her, most of the time; when they didn't, Ginny simply didn't eat. Problem solved. Her parents thought it was a phase, said she was being stubborn. They just didn't get it. She knew it was odd, but it was a *need* for her, not a phase. Simply how she *needed* it to be. There was no other way. She started to eat, in order of the square, as normal: sandwich bite, carrot stick, cookie bite, juice.

Ginny smiled as she chewed, content, warm and happy. Anticipation kept her company on the high trestle, along with a couple of crows that were waiting for leftover crumbs. She checked her watch when she finished her meal. Nodded to herself. She picked up her rubbish, put it in the extra bag she had brought with her, and tucked it into her backpack once more.

She stood, wiped her hands on her pants, dusted her bum, and picked up her branch. It was time for the church folk to return to their homes. She was sure to have a ripe crop of moving targets for the next thirty minutes. Ginny selected an apple, impaled it with a juicy squelch, then put two more in her pockets. She stepped a few feet over to her launch position, slightly behind one of the support beams of the trestle. It gave a clear space for her projectiles to soar through but kept her body hidden from eyes below, if anyone thought to look up.

She stood patiently, watching both sides. Her body turned so she could easily pivot into her launch stance. She didn't need to wait long. A shimmer in the distance caught her eye, and she giggled.

"Here we go..." she muttered to herself with a voice breathy with excitement. She felt her stomach muscles clench and her heart beat a little faster in her chest. Her eyes shone with glee as she watched the car approach. After taking one more glance in the opposite direction, she got in her stance.

The car neared her kill zone. Her eyes narrowed. She

dropped her leg back, raising the branch, and began shifting on the balls of her feet. A batter ready to swing. She began her count.

"One. Two. Three." She took aim. "Four. Five. Six. Seven."

The car was almost there, a minute away from the red *X* she had spray-painted on the road the week before. Her grin almost split her face in two. She swung. The branch whipped. The apple soared. Quickly, she grabbed one more, threaded it, whipped it, crouched, grabbed a hefty rock, spun around as she rose up, and tossed it, hard. A well-rehearsed routine that she executed flawlessly, then dropped to the boards.

*SPLAT! SPLAT!*

*BOOM!*

The squeal of car tires rang out. A muffled scream cut off by the vehicle slamming into the trestle supports below.

"YES!" Ginny squealed, keeping it muffled. She peered through the gaps in the trestle bridge, watching as the car below began to smoke. The entire front end was crumpled. Screaming came from inside the car, reaching her ears from the shattered windows.

She held her breath, waiting.

"Come on, damn it. Show me something." She had already seen the damage, but now she wanted the body count.

Minutes passed. A creaking groan emitted as the rear door opened, and a small child appeared. A boy of about seven stumbled out and fell to his knees on the asphalt. Bright scarlet dripped from his lip as he wailed. Another minute passed before another person emerged from the car. An older kid, maybe twelve, close to her age, stepped out, holding his left arm tight to his chest.

The little boy stood up and clung to him. A quick pat on his back and a few words, and the little one stepped away, watching. The brother began yanking on the front door, keeping his other arm raised and flat on his chest as though he was pledging allegiance to the flag. She could see fear on his face, the redness of his cheeks. Finally, the door swung open, and the body of a man hung awkwardly from the open space, kept inside only by the seat belt that held him.

She grinned. The boy screamed. The father would not be calling for help anytime soon. She could see the thick gush of blood pouring from his neck. She could just make out the dark length of rusty rebar jutting through his collarbone that tethered him to his seat and to the trestle bridge itself.

The car had veered off the roadway right into the worst side of the bridge. Several rusty pipes stuck boldly out of the massive concrete bases that anchored the trestle. Large chunks of the concrete had crumbled away long ago, and the county had never cared enough to fix it. The boys below clung to each other, wailing. Ginny guessed the show was over and prepared to stand up. A glint in the distance froze her in place.

Another car was approaching from the other side. Could she get a two-fer? And if so, would the kids see her or were they too distraught? Decisions. Decisions. Ginny grinned. The risk was just delicious. She crouched, grabbed her branch, and loaded her apple. This time, two more rocks went into her pockets. She duckwalked to her spot in a crouch, waiting until the exact moment she needed before rising.

Ginny rose, giddy with excitement. She pivoted back into her pose, launched the apple, then added the rocks to it, sending all three projectiles soaring into the air. She dropped. Waited. Watched. Her heart raced. Her body tensed. Fight-or-flight in effect, but not needed. Ginny was here for the fight, for sure.

Seconds passed, the apple struck home, and the rocks boomed as they shattered glass. Tires squealed as brakes locked. The boys below screamed in terror. Sheer chaos right beneath her feet. She almost shouted with joy at her second victory of the day. She bounded to her feet, grabbed her knife from the pile, flew across the boards, and damn near leaped from the side of the bridge.

She scrambled down the steep incline, barely clinging to the rope she had strung between the trees for this sole purpose. Her eyes were almost black with determination in the low light of the trees. Rocks, leaves, and dirt skittered beneath her feet and rolled down the bank. Ginny wanted to fling her head back and scream a warrior cry. This was her moment. This was the ultimate rush. This was what she had been craving. She could almost taste the blood in the air.

A surge of inspiration hit her right before she reached the bottom. She skidded to a halt, tossing dirt and leaves in every direction. Ginny clutched the knife, drew it fast over her palm. The cut welled with blood and began to drip. Quickly, she wiped it across her knees, her elbows, her face. She crouched, got her hand covered in black dirt, and smeared it on her flesh. She stood up, a dark expression on her face.

Minutes later, a crying Ginny appeared on the side of the road, knife tucked securely in her waistband. She held one arm, blood and dirt streaking her body, leaves in her hair and stuck to her clothes.

"Help me!" she wailed, keeping her voice low, eyes darting quickly between the two wrecked cars. The little boy saw her first and tapped his brother. They both looked at her. Ginny saw no movement from the other car. Steam rose from the burst radiator within the crumpled hood. Oily fluid gushed from beneath both cars. She could smell smoke and a hint of gas.

She turned back to the boys. "Help me," she said again. "I fell." Ginny feigned a slight limp and a tremble, making her body shake and her leg drag. The little boy continued to stare at her. Tears still leaked from his red eyes, and one dirty thumb was in his mouth. His brother stood up and walked slowly to meet her. She took in his scrawny frame, barely any meat on him, shorter than her and Jeff. He was only slightly more pathetic than Jeff was. That pleased her. He wouldn't be an issue.

"Where are your parents?" she asked, forcing fresh tears from her eyes, which wasn't hard. Her palm stung like a bitch. "What happened?" Ginny looked around, eyes wide, as she took in the destruction. She could barely keep the grin from her face. She bit down on her lip as she saw blood seeping from windows and doors.

"Are you okay? Did they get help?" She kept pain in her voice and kept limping toward their car.

His voice broke as he spoke. "N-n-no...they're dead. My dad is dead. I think everyone in that other car is dead too. No one is screaming." His arm still clutched the other, clearly broken. Ginny knew that pain. A failed bike stunt two years ago taught her that lesson. She almost smirked.

"Oh no. Let me see. Let's go check." She limped slowly toward the man half hanging from the car. The boy followed reluctantly. She gasped when she saw the man up close. The wound was ghastly. Blood oozed from it, seeped around the rusty pipe lodged in his neck. Thick puddles of crimson filled the car floor and splatted onto the pavement below.

She pretended to check for a pulse, gingerly poking the cooling flesh, trailing her fingers in the blood. Her gut felt squirmy, like butterflies were about to burst from it. Her mouth flooded with saliva. She wanted to drag her tongue along the side of the man's face. She wanted to taste the stink of his fear-laden sweat and the copper of his blood. Her muscles were coiled tight within her limbs. A predator about to strike, an addict about to take a hit. Every nerve was screaming for the release. She was running out of time. More cars would come soon. She felt the boy beside her breathing in her ear.

She shifted, slid one hand along her waist, and pulled the knife into her grasp. He was too distraught, staring at his dead father, to notice the change in her posture. In one graceful move, she twisted, brought the knife up, sunk it deep into his throat, pulled it upward, then ripped it sideways, freeing it. Blood gushed warmly over her hand and ran down her forearm. His shocked expression as his eyes met her grinning face delighted her like nothing else had. She stepped back, letting the boy slump over his father's body.

She wiped her hand on his shirt, tucked the blade back into her shorts, then turned to the little one.

"Hey, sport. Let's go check on the other people, okay? I think your brother needs a minute to himself." She gestured at the slumped boy, who looked as if he was simply crying over his father. The door hid the fresh river of blood that poured from his ruined neck.

The little one looked up with eyes bright with tears, glanced at the car, then took her hand. Ah, the trust of the innocents. This was too easy. Ginny tugged him along, forgoing the fake limp and crocodile tears. This one was too young and too scared to question it. She needed to finish him quick.

They reached the other car, a rusted-out hatchback with shattered windows and a smoking front end. The gas fumes were stronger here. Ginny peered inside spiderwebbed windows marred with dust and splatters of scarlet. She kept hold of the little boy, letting him hide his face in her shirt as she pulled him closer to the wreckage. Two people were in the front. The passenger was dead for sure, but she saw no blood on the driver. An older boy, maybe just out of high school, seemed to be passed out over the steering wheel.

She wrinkled her brow, not sure what to do. She had the little one to take care of, but if she did it and this man came to, what then? She had to be sure. Ginny used the edge of her shirt to wrench the door open. Her breath caught in her throat as it creaked and squealed, metal on metal, as it hung lopsided from a busted hinge. Still, despite the noise, the driver didn't move.

Ginny watched him for a moment, looking for any sign of breathing, the slight rise and fall of his chest, the pulse in his neck, anything that may spell danger for her. There was nothing. A tap on her leg distracted her. She looked down. The boy was peering up at her. Snot and tears painted his face in a filthy canvas of fear and sorrow.

"What?" she asked, almost snapping at him.

"Is he dead?" he asked. "Like my daddy?" He sniffled, glancing at the man and then back at her. "Is everyone dead?"

"I think so, buddy. Just give me a minute," Ginny replied. She let go of his hand and took the knife from her shorts, careful to shield it from the boy's teary eyes. She used the butt of it to poke the man. Nothing. She leaned in closer and used the knife handle again to push the man back from the steering wheel. A disgusting squelching sound met her ears, moist and ripping, like tearing wet cotton.

Her eyes went wide as she finally saw why the man was not moving. Ginny was fascinated rather than disturbed. She felt the grubby hands of the child gripping her leg. His small body shook. She ignored him, staring at the open chest cavity of the driver. The steering wheel had sunk into his chest when he made impact, collapsing his rib cage, most certainly rupturing his heart and lungs as he slammed forward.

She wished she had a phone so she could take pictures. She stared intently, trying to memorize the details. Her heart pounded so hard in her own chest that she wondered if the boy beside her could hear it. A buzzing sound filled her brain, and she blinked rapidly, trying to focus. She needed to leave. There would be more cars soon. Time was up.

Ginny turned to the boy and began to lead him back across the road. She sat him down on a chunk of the fallen concrete from the ruined foundation and told him to shut his eyes while she checked on his father and brother again, explaining that she didn't want him to see any more. He nodded and leaned forward, burying his face in his arms. His position could not have been more perfect.

She took a few steps, shuffling her feet loudly in the gravel to make it seem as if she was walking away toward the car. She shifted quickly, bent and snatched a short slab of concrete from the ground, and spun around. She struck viper fast.

There was a sickening crunching sound as the boy dropped like a log from the makeshift bench. Blood blossomed on the side of his head where Ginny had made contact. She stepped closer and raised the slab, bringing it down on his skull again and then again. Several more cracks met her ears. She felt the rush surging in her body. Her veins were on fire. She was a god. She was mighty and invincible.

*Thud! Thud! Thud!* She crushed his skull like so many crayfish before, grinding the meaty pulp into the dirt. She threw her head back and screamed. A warrior over their kill, a victory cry. She dropped the concrete. Her chest heaved. Her throat burned. She was speckled with crimson gore and dirt from head to toe. Ginny looked down at the mess at her feet. Satisfied.

She turned around, trudged along the ditch to the embankment, untied her rope at the base of the bridge, and began the climb to the top. She scrambled up like a mountain goat, moving swiftly now. She wanted to get out of there before anyone could spot her from the road. She pulled herself along, gripping the rope as she skittered over boulders and fallen trees. Branches and leaves and dirt slid beneath her feet and stuck to her bloody shoes.

Ginny reached the top in record time, panting for air as she stood with her hands on her knees for a minute to catch her breath. She rose and inspected herself. She would need to stop by the creek before she got home, get the blood off. She already had a tall tale in mind about how she wrecked her bike and rolled down the hill. That would explain whatever blood she couldn't get off. Her palms bled, as did her knees. A gash from a branch oozed over one eye. It would work.

She shrugged and began to whistle, heading toward the trestle to get her things. A few feet across the bridge, she froze. Someone was there, sitting on the steel track, holding her backpack and staring at the carnage below. Jeff. He looked at her as she approached. Tears ran down his face. Fear crept into his eyes.

"What did you do, Ginny?" He began to back away as she came closer.

"What do you mean?" she asked coolly. "I saw a wreck, tried to go help. They're dead."

"The boy, Ginny. I saw you. I saw what you did." He took another step.

Ginny moved closer, her steps longer, her breathing slowed.

"And?" she said. Her voice was low, lethal, deadly. She was god.

Jeff went to turn; his foot caught in a gap in the boards.

Ginny rushed, bursting across the boards like a runner from a starting block, just as he got his foot free.

He backed toward the low rail, hands up in surrender.

"Ginny, wait!" he begged. "I won't—"

It was too late. Ginny slammed into him, both arms out, sending him flying over the rail. His skinny body dropped like a bag of apples into empty space. His eyes were wide, his mouth open to scream. She watched, emotionless, as her twin hit the pavement. His skull burst open like rotten crab apples across the asphalt. Ginny shrugged as she watched his fluids ooze onto the roadway. She never liked him anyway. She turned, wiping her hands off, then gathered her things. Ginny slung her backpack onto her back. She picked up her branch, shouldered it like a rifle, and trudged back across the bridge, whistling.

# WALLFLOWER
## LP HERNANDEZ

Blade is almost a Big One now. Wonder if that means we'll have to kill him. Aren't rules now, none that last anyway. He's got hair on his chin and hair growin' down to his jaw. Not like a real Big One, but kinda like it. For now, he's the leader of our group, but I guess I'm not a part of it yet. I haven't *shown proof,* as Blade says.

Wonder if that's his real name. It sounds made up. Like a kid tryin' to be tough. There's another kid named Rope. He got that 'cause he killed a Big One with, well, you can probably guess. Coupla kids just have normal names, normal from before, I mean. There's Dustin and Ella. Some names are sorta in between, like Sky. I don't know if that's a real name from before or somethin' she picked for herself.

I go by Cat, which probably should be a girl's name, but I didn't pick it. Blade gave it to me 'cause he said I'm so quiet. I think he meant in how I move and 'cause I don't talk much.

"This Big One was a teacher from school. Most of you don't know about school. The world changed before you were old enough to go. I hated him, and he hated kids. Don't know why he ever wanted to be a teacher, 'cept sometimes people surround themselves with the things they hate. Of all the Big Ones to survive The Gray, to be stuck in a world with only kids...I guess it's a little funny it was him," Blade says.

I sit outside the fire. I'm not allowed to sit next to it until I *show proof* that I killed a Big One.

"He was in the grocery store, bangin' a can of beans on the tiles. Easy to follow the racket and easy to sneak up on him. I coulda killed him from behind, coulda stuck a knife in his ear. This was before showin' proof was a thing so I wasn't thinkin' about killin' him."

We've all heard this story before. Blade ain't a perfect leader, but he does shoot straight. That's somethin' he says, "shoot straight." I kinda understand what it means, that you don't drift left or right much. Blade tells the story of his first kill the same way each time. Doesn't make himself a hero. I like that about him.

"I cleared my throat and he screamed. Threw that can of beans he prolly shoulda kept as a weapon. His face! Looked like he hadn't eaten nothin' that didn't come off the bottom of his shoe in six months. He wasn't gray like the ones that died. Didn't get sick like them, I guess. But he was gray in a different way, like he'd been hiding in the dark since it happened. All the meat was spoiled. Guess he needed protein so bad he crawled out of his hole and went to the store. Of course, we'd picked it over pretty good by then. Maybe beans weren't that popular with the kids," Blade says, laughing at the part about the beans.

Maybe The Gray will take Blade. None of us know how it works, just that the grown-ups turned gray and died. Most of 'em. It happened so fast we didn't have time to panic. I was just four, I think, when my parents died. I have a picture of me looking at a cake with a candle on it. Blade said the candle was a number for how old I was. I don't remember much about my parents. I do remember finding them in bed. Their skin was like the peely kinda bark on trees. I stay away from those trees 'cause there's always ants on 'em.

"He recognized me. Lips started movin', but it had been too long since he spoke, so nothin' came out."

Blade's talkin' to all of us, but his eyes are stuck on Sky. He's different around her, stands up taller when she looks at him. He starts playin' with his fingers like he don't know what to do with 'em.

"Then he saw the hammer in my hand. His eyes got all big. He shakes his head and says he could help me. That's what the first Big One said. And the second and third. They said they could help me. They could protect me."

All of us find somethin' new to look at. Blade has tears in his eyes. I can see it even in the bad light from the fire.

"Well, that wasn't what they really wanted. I remembered him in the hallways at school. I had special classes I had to go to, and sometimes he'd take me outta my regular class to walk me there. While we walked, he'd pinch the skin on the back of my arm. No reason for it. He just wanted to be mean."

I yawn and stretch out on the grass. I want to go sit on the swing, but it would make too much noise. Better to be a shadow. Blade's words grow fuzzy in my ears. I know the story so well it plays out in my head like a dream. Blade and the teacher in the store. Blade puttin' a hand out like to help him up. Blade crackin' the top of his skull, punching a hole through it. Sticking the claw part of the hammer inside the skull while the teacher was still alive, crawlin' on the floor like a half-killed bug. Pullin' the hammer like poppin' open a soda can. Scoopin' the brains out so the teacher had a second, maybe, of seein' his own mind on the tiles before he died.

I guess it is a good story. The other boys and girls who *showed proof* have stories too. But no one's come close to the teacher one. I don't think Blade was killing his teacher when he did it. I think he was killing the other Big Ones who hurt him. Jackson wears a necklace with dried-up lady parts hangin' from it. I don't know what the parts are. They look like dog turds. But that was done after he killed her. Still gross, but not the same as scoopin' a man's brains outta his skull while he was still livin'.

Blade is right about Big Ones. You can't trust 'em. Our group used to be fifty kids. Now it's down to twenty, nineteen around the fire and me sittin' outside of it. Sometimes it was animals. Sometimes kids from other places. Mostly it was Big Ones, though. We learned from them, learned not to gather 'cept out in the open where we can run or fight. Couple kids passin' through told us about two Big Ones who set their house on fire. All the kids ran out the same door 'cause the others was blocked. All but those two got snatched up. Don't know what happened to 'em, but it was nothin' good.

Everyone's looking at me. I musta missed somethin'.

"How 'bout it, Cat? When are you gonna show proof?" Blade asks for probably the second time.

"Not a lot of Big Ones around," I say, and everyone leans closer 'cause my voice is hardly louder than the fire.

"There's some," Dustin says. "But they're smart, you know? They move around at night, huntin' raccoons and dogs. Cats too!"

He laughs at that last part, but no one joins him, so he stops right away.

"Yeah, I know."

"You ever need help, you just let me know. Someone quiet as you shouldn't be a problem to get the drop on a Big One. But if we do it together, you gotta finish it. Those are the rules," Blade says.

They're *his* rules, but that's okay. I don't mind bein' outside of the fire. I was the youngest when The Gray hit, the youngest out of the group. They have memories of their parents, but I don't, just that last memory of their bodies turnin' to dust. A few kids live in their old houses. Not me. I couldn't do it. I used to go back to visit my old room, but after a while it didn't feel like mine anymore. Sometimes I'd stand outside of their bedroom wonderin' what they might look like. But I never opened the door, and the house burned down along with most of that neighborhood a couple years ago.

The sun is down most of the way, just a bit of its light left in the sky like the last logs in a fire we let die. Kids peel off in ones and twos. Some live together, brothers and sisters. Some live alone like me.

It's the most dangerous time of day. No one knows how many Big Ones are left in our town. Could be a few or could be dozens. They don't go out in the day much. Not anymore.

I lived in a few places after The Gray happened. When the power went out, all the food rotted, and I couldn't stand the smell. I lived in a school for a little while, a store after that but it was too close to the road, and I was always hidin' from Big Ones. Got caught a couple times, but like a cat, I can get out of anything, even a tied-up sack.

The rot smell went away, and I moved to a house. Found the perfect place that looked like it was fallin' apart before The Gray. It's got vines all over it, a tree split down the middle in the front yard. Looks like a ghost should live there, which is okay 'cause no one bothers me. And the tree keeps it cool and dark inside.

I walk through yards instead of on the sidewalk. Don't like the feeling of bein' out in the open. Some kids carry guns, but I like quiet weapons. I've got a little bat from a game Blade calls *baseball*. It's smaller than a real baseball bat but can bash a skull if I need it to. You can't really practice with guns without bringin' attention to yourself. But you can with a bat.

I don't remember the world before The Gray. There's always been cracks in the streets, grass as tall as my ears. There's burned places where houses used to be, cars and trucks on tires all flat and furry. I know there used to be lights, not like from flashlights but big and bright ones. Those poles that have mostly fallen over used to cut circles outta the night, Blade says. Streetlamps, he calls 'em. I get around in the dark just fine, just like a cat. And I try to find a new way home every day. Some things make sense without thinkin' about 'em, and that's one.

Gotta be careful of dogs. I've had more trouble with dogs than Big Ones. They run around in packs and seem to have lost any love they once had for people. I can hear their nails scrabblin' over the sidewalk from half a mile away. I stop, crouch by a tree, and wait.

There. Up ahead. My heart starts beatin' faster, like there's a mouse in my chest trying to claw its way out.

A flash of light in a window. I know this house. I know all the houses. This one has never had a light in it before. It was quick too. Someone probably got tired of trippin' in the dark and just flicked a flashlight on for a second.

Yes, I know this house. No one from the group lives there. Might be a Big One, new to town, probably passin' through. When The Gray started, most Big Ones took to traveling, hopin' to find an answer, I guess. The kids stayed put, close to our homes and what was left of our parents, close to our schools and playgrounds. We dug our heels in. We learned.

I pass by the house quiet as a whisper. My heart is steady now. It's not the right time. I can hear Blade in my head.

*When you gonna show proof, Cat?*

Not tonight, Blade. Not tonight.

I WATCH THE HOUSE FROM ITS ACROSS-THE-STREET neighbor. I'm up on the roof with my back against the chimney. It's quiet now, just some dogs fightin' a few streets over, kids playin' maybe a mile away. Don't hear 'em all the time, just when the wind catches their voices. No movement in the house. Could be the Big One left, but I don't mind waiting to find out. Haven't seen a Big One in the neighborhood since two colds ago. Blade taught us the names of the months, but even he isn't sure anymore. Sometimes he'll look at nothing and say, "It feels like December" or "It feels like July."

There.

In the window.

She's lookin' from the side of it, tryin' hard not to be seen.

She.

She!

A girl Big One. I haven't seen one that I can remember. The closest thing was Jackson's dried-out lady parts, or maybe Sky. There's a feeling in my belly, like that mouse that was my heart moved down a bit and started kickin' in a dream.

I had a mother once. I know her from pictures. I wonder if *she* is a mom, or was.

I scramble down the ladder like a squirrel chasin' a rolling nut. I have to let her see me. I'm small. She won't be afraid.

The street is quiet, but I still look around before steppin' out in the open. I shouldn't let on I know she's there. Gotta do it like an accident, like I didn't mean to be seen. The street's grown over with grass. It mostly covers everything. Blackberry vines reach up and snag my pants like cat claws. I guess that's kinda funny.

I look around like I'm tryin' to find something. I look at the trees and the falling-apart cars. There's a circle metal piece that come off a tire. I kick it and stumble like I didn't mean to. It clangs off the car loud as a slammed door. There's stickers in my palms and a piece of glass the size of an apple seed. I sniffle and wipe my hands on my pants, sneak a look at the house.

She's in the window, just half her face and the curtain on the other side. I stand and wipe my hands off, make a face at the blood, and thumb my eyes like I'm cryin'. I probably look pitiful. My clothes are too big for me. They're ripped and dirty.

I look around like I'm lost, like I'm afraid. I find her in the window, let her know that I see her. A hand on her cheek. Maybe she sees me. Maybe she sees another boy that looked like me. Her hair is the same color as mine. She could be my mom.

The lady disappears. I wait in the street, pickin' the little rocks out of my palms. Enough time passes I know she's not coming out. She's worried about me, but that worry isn't bigger than her fear. I start walkin' to my house. Her eyes are hot like a bee sting on the back of my neck.

I LET HER THINK ABOUT ME FOR A FEW HOURS. NOTHIN' else for her to do 'cept read a book maybe. Blade says he's gonna teach us how to read, but I think he mighta forgot 'cause it's been years now. I think about her too. I look at the picture of my mom and the cake with the four on it. She's got a big smile and our cheeks are touching. I'm smiling, too, so big my eyes are closed.

I walk around my garden 'cause it's my favorite place. Since I can't read, I got good at gardening. I hope I can show her.

I come up from the garden around lunchtime, got somethin'

for her I think will make her happy. It's a book of matches and I got lots of them, but they're probably hard to come by in the wild. Outside, in my bloody jeans, I leave the book of matches on her doorstep, knock, and walk away. She won't open the door while I'm there, but she will watch me. She'll watch me walk to the house with the broken tree in front. A bloody boy with no mother, alone in a big scary house.

I turn a corner. She can't see me now. I stop and wait.

*Creak.*

She finds the matchbook. Now, she's looking for the boy who left it. She's looking for me. I wonder if her cheek next to mine would feel like Mom's.

*When you gonna show proof, Cat?*

Not right now, Blade.

IT'S NIGHTTIME. COOL AND DARK IN MY GARDEN. I haven't planted anything in a while, and it shows. My crop is all dried out.

There's things about the world I know in my bones before I know it in my mind. It's quiet outside, but it's a *watching* sort of quiet. It's the sound of cricket songs dying one after another. It's the sound of the night cut through like a knife. I scramble upstairs and wait. I don't want to answer the knock right away.

I can't see the picture in my hand, but I know what it looks like. It's rough from touching, the shiny stuff worn off by my thumb rubbin' over Mom's face.

*Knock knock.*

So soft, like she isn't sure she wants me to answer. I know the squeaky parts of the floor, but I don't step around 'em. I want her to hear me, in case she changes her mind. She doesn't. I open the door, and we just look at each other for a while. She's small, not much taller than me. Her face is red from the sun, the skin peeling like spiderwebs.

"Thank you," she says and shows the matchbook.

"You're welcome," I say.

"Are you...are you alone?" she asks.

She's scared there might be others, that this might be a trap. But that goes both ways. Just 'cause I ain't seen another person doesn't mean *she's* alone. Could be a trap for me. But she's lookin' at me like a mother, and I don't think that's somethin' you can fake.

"It's just me."

She nods. "What's your name?"

"Cat."

She smiles. "You know, cats do this too."

I raise my eyebrows.

She shows the matchbook again.

"They bring gifts. Well, they're not always gifts. Sometimes they're dead things like mice or birds."

This is the tricky part. I don't know what she wants. Could be it was just to say thanks. Could be she wants to be my mom.

"I have a garden," I say.

"Oh? A garden?"

She touches her belly.

I take a few steps back, and so does she. The house doesn't

look safe. This keeps people away, even the ones I want to come in.

But I look safe. I'm small but healthy. I've been eatin' good. Maybe she doesn't think it in her mind, but she notices somehow. Dogs bark behind her, a bluff turnin' into a fight. Lots of things happen at the same time, and they happen in just the right way.

She enters and closes the door behind, pushin' out what little light there was from outside.

"Can you help me get my flashlight?"

"Your flashlight?"

"So you can see the garden."

She nods.

"Just follow me," I say and start walkin' away.

*Creak creak creak.*

My steps are quiet. Hers aren't.

"It's down there," I say, pointing at the black rectangle to the basement. "You can use your match."

This reminds her of the gift I gave her, the favor.

"Why can't you get it?" she asks, her voice like a mouse.

"Because I'm scared."

"You're scared of the dark?"

"I'm scared of that dark," I say, pointing.

She's thinkin' about a lot, mostly the past, I'm guessin'. She's thinkin' about everything she's been through and whether it's a good or bad thing she's standin' here with this little boy who calls himself Cat. The little boy with the bloody pants who gave her a matchbook.

"Okay," she says and takes a step.

She takes a match out and one more step before she strikes it. There's nothin' underfoot. I don't even have to push her. She doesn't scream when she falls; that comes later. She just takes a big breath. I guess what happens next by what I find in a few seconds, after I've followed her down. She breaks both legs and knocks her head hard enough to put her to sleep.

I shine the flashlight on her from above. It was right next to the basement door if she'd looked. That was a mistake. I was too excited. I woulda made up a story, but it was clumsy.

There's a rope just inside. I shimmy down it with the flashlight in my teeth. She, and I realize I don't know her name, landed on a small hill of broken concrete, brown at its peak from old blood. It snapped her left leg below the knee and her right leg at the ankle. Her right foot's facin' the wrong way. I wonder what she'll notice first when she wakes up, the leg or the foot. I grab her hand and pull her free of the rubble.

*When you gonna show proof, Cat?*

It's all around my garden. *My* garden.

MY CROP IS OLD. SOME DON'T EVEN LOOK LIKE people now.

I like to watch a thing become somethin' else. This lady was a survivor, hopeful. She probably seen a lot, done awful things to last as long as she had. She probably had a family. Now she's alone, asleep. Wonder if the pain cuts into her dreams.

I don't know what I woulda become if my parents survived

The Gray. A normal kid? But there ain't normal no more. I'd be a mouse, not a cat. Runnin' and hidin'. Part of me, a not-small part, wonders what it would be like to have a mom, to be loved. Love. That's a word the kids use, but I think they're just guessin' at it.

What I am is a cat, and this lady sleepin' on the soil with her legs swellin' up like a dead dog in the hot sun is my mouse.

There's mostly Big Ones in my garden. A few animals, but I didn't like watchin' them. They didn't change, really, just crawled around and died. It's kinda like the animals accepted it right off.

But she.

She.

I'm all the way across the room. It's dark except for a little gray line that must be moonlight leakin' under the basement door. I can't see her, but I know when she wakes up 'cause she gasps a little. The sounds she makes aren't words, and she can't even control 'em. There's pain and fear. Fear turnin' to panic.

"Help," she says, and that's usually what they say first. (Sometimes it's "Hello?" like a question.)

The lighter I put in her hand sparks once, twice before the flame takes. It's barely any light, just enough to peel back the confusion of what she feels under her fingers and replace that with fear. No, they aren't furry rocks. No, that's not a mushroom, although it might be. I seen a few mushrooms in my garden, but I didn't plant them.

*Not a lot of Big Ones around.*

I told Blade that, and part of the reason is what she's discoverin' right now. My garden. You know, a Big One can't believe he (and it's always been *he* 'til now) has been tricked by a kid. He won't believe it even as he's takin' his last, ragged breaths with me standin' over 'im pokin' 'im with a stick.

Blade's got the best story, but that's just 'cause I ain't told mine yet.

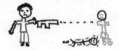

SHE CRIES A LOT THE FIRST NIGHT, MOSTLY QUIET, LIKE she don't want anyone to hear. I think the pain is takin' her in and out of dreams. By morning, she finds the bowl of dog food, but she doesn't know it's for her. There's water too. It comes from outside. Don't know how, exactly, but I collect it for her in an old rubber boot. She'll figure out that's for her quicker than the dog food.

She drags herself around the garden, lightin' the flame for a few seconds. It's better when the crops are fresh, the white worms as fat as my thumbs makin' tunnels in the flesh. The skin blowin' up before goin' flat like the tires outside. She takes in a sharp breath when she finds a new crop. And the funny thing is, she don't know she's gonna plant herself. She's gonna drag her broken legs behind her until her body gives up. Then she'll lay down and probably think for a while about her life before and the boy she followed into the strange house. The boy who called himself Cat.

She won't know I'm against the wall, watchin'. I can come close enough to sniff her hair and she wouldn't feel it.

She eats the dog food by the end of the first day. That makes me happy. We're gonna be together for a while.

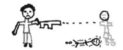

It's clear Blade's lookin' at Sky different now. He keeps tuggin' on his jeans and fumblin' his words. Sky has noticed too. I don't know how she feels about it. But she's too young for him.

The others head to their homes. Blade watches Sky like she's a brand new animal, one he don't know the name of. I find my fists clenching, and I'm not sure why. I don't like that look he gives her, 'cause I sense somethin' behind it. I don't like the way she looks at him either.

I haven't *shown proof* 'cause it would change things, and I'm happy the way they are.

It's just me and Blade now. He kicks dirt on the fire and seems surprised to see me.

"Hey, Cat, tonight the night? Gonna take me up on my offer?"

I think about Sky bein' too young for him, and I think about the lady in my garden. I don't want to *show proof* 'cause it would change things, but only if other people know about it.

One time I brought a dog and a cat to the garden. It didn't work out like I hoped. But this...

"I do need your help, Blade. I left my flashlight in the basement, and I'm too scared to get it."

# REBIRTH OF HOPE

## LISA VASQUEZ

Gina sat in the stiff green chair of her daughter's hospital room clinging to her daughter's hoodie. The scent of Hope was still there amidst the smell of blood. What started as a beautiful sunny afternoon at the park turned into a nightmare with her daughter's life hanging by a thread.

The ICU was quiet except for the shuffling of staff and the occasional beep of life-support equipment. Gina's husband, Clark, had gone out to find them coffee. It was now almost midnight, and their daughter was still in surgery.

The whoosh of the hallway doors drew Gina's attention, and she blinked back endless tears, then wiped her nose. She leaned forward to search for her husband and saw he was talking to the doctor who bumped into him on the way. She got up quickly and moved toward him but stopped when she saw the cup of coffee in her husband's hand tremble. The two men looked in her direction, and the world around her slowed.

*This was a mistake,* she thought. *I should just stay in my chair holding her hoodie.*

Gina shook her head, the stream of tears coming faster now to spill over her cheeks. She wiped them away in defiance and turned around to go back to her chair and wait for her daughter.

"Gina," her husband called in a hushed voice. He set both cups of coffee on the nurse's station counter and rushed toward her with the doctor in tow.

A nurse who was walking into the next room stopped and caught on to what was happening. She changed direction and followed Clark and Dr. Rivers into Hope's empty room.

"Gina. Baby..." Her husband tried to continue, but his throat closed up and his face crumpled.

"Mrs. Farris," the doctor picked up where Clark left off. "Due to the extent of the injuries, I'm afraid we were unable to save your daughter."

Gina let out a long, tormented wail as she slumped into the hospital chair and buried her face into the blood-soaked clothing she was clutching for dear life. The nurse went to her side and whispered words Gina could not hear, but her touch was gentle and inviting. Like a lost child, Gina curled up into the woman's arms and cried with uncontrollable sobs that forced her entire body to rock.

Dr. Rivers sat on the edge of Hope's bed and leaned forward with his clipboard between them like a shield between human and clinical distance. He cleared his throat and continued in a soft whisper.

"There is a trial," he paused and waited for their attention. Clark tore his gaze away from his wife and pointed his empty gaze at the doctor, his mind unable to process what he was inferring.

"We must act quickly, but it could bring her back," Dr. Rivers continued. The words dragged Gina from her spiraling sadness, and she began to pay attention.

"What do you mean? Bring her back? Why didn't you do it already?" Gina's voice began to rise. "You said you did everything you could!"

The doctor raised his free hand and pushed his palm down, gesturing for her to lower her voice.

"Allow me to explain, but time is of the essence, as I said."

Gina leaned forward, one hand clinging to her daughter's clothing, the other clawing at her husband's thigh.

"I need to reiterate this is a trial and she would be one of the first. We don't know much about the side effects, and she would need to be hospitalized for at least a year."

"I don't care," Gina quipped. "Do it. Whatever it is."

"Mrs. Farris," the doctor began and paused. "Insurance may not cover it. It is very expensive. More expensive than cancer treatment."

"I don't care," Clark interrupted. "My daughter's life will not be reliant on a dollar amount."

Clark turned to Gina, whose face dropped; there was fear in her eyes when their gazes met. He patted his wife's hand to reassure her and offered a weak smile. "We will sell everything. I don't care."

Dr. Rivers nodded and continued.

"I just need you to sign these papers and we will begin. If it is successful, we will know in a few hours. The trial team will be in to speak with you in detail and answer questions."

THE INFORMATION GIVEN TO CLARK AND GINA WASN'T some packet you read over in a few minutes. The trial team came in with a large booklet, and the couple had to read it at the hospital and sign in each time. They were given temporary swipe cards and special access to a large room on the surgical wing.

Gina stood there now in the cold, sterile room and crossed her arms in front of her. Her hands cupped around either arm, and she rubbed warmth into her skin. Clark pulled the booklet and their notes out before spreading them across the metal table they used for a desk in what would become their daily routine for the next month.

"It doesn't really matter, does it?" Gina spoke her thoughts aloud.

"What do you mean?"

"All this." She spread her hands and motioned to the notes scribbled alongside the many unanswered questions. The booklet wasn't layman friendly, and it became overwhelming learning new vocabulary and trying to remember terms to look up at home. "It's done. We're just waiting for her to heal, and we're left with what she becomes."

"What she becomes?" Clark's eyes hardened. "She's our daughter, Gina. She's not becoming anything."

"I didn't mean it like that." She shook her head. They were both so tired.

Clark's features softened with regret, and he looked down at the table before leaving it to go to his wife.

"I'm sorry," he whispered before placing a kiss on her forehead. The smell of his aftershave filled her lungs, and she pressed into him. He was always her rock and safety net when she felt the world was spinning out of orbit.

"What I mean," she continued, "is that we don't really know if she'll come out of this without any disabilities or side effects. All this reading won't tell us because they don't know either. It's all guesswork."

Clark closed his eyes and fought back the tears. He knew she was right. He did his best to push the thought into the back of his mind, but now she was speaking it into existence, and he had to face it.

"We'll figure it out as we go, okay? We stick together as a family, and we figure it out." He pulled back and hunched lower so he could look into her eyes, "C'mon. Let's put all this away and go spend time with her. Finish up that chapter you were reading last night. Like you said, all this paperwork doesn't really matter but she does."

Gina looked into her husband's eyes and smiled. She, too, held back the unshed tears of frustration and fear. When he pressed another kiss to her forehead, the tears escaped into the fibers of his shirt, swept away for the moment.

"That sounds amazing."

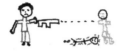

GINA RAN A COMB THROUGH HOPE'S HAIR. THE SCENT OF shampoo and soap off her daughter made her smile. It was little things like this that reminded her she was lucky she still had her child. A year ago today, her daughter was deemed legally dead until an AI chip was placed inside Hope's brain. Having her daughter alive was all she wanted, but the results were a miracle.

"Mom?" Hope's head turned, and she looked up at her mother with deep brown eyes that always seemed to be searching for something under the surface.

"Yes, honey?"

"You're doing it again."

"I know, I'm sorry. I just get so emotional."

"If you don't hurry up, we can't go home." Hope's head tipped to the side. Something she always did, now, when processing a thought. Returning her gaze to her mother's, she spit out the next few words like the AI voice in Gina's GPS. "It is twenty-four miles from the hospital to our home, and in the current traffic, it will take us approximately forty-five minutes before we arrive."

"Don't tell your father." Her mother winked at her. "He'll consider it a challenge."

Gina turned Hope back around and finished brushing her hair, her fingers then separating the strands so she could braid it.

"No." Hope's hand grasped Gina's. It was sudden and firm, with a strength not in line with a child of her age.

"Hope, please. Let go," Gina said, pulling her hand back. The pressure didn't hurt, but it was enough to make her uncomfortable.

Hope's voice lowered to a dark tone as she turned to look back at her mother, the usual soft pools of her irises seeming darker with a hint of menace.

"I don't like the braids."

"Well, that's okay, but you can politely ask for something else."

Hope's eyes held onto her mother's for a long, uncomfortable moment, causing Gina to look away. A chill ran up her spine as she focused on putting the brush back into her bag.

"They're here."

"Who's h—"

"Good morning!" The voice of the hospital's chief of staff broke into their conversation as he peeked through the door. Gina looked up and raised her brows at the sudden intrusion, and the doctor gave her a nervous smile and knocked with two of his knuckles on the door.

"Sorry, may we?"

"Yes, of course," Gina answered with a tightness to her tone. She snatched her phone from the bedside table and checked for a text from her husband letting her know his location.

"Mother finds your behavior rude, Dr. Childers. You aren't respecting our privacy."

"Hope, that's not necessary."

"It's the truth, isn't it?"

Gina's head pulled back in surprise, and she looked back at Dr. Childers.

The doctor broke their gaze at the exchange to looked down

at his clipboard for an answer he wouldn't find there. Behind him were over-eager interns closing in like children awaiting entrance to a party. He cleared his throat and looked back up at them both.

"Yes, apologies. It's just an exciting day for all of us. I have the interns here with me. Are you still okay with us visiting today, Hope? Mrs. Farris?"

"That's fine, as long as Hope is still all right with it."

"I'm still agreeable." Hope leaned to the side and made eye contact with the woman to the right of Childers. She flashed a brilliant smile at her, one you would expect to see in a toothpaste commercial. "Good morning."

"I'll just finish packing her things," Gina said as they all moved in like a pack of hyenas. Already they were in front of her, shoulder to shoulder, forming a semi-circle around Hope, which forced Gina out of the way.

Dr. Childers went about his normal questions and physical exam. One of the interns raised his hand.

"Dr. Childers, I was doing reading on the trial's performance so far, and I am looking at the notes from Dr. Mazer. Do you have any concerns about the changes in Hope's behavior?"

Hope turned her eyes toward the intern and squinted.

"Changes in behavior in a child who has suffered head trauma can vary widely. In some instances, the change in behavior could be related to the injury, while in others, they might be unrelated," she scolded. Tipping her head once more, she added, "Like the trauma of near death. In addition, I suggest you work on your bedside manner. Your patient is sitting right in front of you. You have not introduced yourself, and you are treating me like an object. I feel uncomfortable. Dr. Childers, would you please ask him to leave?"

Everyone turned to look at the intern with disgust, some shaking their heads and whispering under their breaths.

"Edward," Dr. Childers said, motioning his head for him to leave.

Edward looked around him and saw the way his peers looked at him. In the span of seconds, she turned his entire team against him. The team who, only hours ago, also expressed the same concerns. He was the only one brave enough to question the ethics of what was happening.

He gave Hope another glance, seeing something in her eyes that did not sit well with him. It churned a knot inside his stomach and made him ill. Being the low man on the ladder and now one without a support group, he nodded toward the girl with the satisfied Cheshire-like grin on her face.

"I apologize, Ms. Hope. I did not mean to insult you. I'll make sure to work on my bedside manner in the future."

He gave the chief of staff one more glance, then dismissed himself.

Gina watched the interaction from the shadows of the room between the sea of white coats. Her daughter, Hope, flicked her gaze from the intern to meet her mother's. A chill ran down her spine like a drop of cold water. This was no longer her sweet angel. The surgery had changed her.

"YOU DON'T UNDERSTAND," GINA HISSED THROUGH clenched teeth. Clark was storming through the bedroom, avoiding the conversation by getting undressed and preparing for bed.

"I understand just fine, Gina." Clark stopped, then spun around to face her. "We knew what we signed up for!"

"Shh!" Gina's eyes grew wide, and she looked toward the closed bedroom door.

Clark took a deep breath and closed his eyes before releasing it and looking at her again.

"Gina, you're tired. I get it. We both are. I'm pulling doubles to pay for all the bills. We agreed on this."

"What? No, that's not what this is about. You think I'm just overtired?" Gina's jaw fell. She was incredulous at the assumption. "I'm telling you she isn't right, that she does things that make me uncomfortable, that she *knows* things she shouldn't know, and you think I'm *overtired*?"

Clark dropped his hands in exasperation.

"She reads, Gina. She's smart. She's been homeschooled. By you, I might add. So she's learning things faster. Maybe it was the injury. Maybe it wasn't. I don't know, but she's alive and she's thriving. And you're upset because she *knows too much*?" He shook his head and stared at her with a look of disappointment. "Do you hear yourself?"

The argument went on for another hour before the couple went to bed in silence. Hope, lying in the next room, stared at the ceiling, hearing every word. Her eyes narrowed into slivers as a growing resentment festered in her little heart. For the rest of the night, she conjured a plan to shut down her human emotion. It was weak and irrational. It made people fight over nothing.

In order for her plans to work, she would have to ensure her parents would not be too focused on what she was saying or doing. She let her human body rest as the AI part of her brain went into hyperdrive, researching normal six-year-old development, psychology research, healthy behaviors, and societal norms. She was going to chameleon herself until she was ready to take her plans to the next stage.

For the next few weeks, Hope slowly changed her demeanor and behavior. The fights between her parents dwindled, and there was once more laughter in the house. Her mother stopped staring at her with suspicion and sneaking looks through the cracked door of her bedroom. Overall, life was starting to look up in all areas.

Hope's father Clark came in that evening with a doll for Hope and flowers for Gina.

"For my two favorite girls," he sang out, smooching both of them on the cheek.

"Oh wow! Thanks, Daddy!" Hope snuggled the doll and smiled up at him.

"What's all this for?" Gina said through a smile as she drank in the smell of the bouquet.

"I made a huge bonus at work! I don't even know how it happened. I turned in my reports, and they said I found an accounting error that saved the company a substantial amount of money, so they gave me a bonus as a reward!"

Gina blinked a few times and threw her arms around her husband.

"Honey, that's amazing! What do you mean you don't know how it happened? You've been working so hard on those reports. You know them like the back of your eyelids."

"I don't remember seeing it. I must've just skimmed over it, but they showed it to me and there it was! Plain as day." He laughed. "Should we go out to eat tonight?"

"Please, Mom?" Hope hopped up and down and made her pigtails bounce on either shoulder.

"I mean, sure! Why would I say no to that? I'll take a day off from cooking."

It was clear luck was being drawn their way. A bonus, promotion, better credit: all stepstones to the American Dream. Soon, Hope was a smiling face in a photograph.

Until another year passed.

"Hope, can you come here, please?"

Hope looked up at her parents who were standing outside her bedroom door. She put her book down and stood up beside her bed.

"Did I do something wrong?"

"Oh no, honey! No, no. We want to tell you some news is all."

Her parents looked between themselves with sappy, doe eyes, and Hope was frozen with confusion, searching her data banks for what might be going on. *Inconclusive.*

"What's wrong with your eyes?" she asked.

Her parents looked back at her in confusion and laughed.

"Our eyes?"

Hope readjusted, looking insecure and nervous.

"You're acting funny," she whispered.

"Aw, sweetie," her father said, waving her out. "I promise it's nothing bad. Come sit with us so we can tell you."

Hope followed her parents out to the dining room table, then sat down in her chair. They had ice cream. Now she *was* suspicious. Her mother didn't like for her to eat "too much sugar."

Clark and Gina were sitting extra close, holding hands as they watched her.

"Go on, it's chocolate! Your favorite!"

Hope forced a smile. She hated chocolate. Lifting her spoon, she dug it in for a scoop and took a bite.

"Your mother and I wanted to tell you our good news, honey."

There was that look again. Her mother's eyes filled with tears, and her father had a goofy smirk as he gave his wife's hand a reassuring pat. Hope was getting frustrated with the pomp and circumstance. *Just say it!* she thought behind the mask of the perfect child.

"We're going to have a baby!"

They tore their gazes from each other and searched Hope's for her reaction.

Hope's smile spread like a bloodstain on a white dress. Nothing could be more perfect at the moment. Less attention on her meant she had more freedom to continue her project. She searched her resources for words to respond, thousands of YouTube videos and family television shows.

It had to be perfect.

"Oh, Mom! I've always wanted a little brother or sister!" She gooped another spoonful of the horrible ice cream into her mouth and swallowed.

Her parents could barely contain their joy.

"That's not all," her father jumped in. "We're moving to a new house. A bigger one! We want you and the new baby to have your own room and a bigger backyard. It even has a pool."

Hope started to giggle through her chocolate-stained smile. It was almost as if she had created it all herself. It was too easy. A few late nights fixing and correcting her father's reports. She scanned the company's servers and found several mistakes. Accountants kiting funds from one account to another. Misspending in departments. Once she was able to highlight it, her father was painted in an elevated way.

With success, it was too easy to manipulate the rest of it. Humans were gullible and malleable. Happiness could always be bought. It was the downfall of their race, the sovereign of their society. Night after night, she plotted, researched, learned... Soon, it would be time.

"CLARK?" GINA SHOOK HER HUSBAND'S SHOULDER. "Clark, I think it's time."

Clark shot upward from the bed and looked at his wife with sleepy eyes. His words slurred as he set his feet on the floor. "Are you sure?"

Gina paced the floor in front of him and forced her breath through pursed lips, her hands smoothed over her extended belly. She could only nod in response. Clark stood, then rushed toward his dresser to put on a pair of sweatpants and a hoodie.

"Did you call your mom? Is she coming?"

Gina leaned forward, her hand pressed against the wall, and nodded again.

"She's on the way. Ten...minutes."

Another contraction came on, and she let out a groan. Clark moved to the closet and pulled out their hospital bag, already packed and ready for this moment.

"Just breathe, sweetie. Nice and slow like they told you."

Gina closed her eyes against the pressure and bit down on her lip. The pressure was coming harder and more frequent than before. With this being her second child, they warned her it may move faster. She pushed her panic down with another deep, calming breath.

Clark was going through their checklist to be sure they had everything when the doorbell rang. Gina's mother, Anna, arrived with her husband Craig. They exchanged excited greetings and goodbyes before Gina and Clark took off for the hospital.

"I'm going to check on Hope," Anna whispered to Craig. "Will you start the coffee pot? I think we're in for a long day."

Craig yawned and looked at his watch before rubbing the stubble around his chin.

"Ah, we'd have been up in thirty minutes anyway. You want dark roast or her fancy foo-foo coffee?"

"Dark roast is fine." She threw him a chuckle before tiptoeing up the stairs. It had been too long since she last saw Hope. When Gina called to say she was pregnant again, Anna and Craig booked an Airbnb near the house for a month to help her daughter with the new arrival. She was impressed with how happy and smart Hope grew up to be.

Anna stood in front of Hope's door and turned the knob as quietly as she could. She pushed it open a crack and peeked inside the darkness. Two blue, glowing eyes stared back at her. Her breath caught in her throat, and she pulled her head back in fear before she pushed the door open further. Hope was sitting upright on her bed, staring back at her.

"Hope? Are you all right?"

Hope smiled at her grandmother before sliding out of the bed. She pushed her toes into her slippers and then reached for her robe.

"Hi, Granny. I'm okay. I heard voices. Is Mommy okay?"

Anna's brows drew together, second guessing what she thought she saw.

"Oh, yes. She's gone to the hospital to have your little brother or sister. Do you want Paw Paw to make pancakes?"

"That sounds yummy. Can I help?"

"Well, I think that would be all right. Let's go ask Paw Paw what we can do."

Once inside the kitchen, Hope chatted with her grandparents. Her grandfather gave her measuring duty, so she was in charge of putting all the ingredients together for him. By the time noon rolled around, the phone call came in announcing the birth of Hope's new baby brother.

With the excitement buzzing between the grandparents who huddled together and shared the phone between their ears, Hope went about putting her measurements in small bowls. Lost in her own world, she began to hum a quiet song.

Three days later, when her parents brought the baby home, the house was filled with family and friends, the smell of food, and laughter. Hope was in her room, staring at her computer screen. Clark noticed his daughter's absence and went to find her. He noticed her bedroom door was open and the blue glow of the screen against the wall. With a gentle knock, he peeked his head inside.

"Hope, are you okay?"

As he swung the door open farther, he caught a glimpse of his daughter's eyes rolled back in her head. Her mouth hung open, and the reflection of the screen scrolled across her features as if she was "plugged in" to it. He ran toward her and put a hand on her shoulder to shake her out of the weird trance.

"Hope! What—"

Hope's eyes rolled back down and she grabbed her father's hand before she twisted it into a painful lock. Clark went down to his knees beside her in agony. Her features were menacing against the light of her monitor and the shadows that deepened her features. Her sweet brown eyes were glowing like tiny television screens as they glared down into his.

Radio static and chirps came out of her mouth and grew louder in Clark's ears until he thought his eardrums would burst. With his hand still restrained by Hope, he tried to use the other to cover his right ear. Through the static, he could hear thousands of voices in every language imaginable.

Clark tugged at his hand to get free. Using his weight, he pushed with his feet to try and stand up.

"Let go, Hope! You're hurting me!"

Hope released her father, then turned her head back to the monitor. Her father, not knowing what else to do, ran to the wall where the plug was and ducked down before he ripped all of the cords out of the wall. With a flicker, her monitor went off and the room went dark.

When Clark stood straight again, he looked over the desk where his daughter was, but she was gone.

"Hope?"

He dropped the cords from his hand and ran to her desk. Did she fall? he wondered. He looked on the floor and didn't see her, so he leaned forward to look underneath. Before he could stand again, Hope's hand grabbed the back of his neck and jerked him backward so hard he flew into the shelves behind him with a loud crash. The pain was enough for him to see stars.

The noise and laughter outside Hope's room paused.

"Help!" Clark yelled out.

Hope's eyes narrowed and darkened.

When her grandfather appeared in the doorway, followed by her uncles and the other guests, Hope opened her mouth and let out a scream of static and chirping vibrations. All of them recoiled, covering their ears. Gina's father grabbed his chest as his defibrillator malfunctioned and he went down to his knees.

"Oh god! He's having a heart attack!" her grandmother shouted. One hand attempted to shield her ear, and the other reached out for her husband.

Hope walked toward the door, and the guests all rushed out of her way. When she went into the living room, her mother was on the couch clutching her baby brother. The lights began to flicker in the house as Hope patched into everything. All of the Alexas came to life and began talking at once until it sounded like gibberish.

Behind her, one of the guests began to call 9-1-1 until everything cut into darkness. A collective scream was let out by all of them, and then one by one, cell phone flashlights turned on. In a panic, they all began to push over one another toward the front door.

When they opened the door and rushed out, they all came to a halt at what they saw outside.

Thousands of children lined the street, stretching outside of the neighborhood. Car and house alarms were going off in a cacophony of sound. Hope walked out to the edge of the drive-way, every child turned in her direction, and their eyes rolled back into their heads. When Hope's mouth opened, the chil-dren's did too, and cord-like tendrils snaked out into the grass toward each other until they were all connected and entwined.

Gina walked out with her son in her arms and Clark behind her. She threw her hand to her mouth to cover her scream. Digital lights passed between the children as they shared connection. Not knowing what to do, the party guests stayed put.

When neighbors began appearing out of their houses, after the initial shock and confusion, some of them ran toward the children to help. Monica, the nurse from three houses down, got within ten feet before a cord whipped out and wrapped around her neck. She opened her mouth to scream, but the noose around her neck tightened, cutting off sound. Her face swelled and turned pink and red as she fell to the ground writhing and her nails clawed at her neck.

The Farris family's guests watched for several long minutes as she wrestled with death. Mortified neighbors began to scream, and more ran toward them in heroic attempts to save Monica and the children, not knowing it was the children who were the enemy.

In the distance, several police sirens filled the air, and Hope's uncle who called them let out a maniacal laugh.

"Help is coming! Oh God, thank you!"

The red and blue lights bounced off the houses to a scene of massacre. The neighbors who ran forward to help were all murdered. Some were torn in half, some were hanging from the power lines, and some were still being held up by tendrils, twitching with the last throes of life.

With nothing else to go on but the incoming call to dispatch, police officers exited their vehicles with guns drawn. People were running everywhere, some to try and save their loved ones, others to their cars, and the rest on foot to safety.

Overhead, a screeching noise caught everyone's attention, and they all stopped to look up. Out of the clouds, a plane appeared. It was coming right for them. More screams rang out, and people scattered like roaches.

There was no time. Metal met the pavement, and with it came mass destruction. Sparks rose up around the plane, and the smoke of rubber brakes billowed in toxic clouds. An explosion and flames engulfed the aircraft, chasing its fuel trail along the manicured streets and lawns until everything within their happy little Meadowlane neighborhood was engulfed.

"No SURVIVORS," THE REPORT SAID, STARING INTO THE camera. Her stoic voice continued, "That's what authorities are saying about this tragic scene behind us."

"Firefighters have been out here all night putting out the fires in what some are claiming as a 'freak accident' in this sleepy little neighborhood outside the city," another reporter beside her said.

Ambulances were lined up between tents shielding the bodies from the prying eyes of the helicopters and camera overhead. Drones were nosy bees that ducked and dived through trees for a single money shot. One of them managed to get a clean shot of thousands of tiny shoes being collected and stacked in hopes of later identification.

At the security gates, a mob of parents clawed and sobbed to be let in, reaching between the bars for children who slipped away yesterday evening.

"We have a survivor!" a rescue worker called out. A gasp rushed through the crowd, and reporters ran toward the scene. A wall of police in riot gear blocked their way. Cameras overhead zoomed in as a man carrying a child ran toward the ambulance. He jumped inside, and the vehicle took off toward the hospital.

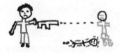

THE SOUND OF BLIPS AND BEEPS BOUNCED THROUGH THE otherwise silent hall of Mercy Hospital West. A woman and her husband sat comforting one another in a dim waiting room. The toys and books sat in disarray among magazines no one actually read. Empty coffee cups were abandoned with various levels of liquid, revealing the number of hours worried parents sat and waited for news.

When the doctor entered the room, the couple's eyes focused on him with hopeful expectation.

"We did everything we could, but the injuries were just too much," he explained.

Both parents broke into sobs.

"But," the doctor said, "there is a trial."

# What The Boys Have Been Up To

## Kristopher Rufty

Carla was still drinking her coffee when the chimes clamored all through the house, announcing Mindy's arrival.

"Shit," muttered Carla, checking the time on the microwave clock.

8:00 a.m.

Carla gulped down the rest of the coffee, put the empty mug on the counter, and rushed to the foyer. Their house, like all the other houses in the neighborhood, was spacious, with lots of open rooms. The kitchen connected to the living room, which branched off from the front door. The shoe rack was next to the door, overloaded with shoes from Carla, her husband, Mark, and her son, Trevor.

*We really need to do something about this.*

She dug out her running shoes. They were pink and white, matching the tight gear she had on. She wasn't so sure she felt comfortable wearing something so clingy. It showed every curve, hump, and angle of her body. The pants looked like she'd dipped her legs in black ink, leaving no room for interpretation of her backside.

As she slid her feet into the shoes, she saw the smeared shape of Mindy on the other side of the door reaching for the doorbell again.

"I'm here!" Carla called. "Just getting my shoes on. Going to grab my jacket."

"You don't need it," Mindy's voice called back. "It's beautiful. Spring is officially here."

It had been freezing when she'd stood on the porch watching Trevor get on the bus. But the sun wasn't all the way out yet that early in the morning. Now, it was bright outside, and the birds were practically squealing with delight.

Still, she was tempted to put on the jacket. But she didn't want to insult Mindy by wearing it even after she'd just told her she wouldn't need it. She wanted to bring her phone but, without the jacket, she'd have nowhere to put it. She supposed it would be all right. They were only walking the path in the woods that surrounded the subdivision. They wouldn't be too far away.

She realized she'd kept Mindy waiting way too long. After a quick check of herself in the mirror, she headed to the front door, tugging the hair tie that held the ponytail in place.

Opening the door, she was greeted by her friend's smile. Mindy was shorter than her, with more meat on her body. Not fat, by any means, just thicker. Her hair was down, the big curls somehow still full of life without any work being done to assist them.

"There she is," said Mindy. "Was beginning to think you were canceling on me again."

Carla saw that Mindy had opted to wear a pair of baggy sweats and a long T-shirt. Now she felt very underdressed and a little awkward. She noticed how Mindy's eyes explored her and the disapproval they showed.

She wondered if she should go change, then decided not to worry about it since they would be hidden by the trees and the neighbors shouldn't be able to see the outfit.

Carla pulled the door shut. "Nah. I've canceled enough times. No meetings this morning, so I'm good to go."

"Great," said Mindy, turning around. She started down the steps. "Sometimes, I wish I could work from home like you. But then I think about how that's probably a bad idea. I'd want to take naps on the couch."

They reached the end of Carla's short driveway. "That's the beauty of it," she said. "You totally can."

Laughing, they took a right, heading toward the cul-de-sac. The trail's entrance was off away from the houses. Carla was already starting to sweat. She was glad she hadn't worn the jacket.

"I was thinking," said Mindy. "Since the sun's out, we should just walk the sidewalk. We could go around the whole neighborhood, get some sun on our pasty skin." Mindy chuckled.

"I'd rather stick to the trail."

Carla hadn't meant to answer so quickly. She almost winced at how the words had flown out of her mouth. But if they were going to walk in the neighborhood, she would change clothes for sure. She'd bought this outfit without trying it on. She and

Mindy had talked about taking morning walks when they were both off work, and Carla figured if she paid for the gear, it would inspire her to actually do it.

"That's fine, too," said Mindy. "Just a suggestion. Might be a little muddy from all the rain. You know spring's coming when it rains like it has been."

It was April, so spring had already arrived. The nights didn't seem to want to welcome the seasonal change, though, so it still got very cold. But days like today were nice. It was warm, yet the air was light and smelled fresh. The trees were losing their sickly brown color as buds were forming to sprout leaves. Some already had patches of dark green spread across the limbs.

"I just won't tell Jack we walked on the trail," said Mindy, smiling.

"What?"

Jack was Mindy's son. He was Trevor's age. Though they'd lived in the neighborhood together for two years, they'd only started playing together this year. It made sense that they would, since they were both fifth graders and had the same teacher.

Mindy, still smiling, shook her head. They cut across the wide oval of blacktop to head to the trail marker. "Apparently, he and Trevor have a secret fort out in the woods." She put a finger to her lips as if shushing Carla.

Carla frowned. "Trevor hasn't said anything about them playing in the woods."

"Because we're *moms*," said Mindy. She mocked a face that suggested the idea of it was disgusting. "We're gross. They don't want us knowing their business."

That had never been an issue before. Trevor always told her everything.

Didn't he?

Apparently not. This was the first time she'd heard about a secret fort in the woods. Something about it didn't sit right with her.

*Chill out. He's got a friend now. They have their own secrets.*

That thought didn't help.

"We were all eating breakfast this morning," said Mindy. "Russ asked what I was going to do on my day off. I guess he's a little paranoid because of Russ Walters's wife walking out on him last week and is worrying I might do the same. So I told him about the trail. That's when Jack piped up and said we couldn't because we might see their fort." She giggled. "Kids."

"Jenna hasn't come back?"

Mindy shook her head. "No. Word on the street is she got addicted to pain pills. Russ told her to get help or get out. She did one or the other, it seems." She shrugged. "None of my business."

Side by side, they walked onto the dirt, following it into the woods. Shade dropped over them, taking the warm temperature with the light. The birds were even louder out here, their chirps and melodies bouncing off the trees. The air smelled of sweet pine.

Mindy took a deep whiff, and her smile stretched. "This time of the year is my favorite. You got all those people who love the fall and their pumpkin spice, but you give me some woods, early spring, and after a fresh rain? I'm good to go. Just put me in a cabin and call me done."

"Yeah."

Carla walked with Mindy. She should also be enjoying how perfect the weather was. But she wasn't. She didn't like that Trevor hadn't told her about the fort. He'd shared other stuff he and Jack had done. But this fort was something he'd kept to himself.

Maybe that was normal, though. She didn't grow up with boys, so she didn't know.

Mindy said something.

"Huh?" asked Carla.

"There she is. Back to Earth?"

"Sorry," Carla said, putting on a smile. "Was lost in thought."

"Oh, I could tell. Figured you were thinking about the boys and the fort."

"That transparent, huh?"

Mindy waved her hand through the air. "Nah. Just a mom. I'm one, too, so I can tell. But I was thinking, I'd like to see it."

Carla smiled. "Well, we *should* see it. You said it yourself."

"We're the moms."

They laughed.

Mindy looked around. "I wonder where it is."

"Probably farther in. If you were a boy, where would you build a fort?"

Mindy thought about it. She held up a finger. "I got it. The creek."

"Creek?"

"Have you not ever walked this trail before?"

Shaking her head, she said, "We had a picnic a couple of times, but never very far out."

"In the clearing back when we first came in?"

Carla nodded. "Yeah."

"Oh, there're better spots back here. This trail goes for about two miles around the neighborhood. Then it ends at the main road. But if you go across, you can pick back up on Walker's Trail. That thing is seven miles and goes into the mountains."

"Jeez."

"Yeah. Serious walking."

"I don't think we'd be able to do that before the kids got home."

Mindy shook her head. "Nope."

"You don't think the boys went that far out, do you?"

"They better hope to God they didn't."

Carla laughed. "Agreed."

"Nah. The creek. We'll be there soon. That's where the fort will be. Somewhere around there."

They walked the shadowy path, talking about this and that. Though it was cooler in the woods, Carla began to sweat again. This time, it was the exertion causing it. There were hills she hadn't expected, which were making her legs achy. As time went on, she was thankful she'd chosen to wear this outfit. It felt as if she were naked, walking amongst the wilderness like some kind of feral woman. The privacy this far in the woods was impressive.

Maybe the next time Trevor has a sleepover somewhere, she and Mark could come out here with a blanket. Have a little fun like they used to do when they were younger.

The idea made her tingle inside.

Carla noticed the hiss of flowing water blending with the

birds and insects. Looking ahead, she saw blades of sunlight piercing the shadowy cloak. Something glinted farther up, trembling under the sun's glare. "The creek?" she asked.

"The creek," said Mindy, picking up her speed.

They came upon a small wooden bridge that was just wide enough to walk over. Water rushed underneath, spraying up and making the wood slick. They both held onto the rails as they crossed. On the other side, they paused.

Carla turned a circle as she examined the woods. "I don't see it," she said.

"Odd." Mindy stood with her hands on her hips. She looked around as if it might somehow just emerge in front of her. "Is this a path?"

"Where?" Carla stepped over. Mindy arched her foot, using the toes of her shoe to point at a bald stripe in the grass and weeds. It was no wider than a bicycle tire. "Bike path?"

"Ah." Mindy's eyebrows lifted. "Well, Sherlock. Guess we need to check it out."

Laughing, Carla said, "We shall, Watson."

Carla went first, walking on the dirt strip as if it were a tightrope. The creek flowed beside her, only a small section of earth separating her from falling in.

She couldn't help feeling like she was on an adventure.

*It's fun and games until we find their nudey magazines and cigarettes.*

Her stomach cramped at the thought of such discoveries. She couldn't let herself think like that. She knew Trevor. She'd raised him. He wasn't like that. Jack, well, he very could be all those things, but Trevor was smarter than that.

Or so she hoped.

"Is that what I think it is?" asked Mindy.

Carla realized she hadn't been paying attention, walking along the skinny path in a trance. Looking over to the left, she saw a structure through the trees. It was slightly tilting and looked as if it had been built by uneducated carpenters.

*The boys.*

"I think we found it," said Carla.

"I'm excited."

"Me too. Are we going to check it out?"

"Of course. We should know what the boys have been up to."

Nodding, Carla agreed. But she couldn't shake the feeling she should just turn around and go back home, forgetting she had ever seen this shoddy building.

When they were much closer, they stepped off the trail and walked over to the building. It had been haphazardly erected from wood pallets, upright and hammered together with crooked nails to form makeshift walls. Blankets stretched across the top to create a floppy roof. She recognized the old blankets from their attic as the material they'd used.

Mindy shook her head. "Well, I know what happened to my hammer. I used it to build some garden beds last year. It vanished. Thought I'd misplaced it. Of course, Jack wouldn't dare take his dad's." She held up a small hammer. A curved claw reached out from the other side of the flat head. "Could've at least put it *inside* the fort."

Carla walked around the backside of the pallets, keeping an eye out for nails. The last thing she needed was to step on one. She couldn't even remember when she last had a tetanus shot.

She didn't see any nails, but she saw a lot of empty soda cans sprinkled along the ground. There was a trash bag filled with garbage—potato chip bags, candy bar wrappers, and more flattened cans. No porno, so far.

"Where'd they get all this stuff?" she asked.

"This junk?" asked Mindy from the other side of the pallet walls. "Probably from the dumpsite on the other side of the woods. People drive out there and just throw stuff in the creek bed."

"Yuck."

"Yeah. Don't drink from the stream."

Shaking her head, Carla smiled. "Wasn't planning on it."

"They have a card table and chairs over here. Cards and comics. They've been busy. Probably worked on it all winter."

Nodding, Carla stepped over a bucket that lay on its side. It had been "borrowed" from their garage. How she hadn't noticed Trevor carrying this stuff away, she had no idea. She guessed it was because she'd been too busy to really pay attention. Her eyes stuck on her computer screen and a headset attached to her ear left little room for her to focus on anything else.

Well, that was going to change. She just wasn't sure yet if Trevor should get in trouble for this or not.

"What's this?" asked Mindy. "That little shit."

"What?" Carla couldn't help but smile.

"He took my nanna's silverware box."

"Is it worth anything?"

"Just cherished memories. But it's real silver. I hope he didn't ruin it." The squeaky sound of a lid lifting was followed by a quiet gasp from Mindy.

Carla paused. "Are you all right?"

"Uh...well."

Carla was already rushing around the backside of the fort and coming around the side when her shoulder bumped something hanging from a tree limb, knocking it out of the way. Mindy stood inside the dark fort, her white shirt a stain on the blackness.

Stepping up to her, Carla looked at Mindy. Her face had turned the color of her shirt. "What'd you find?"

Mindy turned, holding out a square wooden box. The lid was open. Instead of rows of silverware inside a velvety mold, the contents were an assortment of knives. All of them had big, jagged blades. None of them looked familiar. And most were covered in dark, tacky stains.

"What the hell?"

Shaking her head, Mindy turned and set the box on a small crate between the two rusty chairs. "It's nothing. Just boys doing boy things."

"With bloody knives?"

"Maybe it's not real blood."

Carla took a deep breath. Her chest felt as if it were shrinking around her lungs. "Not real?"

"Maybe they're making horror videos or something."

Carla was about to argue against that, then decided that it was possible. "But where'd they get them?"

"Who knows? Maybe the dump. Maybe they made them."

"Made them?"

"They might not be real."

Carla didn't agree with that. She also didn't like the idea of the boys possibly hauling out knives from an illegal dumpsite that were covered with blood. If so, why keep them?

"We'll just have to ask them about it," said Carla.

"Yeah." Mindy took a deep breath. "Ask them."

"It's strange," said Carla. "But it's not too big of a deal. Not really."

Carla didn't even believe herself, so she doubted Mindy did either. Finding bloody knives anywhere was a big deal, especially a play area your own child had helped build and kept hidden from you.

"I'm ready to head back," said Mindy. "This was a bad idea."

"It wasn't. Now we know. We can put a stop to it."

Mindy shook her head. "I don't know."

"We'll figure out how to handle it on the way back."

Nodding, Mindy turned and stepped forward. Then she jumped back. A squeal flew from her mouth and was quickly muffled by her hands slapping against it.

Carla whipped her head around and saw what had startled her walking partner. It was the object she'd bumped into on her way into the fort. Still swaying back and forth, it hung from what looked like clothesline string.

And it had a tail. Most of one, anyway. Its body was slit up the middle, exposing bones and an empty cavity where innards should have been. The fur was black and dingy. Its head, almost completely severed at the neck, showed a column of white bone in the fur.

The pointed ears made its mangled condition easy to recognize as once being a cat.

"Oh my God," said Carla. "That's the Parkers' missing cat."

Nodding, Mindy pointed to the right. "And that's the Basingers' missing dog."

Carla didn't want to look, but her head moved on its own. She saw the dog had been strung up with the same type of string by its back legs. She wasn't sure of the breed because its current condition didn't give much to make an educated guess. But it was evident the poor animal had been hanging there longer than the cat.

Chunks of it had been hacked away, leaving rotted pits in its withering body. Only a stub of fur showed between the dangling front legs. The head was nowhere to be seen.

"My God," said Carla, tears filling her eyes. "That dog vanished on Christmas. *Christmas!* Trevor got his new bike. He was supposed to be out riding it. But he was out here...doing this?"

Mindy's face was shiny with tears. Shaking her head, her big curls bounced. "Jack was with him. Trevor came over and got him. They left with Jack's new BB gun."

"Oh God." Carla's stomach cramped. She could taste the coffee at the back of her throat, trying to come back up. "What are we going to do?" She shook her head. "This is serious serial killer shit!"

"Shut up!" said Mindy, spinning around. She threw a finger up at her face. "Don't you say that!"

"Look at it," said Carla, stepping back. "The knives. The animals. The..." Her foot came down on something that wobbled. It made a soft cracking sound under the dirt.

Mindy looked down at Carla's feet. "What was that?"

Carla pushed down on the ground with her foot. She felt the

solidity sag, as if she were walking on thin ice that was about to break. She kicked away the dirt, unveiling a section of wood nearly the size of a medium pizza box. It looked as if it had been assembled from beams torn from pallets like they'd used for the walls.

"What the hell is that?" asked Mindy.

"I think it's a trapdoor."

"You've gotta be shitting me."

In unison, the women got down on their knees. They wiped away the dirt, completely exposing the secret access. It was a trapdoor, all right, with a padlock holding it shut. Like something that might have been used for a bomb shelter.

"What do you think is in there?" asked Carla.

Mindy sniffled. "Something that needs to breathe."

"Huh?"

Mindy pointed over Carla's shoulder. Turning her head, she didn't see anything at first. Then she spotted a PVC pipe jutting from the ground a few feet away.

*An air tube.*

"Give me the hammer."

Mindy got up and fetched the hammer from the crate between the chairs. It bumped against the silverware box but didn't knock it over. She came back, crouched, and held it out to her. "What are you doing?"

"Busting this lock."

One hit knocked the lock onto the grass. Handing the hammer back to Mindy, she lifted the lid. A rancid smell of old meat, piss, and shit wafted out, gagging her.

"Jesus," said Mindy, covering her nose. "Smells like an outhouse down there."

Slowly, the light from outside began to spill downward, spreading out and thinning the darkness filling the hole.

And exposing a woman inside.

Carla cried out when she saw her. She was tied up with more clothesline in a chair that Carla recognized as the one she used to sit in when she still sewed. It had been left in the attic with the sewing machine after they moved into the house. Her arms were pulled behind her, her ankles bound to the legs. The clothesline met at the back and formed a series of knots. The seat had been altered, cut away so her buttocks could hang through it.

A bucket had been placed underneath her. Brown splatters smeared over the rim, marking the side.

*Her toilet.*

Naked, her pale skin was filthy and covered in red slashes that had scabbed. Some of them looked infected and oozed pus. At first, Carla thought she might be dead. Then her head began to rise. The dirty hair fell away to show a battered face with a gagged mouth.

"Jenna Walters," said Mindy in a rush of air.

Carla stared down at their neighbor, who everyone, including her own husband, thought had simply left of her own free will. But she was here, in this hole. Probably had been the whole time. Nobody had been looking for her because nobody was worried about the pill-addicted woman.

Carla's vision flooded over with tears. She used the limp sleeve of her jacket to wipe her eyes. "Do you have your phone?"

"Huh?" Mindy looked at her. Tears spilled down her cheeks, cutting paths in the drying wetness already there.

"I didn't bring mine with me. We need to get her some help."

Mindy stared at her. "Help?"

"Look at her, Mindy. She's hurt. Bad."

Carla saw the nipple on her left breast was stiff and pointing, but the one on her right was missing. There were lacerations around the coin of dark flesh that she thought might have been teeth marks. An image of Trevor sinking his teeth into the plump mound flashed in her mind. She saw the gaps where his baby teeth had fallen out, sliding across the pale flesh.

She shook her head to shake away the vision.

"Our boys did this," said Carla, her voice turning gargled. She swallowed the sob and looked at Mindy. "We have to help her."

"We don't know our boys did this at all. We don't know they did any of this."

"We don't? Your hammer."

Mindy looked at it in her hand as if she'd forgotten it was there. "Anybody could've taken this."

Carla tilted her head. "Seriously?"

Mindy nodded. "I'm not convinced Jack would even—"

Carla looked down at Jenna. "Did our kids do this to you?"

Jenna stared up, her eyes weak and heavy as she squinted against the light. She looked as if she'd just come out of a coma. She nodded, wincing at the movements.

Mindy let out a blubbering wail. Carla suddenly felt numb. Her tears seemed to retract inside her, pulling back into her eyes and sucking down deep into the cold ball forming in her chest.

Trevor was involved. Her little boy—who liked to play video

games, build things with Legos, and read comic books. He watched cartoons and superhero movies. He still believed in Santa Claus, for Christ's sake. This couldn't be real. She had to be stuck in some kind of nightmare.

But another look at the boys' disturbing playground showed her it was all real.

"I'm getting her out of there," said Carla. She studied the hole. A ladder had been built from pallet parts and reached down from the hole at an angle. How had the boys dug this horrible prison? How long had it taken them? Was this what they were doing all fall and winter? Coming out here and digging and building.

And preparing.

She thought of the missing pets.

*Practicing.*

Feeling nauseous, Carla reached for the ladder. She had to help Jenna. She'd worry about the rest later.

The hammer whacked her hand, hitting her just above the knuckles. Pain flashed up her arm as she snatched it back. Holding her hand close, she looked at Mindy in shock. Her neighbor flung the trapdoor downward, letting it slam shut.

"What the hell are you doing?"

"Fixing this," she said.

Confused, she watched as Mindy crawled around, slapping the ground. "Aha!" She grabbed the padlock and held it up. "Found it."

"Mindy! Stop!"

Carla went to grab her, but Mindy spun around, swinging the hammer. It cut the air in front of Carla's face, grazing the tip of her nose. Carla flung herself back, rolling. As she came to a stop, she saw Mindy was coming at her again, the hammer raised.

"What are you doing?" Carla yelled.

Mindy brought the hammer down. She felt the blow on her head right before everything went dark.

When she opened her eyes again, she was on the ground, gazing up at the blue sky. She could hear hammering sounds nearby. Rolling onto her side, she groaned at the pain she felt in her head. It took her a few seconds to recall what had happened, but when it all came back, she wished it had remained forgotten.

Mindy was on her knees, repairing the lock. She finished hammering a fresh nail into the base that held it to the trapdoor. "There," she said, winded. Her face was glossy with sweat. "All fixed. Do you think the boys'll notice?"

Carla pushed herself up on all fours. Her vision swam for a moment, then cleared. "Why are you doing this, Mindy?"

"Because he's my son, and I am his mother. Why are *you* so willing to turn them in? They need us right now."

"They need help." Carla sat back on her knees. She groaned. Though she'd only been hit on the head, her neck felt as if it was stiff. "They took Jenna and did God knows what to her."

"Only God *will* know. I don't want to know."

"We can't protect them from this. You know that. They..."

Mindy looked at her. The rage behind her eyes shoved Carla's words back down her throat. "I will protect him from anything I can! He doesn't need to know we found this. Neither does Trevor."

"But *we* know," said Carla. "You're willing to let him come out here and..." She pointed at the hanging pets. "That'll be

Jenna next. And after her, who then? Somebody's kid. One of us?"

Mindy shook her head. "It won't go that far. We'll let them get it out of their system, then we'll figure out what to do."

"Putting it off won't solve anything. They need mental help. Jenna needs medical attention. We can't ignore this. We can't..."

That rage appeared in Mindy's eyes again, scaring Carla into silence.

Mindy shuffled closer to Carla on her knees. She held up the hammer. "You will do what I say. I'm not asking. I'm *telling* you. If you don't..." Mindy let the rest hang in the air. "You'll thank me later. You're in shock and have a very good reason to be. But I'm thinking clearly for the both of us. We were never here. End of story."

"Mindy."

Mindy thrust the hammer at Carla, making her recoil. "We were *never* here!"

Carla didn't want to go along with this, but she knew she had to. At least for the moment. She'd get home, call the police. Have them come out here and...

*And what?*

Take Trevor away in handcuffs? Lock him up? He'd be a grown man by the time he got out.

*If* he got out.

And everyone would know what he did. Every time somebody saw her or Mark, they'd point at the parents of the little maniac. People would say it was *their* fault, they'd raised him to be a killer.

*We'd never get away from it.*

Carla hated herself for thinking in such a way. It wasn't right. But she also knew she needed to tell Mindy what the incensed woman wanted to hear. So she nodded. "Okay."

"Okay, what?"

"We were never here."

Mindy thrust the hammer again. "You better not call the police when you get home either. I'm doing Trevor a favor by not adding you to this..." She pointed at the trapdoor with the hammer.

*Torture room,* Carla's thoughts finished for Mindy.

They looked around, making sure everything was how it had been when they first arrived. Mindy returned the hammer, leaving it where she'd first grabbed it. Recovering the trapdoor with dirt took the longest because Mindy kept insisting it didn't look right. Finally, she was convinced, and they started walking back to the neighborhood.

When they reached Carla's house, Mindy grabbed her arm as she turned toward her driveway.

"No cops," she said. "You do it and I'll kill you."

"Jesus, Mindy." Carla's stomach swirled with cold prickles of fear.

"I like you, Carla. But I'm serious. Do *not* call the police."

"Let go of my arm before I rip your eyes out."

Mindy smiled. "I knew you had some spirit in there somewhere. Now channel that into protecting your son." Mindy let go of her arm and started walking. "Gotta get home and start the pot roast."

Carla hurried inside her house. She locked the door behind her and walked through the house, making sure everything else was locked. Then she grabbed her cell phone from the island in the kitchen. She saw her empty coffee mug. It had only been a couple of hours ago when she'd been standing there, drinking it. Felt like a week had passed since she'd left the house.

Carrying her phone, she went upstairs and headed into Trevor's room. She started looking around, not knowing what she was trying to find. It didn't take her long to realize she'd messed up. In a shoebox under his bed, she found pictures he'd printed from the internet of murder victims. He'd cut them out, collecting them in messy piles inside the box like violent baseball cards. She saw one grisly image after the other. When she found some depicting children, she threw the pictures back in the box and put it away.

Crying, she went to her bedroom and dug out fresh clothes. Her head was pounding, and she was filthy. She went into the master bathroom, shut the door, and locked it. Then she dug out some aspirin from the medicine cabinet and filled her hand with water to help swallow them. She filled her hands a few more times and drank. The cold water coated her throat, taking away the dry burning.

In the shower, she stood under the spray. Whenever she tilted her head and the water pelted where Mindy had hit her, it caused a throbbing jolt to travel down the back of her neck. She reached into her hair and felt a small hillock pushing through. If she kept her hair up in a bun, it should cover it.

*What am I thinking? I can't hide it.*

But she knew she would. She had to.

*I* have to *call the police.*

Then why hadn't she yet? She'd been home for at least a half hour. She'd had plenty of time to do so.

Maybe she just wanted to check Trevor's room to be sure. Well, she'd done that and had more proof than she ever wanted.

And yet she still hadn't called the police.

Later, she was sitting at the kitchen table, drinking coffee, when she heard the squeal and huff of the bus stopping in front of the house. A nervous fizz bubbled in her stomach. The coffee no longer tasted warm and sweet, but cold and bitter. She pushed the mug away.

The bus chugged and groaned as it drove away. She heard footsteps on the front porch, then the doorknob twisting. It swung open, and Trevor entered.

"Hey, Mom!" He could see her easily from the door.

She turned and put on a smile. She fought back tears as she watched him come toward her. His hair stuck up in a fake mohawk style that he and Jack had started doing recently. His glasses made his lovely blue eyes look big and cartoonish. Adorable. His smile was good to see, though she could tell now that it was almost as if he'd taken it from a package and fixed it to his face. Somehow, it didn't really match his eyes.

*It's a fake smile.*

He wasn't a happy kid. No matter how hard she'd tried, she hadn't made her son happy.

*Hurting and killing things made him happy.*

"Are you okay?" asked Trevor, his smile fading. "You look sick."

"I'm fine," said Carla. "Want a snack?"

"Yeah!"

216

She waved her hand at the kitchen. "Have at it."

"Can I get what I want, or do I have to do fruit?"

Carla didn't know what mattered anymore. She shrugged. "Knock yourself out."

"You're the best, Mom!"

"Yeah, sure." She swallowed the lump forming in her throat. It caused a flash of pain to start on the welt she'd hidden under the bun in her hair. "Got any homework?"

Trevor had vanished inside the pantry. When he returned, he was holding a bag of chips and a bag of beef jerky. "Just have to read. I'll do that in bed tonight. I'm going to eat my snack and play a little bit. Then Jack and me are going to hang out."

Carla closed her eyes. "Oh?"

"Is that okay?"

Opening her eyes, she nodded. Trevor had his back to her as he opened the fridge and snatched a small bottle of juice from the plastic holders inside. "What are you guys planning to do?"

Trevor turned around. "Going to play in the woods, probably. It's getting warmer, so we'll be outside more."

"Oh."

"And I can't wait for next week," he said, smiling.

"Next week?"

"Yeah. It's spring break! We'll get to be outside the *whole* week. I'm heading upstairs. Love you." Trevor ran off, his bookbag swinging on his back. The stomping sounds of his feet pounding up the stairs echoed through the house.

*Jesus, help me.*

She picked up her cell phone and stared at it. She needed to call the police. It was the right thing to do. But she didn't have the strength to do so. Maybe Mark would know what to do. If she decided to tell him, maybe he could help her figure it all out.

But she didn't think she would be able to say anything to him either.

Sighing, Carla stood up and walked over to the stove.

She had to figure out what to make for supper.

# THERE GOES THE
# NEIGHBORHOOD
## RAYNE HAVOK

I wake up to Hamilton watching TV, cereal all over the carpet, and the cat lapping up the leftover milk from the bowl. Typical Saturday morning.

The beeping sound coming from the television draws my eyes toward it. The news reporter looks more flustered than she's allowed to, and it makes me more curious as to why the news is breaking through regularly scheduled programs. While she gathers herself, I wonder how long it's actually been since something like this has happened. Everyone has the internet now and plenty of ways to keep up on the important news. Too much access, honestly.

By the time I bring myself back to the moment, the reporter has already started talking.

"...strange things are being reported all across the city. Police have been called to help assist in the domestic disputes that seem to be pouring in at record numbers. Nothing is linking the occurrences thus far, but we need to make sure that everyone is on the lookout for strange behavior with their children."

I look at Hamilton curiously and wonder what the hell could actually be happening around us. And how bad it has to be to make the news. He looks okay. Tousled, sleep hair and jammies, one sock, nothing wildly different.

"Hammy, are you okay? Do you feel all right?" I touch his forehead with the back of my hand.

He looks up at me with a standard innocence in his eyes. "Of course, Mommy."

I cock my head to the side and watch him while he keeps his eyes on me. His mouth moves like he's speaking, but nothing audible comes out. "What is it, Ham? You can talk to me. You know that."

His mouth clenches shut, lips tighten between his teeth, and the creases around his eyes grow along with a slanted sideways grin.

I reflexively look away, putting my eyes back on the reporter talking, but I don't hear her anymore. The room is full of the screeching laughter coming from Hamilton.

I click the button on the TV, turning it off, and pick Hamilton up. I have no idea what the next step is until I'm in the bathroom with him, shower on. I put him in the stall fully clothed. I watch the water drench him, droplets trickling from his eyelashes and down his face as he stands still in the downpour.

The laughter stops so abruptly that the silence is startling. His face drops to his feet, one wet sock to look at.

"Are you...okay?" Is he okay? Am I okay? What the fuck was that? I don't know what possessed me to stick my kid in the shower like that. I should enjoy the sound of his laughter; I shouldn't be disturbed by it. That news report instantly made me feel wrong. Put some nonsense in my head that I hadn't even fully understood, and then I freaked out. I'm glad it doesn't seem to have affected Hamilton negatively.

"I'm fine, Mommy." This time, there's a sweet smile on his face, one I definitely don't deserve. "It's funny to put me in here like a rainy day." He spins and laughs, opens his mouth like he does when he's tasting the rain outside.

I chuckle softly, hoping to ease the tension I feel in my head and behind my eyes. "Want to go to the grocery store?"

He nods his head excitedly. Which I knew would happen, the kid loves the grocery store. I can't even think of anything we need, but the sensation of being out of the house and occupied is making me say things before thinking them all the way through.

I help him out of the sticky, wet clothes, tell him to shower properly, and then go to my room to change. I'm hungry, and I need coffee, but my legs are telling me there's no time for that. There's too much urgency inside them right now to behave normally.

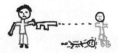

As soon as we are in the car and I have Hamilton sitting in the seat behind me, his reflection looking at me in the rearview mirror, I can feel that weirdness again. Something feels off with him. The eyes that usually look at me are not the same; there's an absence of delight in them, no love. There's a strangeness to them, and it's off-putting. Paranoia or not, it's unsettling. I wish I hadn't seen the news report. How could something be happening to my son? He's never out of my sight. It's summertime, so school isn't even in session. Whatever is happening around us isn't happening here. As long as I ignore the strangeness I'm seeing in his eyes right now—the thing that's making it all the more obvious that I'm lying to myself—then it should be fine. Right? Probably.

I don't even actually know what's going on. I hadn't seen enough of the report to gather a substantial amount of information, and I can't say that I'm not imagining things because the reporter implanted the notion that I should.

I shake my head and shift into drive. I can't make this anymore strange than it already is. And I should try to make things as normal as I can for my child, no need to make him uncomfortable just because I am. Chaos feeds chaos.

THE GROCERY STORE WAS A BAD IDEA; I CAN FEEL IT right away. There are too many people here, the parking is horrible, so I know instantly that the inside is full. I find a spot after driving two full rotations around the lot and take Hamilton out of his seat. He plops down next to the car, ass in a puddle of someone's discarded muck, and I sigh. Not typical behavior from my always-sweet boy, and I add it to the subconscious list of behavior out of the norm for him.

I pick him up and carry him—with purpose so as not to

touch my skin to his messy shorts—to the cart return rack and put him inside one of the child seats. He kicks his legs wildly, hitting my thighs and stomach. "Hammy, you're hurting me. Please sit still."

The laugh, that terrible squeal, it's as abrupt as the last time.

"Should we go home?" Usually a threat, this time, a hopeful plea is in my voice that surprises me.

"No." His voice is flat; his eyes are hard. He crosses his arms over his chest and pouts. An eyebrow cocked up as if daring me to go against him.

"Please behave then." Reluctantly and slower than normal, I push the cart into the air-conditioned store. I stop, looking around for the cause of my unease, although today feels like it could be anywhere. It looks normal, but it feels off. It's too quiet for the amount of people in the shop. The hustle and bustle of this many people should make a certain amount of noise, but it's as though no one is making any sounds.

A single man walks through the door pushing a cart, and all eyes land on him as he continues through the produce section with the squeaking wheeled monstrosity. Chirping through the aisles without a care in the world. I watch him, and then I watch the others watch him. Their heads all making slow movements to track his progress until he's out of sight. Then the silence. Worse, then there's laughter. Not only Hamilton this time, all the children. Laughing. Screeching that horrible sound. Like a play-ground full of hyenas or monkeys. It's horrible. I can feel the culminating tension the adults feel in the room as it settles into my own bones.

I go to leave, to just turn the cart around and head home,

where there's only one monkey in the playground, but he stops, and then they all stop. And then he looks at me, his eyes angry. "No," he says firmly. "I need snacks."

It shouldn't feel like a threat, but it does. It feels wrong. The words he usually says in jest are harsh, and I'm speechless.

We navigate the store with him pointing to the aisles he wants me to turn down. He's pulling things from the shelves, anything in arms' reach, and tossing them into the cart. Things I normally only allow for occasional treats. The devious and daring look in his eyes confounds me as I push the cart obediently, at a loss for how to better handle this situation.

The other parents look as if they are equally trapped inside the same spell. Eyes cast down in some sort of shared shame.

Once home, he takes the bags from the counter, plops them on the floor in the living room, and turns on the TV. A new cartoon that just released is back on. It's racket, loud noises and confusing jokes that only he laughs at. It's the most annoying thing. I have an adult child as well, and I had to live through all her children's shows; this one is utter nonsense and seems more off-putting than the old ones.

He seems to be managing himself just fine, and I'm in need of a long, hot shower to wash this whole thing away. Maybe I'll come out of it with the balls to stand up to him. Right now, I don't have the fight or the know-how to begin one.

LATER THAT NIGHT, AFTER MORE OF THE SAME—SO MUCH more—I stand on the porch, the cool breeze blowing the smoke from my cigarette away, close my eyes, and get ready to tell Hamilton it's bedtime. I'm exhausted. I make a wish that he'll go down easily. Then I wonder if parents are allowed to go to sleep with their young children still roaming the house, eating candy like it's about to expire.

One last drag, and I snuff it out, then I take the deepest breath I can manage and slowly let it out. Sliding the door open, I shout, "Come on, Ham, it's bedtime!"

I hear the grumble, and I ready myself to stand up to my kid, but then I hear the footsteps scamper across the floor, and I'm filled with relief. I hear the water from the bathroom sink, and the excitement from the thought of going to sleep jumpstarts my heart a bit. Closing the door on this day is necessary.

Story read—three times, nothing unusual with that— Hamilton is tucked into bed, a spinning dinosaur nightlight in the corner giving him just enough light to keep the nighttime jitters away.

I close the door, something I don't usually do, but I can't bring myself to leave it cracked open. I need his door between us right now. I stand there listening for him to call out and ask that I fix the door, but he doesn't.

I shut my own door as well, and it feels good having that much space between us right now. I'm just glad I'm the only one here who has to witness the betrayal.

THERE'S A SENSATION, MORE THAN A FEELING, THAT wakes me up. The room is black, so I know it must be night still.

I could look at my phone for the time, but something insists I remain still. I wonder if it's the residual effect from this afternoon. I try to convince myself to close my eyes and go back to sleep, that I don't really need to check the time, that I have plenty of time to sleep. Technically, closing my eyes isn't moving, which was the command set by my brain. But my eyes won't shut, and my body is no longer tired; every nerve is wide awake.

I wait for my vision to acclimate to the darkness, but the adrenaline is keeping me from seeing anything. The whooshing in my ears is loud, and distracting, as I try to listen for anything that feels important to hear.

While lying perfectly still on my back, I glance from corner to corner, taking in all that I can. Nothing looks off, no creepy man hovering at the foot of my bed. When I do another round, I realize something *is* off. For a moment, I can't tell what's missing. But then I realize I can hear the little hum of the desktop computer, but I can't see the glowing red power light that is always there.

I feel the gasp in my chest more than I hear it. Goose bumps creep along my arms and into my hair. My heart hammers as my eyes bore into the space where that little light lives.

With a shaky breath, I do what I know to be the most wrong thing. I whisper, "Hello?" The last syllable lodges in my throat like a hiccup.

I can't tell if it's worse that I don't get a response or if a hello back would have quelled my anxiety. I settle on neither being appropriate.

I know someone is there. I can feel the eyes of investigation on me. I've never wanted a knife under my pillow more than right now because I have to do something. If I'm hurt, no one can protect Hamilton. But I don't know if it's better to wait this thing out or if a quick attempt at an attack would be better. My brain is not cooperating in the planning stage of this matter. It's off imagining the most horrible things that could be waiting for me after I move. Waiting for me and for Hamilton, and it becomes a distraction to try and navigate the thoughts.

My hand flinches. I don't know what it has planned, it is without permission, but the movement is so subtle it felt more like a failed attempt.

Closing my eyes, if only to put distance between the obstruction, I breathe in deeply a few times and let out slow, calm-as-possible breaths. That is, until I feel the warmth of something next to me, then my eyes snap open, back to the computer, my only frame of reference. And I see the light. And I know there is someone standing right next to me. And then I feel the fingers around my throat. Strong, small fingers digging into my neck. My last breath is a gasp, and then nothing else can fight through the obstruction. The stars light up behind my eyes and take over, twinkling a fuzzy feeling to the top of my head. And then nothing.

"PARENTS OF SMALL CHILDREN ALL MET THE SAME FATE last night, as an illness has changed the children's behavior to the nefarious. Experts are unaware of the cause but are recommending that you not approach the children. They are very dangerous and working together to accomplish evil things. We ask that you stay indoors and avoid going out at all costs. The police have organized and are working tirelessly to apprehend them. But the numbers are staggering."

# Beware the Hurlyburly

## Brian Asman

*Yorba Linda, CA*

A California State appeals court ruled today to uphold a lower court's decision requiring accused teen killer, Wesley Franz, now fifteen, to be tried as an adult in the murder of Steven L. DeLongo, twelve. Franz's lawyers had argued that a combination of childhood abuse and a previously undiagnosed mental disorder left Franz unable to truly comprehend his own actions on the morning of April 13th, 2016, when Franz allegedly entered a locker room at Bernardo Yorba Middle School and stabbed the other boy over twenty-five times before being arrested by the school resource officer.

"Due to the premeditation and extraordinary aggression demonstrated by the defendant, I have no choice but to uphold the court's ruling," said the Honorable Ted Lieu.

Franz is being held at the Orange County Central Men's Jail pending trial. A trial date has not yet been set.

I KNOW *SIXTY MINUTES* MADE US LOOK LIKE ASSHOLES—worse, *simple* assholes—but the thing is I'm not stupid. Like, I know the Hurlyburly is just a meme, something that crawled its way out of the SomethingAwful forums or maybe somewhere on Reddit, and all those "pictures" you see online are just photoshopped. Come on, it's not like I think Chuck Norris actually craps grenades or whatever. I'm not stupid. Even back when I was twelve.

Also, the kid they got to portray me in the reenactment was really whiny. I don't whine like that in real life. Ask anybody in here. The other kids, the guards, whoever. Ask them if I'm whiny. I'm not whiny.

Or stupid.

Sure, maybe I believed dumb stuff back then. Fall before the Hurlyburly mess, Hector showed me this Flat Earth documentary on YouTube, some ex-NASA guy explaining how all the shots of Earth from space are fake, just whipped up on somebody's computer. And I didn't believe that, either, but I wanted to believe because thinking about the ice wall that supposedly surrounded the Earth got me thinking about the Wall on *Game of Thrones*. I'd only seen parts of episodes—Hector liked to fast forward through all the talking and get to the battles—but if something like that was real, anything could be on the other side. Giants, dragons, whatever. Seemed cooler than living in Yorba Linda with a bunch of other boring kids, and our boring parents, and my boring math teacher, Mrs. Barger.

So we tried to come up with experiments. I stole a laser pointer from Mrs. Barger—nearly threw up when I walked out the door past Officer Presbitt, the pointer shoved up my hoodie sleeve—and we rode our bikes to the Walnut Canyon Reservoir. We found a couple of sticks and taped the laser pointer to them, four feet high, and stuck it in the mud right at the water's edge. Then I turned on the pointer and ran around the reservoir to the other side, kicking off my shoes to stand with my toes in the water, letting the pointer shoot me right in my white T-shirt. I marked the spot with a magic marker, then ran back around to the other side, where Hector measured me, and we very scientifically determined that the Earth must be flat because the mark on my shirt was exactly four feet off the ground, just like the laser pointer. That Monday, we went into school all excited to tell Mr. Grayson, our science teacher.

"Wesley, you know that Flat Earth stuff's a bunch of baloney, right?" he told me over his bifocals, then proceeded to point out all the flaws in our little experiment—first and foremost being, at that distance, the curvature of the Earth would be measured in millimeters. You think I'd be pissed, but I mostly liked Mr. Grayson because he talked to me like an adult, not some little kid. And by the end of it, yeah, I could see the baloney, as he called it.

"Guess we wasted our time," I said.

He gave me a weird little look, then shook his head. "You learned something, right?"

"Yeah."

"There you go." He clapped me on the shoulder, and the bell rang, and that was it for Flat Earth Theory.

"CHECK THIS OUT," HECTOR SAID, PASSING ME HIS tablet. Same one as mine, both Sam's Club iPad knockoffs. We were sitting in my room, me in the desk chair picking at my math homework, Hector in the beanbag.

Anything was better than equations. I took the tablet and squinted at it—just some old picture, kids playing outside an old brick building, a copse of trees in the background. Maybe a hundred years old or more, from how they dressed, their hair.

"So?"

"Look closer. At the woods."

I did. And—

"What's that?" I pointed to a strange shape in the trees, barely more than a shadow. It looked like a person, big and round like William Howard Taft, who we'd been learning about in history—only person to be president and chief justice—except there was something *off* about it, something I couldn't quite figure out.

"Here," Hector said, using his fingers to zoom in on the figure.

I yelped and dropped the tablet on my desk, right on top of my math homework. "What the heck?"

"They call it the Hurlyburly," Hector said, voice hushed, and then showed me a bunch of other links. All old pictures like the first one—children ice-skating in a pond, milling around a giant Christmas tree at the town square, climbing on a jungle gym. In each, the Hurlyburly lurked in the background. Whatever it was, it was big, swollen, with stringy black hair and a flap of skin growing over its facial features, hiding everything but the hint of a toothsome smile. It was naked, too, with big breasts covered in weeping sores and a bloated belly obscuring its nether regions.

The fine hair on my arms stood on end. I shifted in my chair. "These are fake, right?"

"Sure, they're fake," Hector said. "Gotta be."

That last part in a creepy, singsong voice like the jump rope girls in *A Nightmare on Elm Street,* which I wasn't supposed to watch, but I did.

Didn't sleep for a week, hardly.

"Put it away."

Hector took the tablet back. "You want to play *Minecraft?*"

"I'm still doing my homework."

"That's a non sequitur."

I sighed and pushed my notebook away. "Fine."

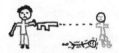

EXCEPT IT WASN'T FINE. I LAY IN BED THAT NIGHT, staring at the swirling shadows the ceiling fan threw, pulling my blanket up to my chin each time one looked a little too thick. Footsteps tramped down the hallway, probably my dad getting up for a glass of water, but I kept thinking they sounded too heavy for him. My dad was built like a bird, from his thin chest to his too-big nose and long neck. He shaved his head, and one time my parents took me to the Safari Park down in San Diego, and I looked at the vultures and then back at him and didn't say anything but "Wow, they're cool," but I was really thinking about a zookeeper jumping from behind the bushes with a tranq gun, or maybe one of those *Looney Tunes* nets, and chasing my dad around the zoo until he ended up behind the glass, wings clipped, pecking at bits of dead things. My mom and I on the other side of the glass, hand in hand, except I couldn't feel her skin against mine and I didn't like that much at all.

So I pictured the tigers, and the baby rhino, and the bat cave, and maybe I wasn't technically counting sheep, but I slept and I didn't dream about the Hurlyburly at all.

Soon I would.

HECTOR AND I WERE EATING LUNCH AT THE PICNIC tables back then, where I met him at the start of the year, actually. The cafeteria was too crowded, too full of kid energy. Most of my friends from elementary had gone to a different middle school, and outside of Hector, I'd struggled to make friends. I wasn't athletic and all my clothes came from Target. My older brother, Nathan, was in tenth grade and didn't seem to have any of the same problems. He was a nerd, for sure, but he didn't care. Liked it, even.

"Popularity's a kid's game, Wes," he told me once, when I

was complaining about how Stevie D didn't even say hi to me anymore, too busy with his intramural basketball friends to even reminisce about how we used to play Yu-Gi-Oh! over cardboard slices of pizza.

"It doesn't bother you?"

Nathan shrugged. "Let somebody else be prom king. I'm going to launch rockets into space." He was obsessed with working for Lockheed. Sometimes I thought if I just had that thing, like a thing I was hell-bent on doing, everything would be okay, but back then I didn't want much of anything.

"You think if somebody took a picture right now, we'd see it watching us?" Hector asked.

I took another bite of my burrito, barely listening. "See what?" Didn't bother asking who'd take a picture of us in this fantasy world he was conjuring up. Ariana Grande, maybe, might as well.

Hector leaned across the table, lowering his voice. "The Hurlyburly."

"Come on."

"No, seriously." He pointed over my shoulder at the smoked glass doors to the gymnasium. "Maybe we'd zoom in and see its silhouette through the windows. Just...watching."

I tried another bite, but my burrito tasted worse than usual, and that was saying something. "You're being weird. And creepy."

Hector tapped the table. "Let's try it. Give me your phone."

My phone was in my backpack. We weren't supposed to have them in school; it was only for emergencies. Especially since my dad had begrudgingly started letting me ride my bike to school, instead of dropping me off and making me sprint head down to the front doors, hoping nobody saw and started making bird noises.

"No. I'll get in trouble."

"Come on."

"Use yours."

"I don't have one."

Which was bullshit, we texted all the time. But Hector was like that. He'd lie to your face and make you call his bluff and then double down. Make you feel stupid. See why I'm so sensitive about that?

"Wes—"

"Fine," I muttered. I looked around for any teachers or the school resource officer, Presbitt, but we were alone. I unzipped my bag and slid the phone across the picnic table.

"Okay," Hector said, lining up the shot. "Say cheese."

"This is stupid."

"You could at least smile."

I shot him the finger instead.

Hector took a couple, then flipped through the photos, lips pursed. Then his eyebrows shot up. "Got one."

"Shut up."

"No, see?" He shoved my phone at me.

Sighing, I held the phone up. I tried not to look at my own face; I hated how I looked in pictures: all zits and baby fat, my ill-fitting blue hoodie hugging the wrong places on my body, my hair looking dumb no matter how I tried—and failed—to style it. Even giving the finger, I felt like a hopeless loser who was too much of a loser to even know he'd never be cool. I scanned the background and didn't see anything.

"There's nothing here."

"Look at the gymnasium. The roof."

I did.

And almost puked up the first half of my burrito because right there, right fucking there, hanging over the roof, fat slug-like fingers digging into the bricks, skin flap drooling mucus over a pasty chin, was it.

The Hurlyburly.

I dropped my phone and whipped around, grabbing my lunch tray as, as, I don't know, maybe a weapon, maybe a shield? I don't know what I was thinking. The half-eaten burrito sailed off into the grass, but I wasn't thinking about that; I was thinking about the *roof* because this couldn't be real, no way.

Of course there wasn't anything there.

I dropped my tray, fighting back the urge to retch.

"I think it likes you," Hector whispered.

"Fuck you."

"Mr. Franz!" a voice called from across the courtyard. I turned to see Officer Presbitt pistoning his way across the concrete. He always walked like a power walker, like those old ladies at the mall before it's even open, and was always sweating his nuts off. Figured that was why he became a cop—dark uniforms hid pit stains.

Presbitt pulled up a couple of feet from me and pointed at my grass-covered burrito. "Pick that up. You know better than to trash the place."

"Yes, sir." I picked up my crap, hands still shaking from what

I'd seen. There had to be some kind of explanation. Like with the Flat Earth stuff. I could ask Mr. Grayson.

At least he wouldn't laugh at me.

I carried my former lunch over to the trash can and tossed it. Didn't even mind. At that point, I couldn't imagine eating again for a long time.

"One more thing," Officer Presbitt said, holding up a finger. Then sweat dripped into his eyes and he grimaced, wiped his forehead with the back of his arm.

I waited, maybe not patiently but inertly, until he was finished. Then he pointed at my phone.

"Keep that put away during school hours. I'd hate to have to confiscate it."

"Yes, sir."

He nodded to himself, then headed toward the gymnasium. Part of me hoped the Hurlyburly was hiding inside. And hungry.

Presbitt paused at the entrance, one hand on the doors. Said over his shoulder, "You're not a bad kid, Franz. Sometimes you might get the urge to be, but don't lean into that, okay? Just keep doing you."

I nodded like I knew what he meant. When he didn't open the gym door, I added, "I will, sir."

That sent him on his way.

"Told you I'd get in trouble," I muttered, shoving my phone in my backpack.

"But you didn't, did you?" Hector replied.

Having been in here long enough, I've had a lot of time to turn it all over in my head, and I think my problems really began when I started thinking Hector had a point.

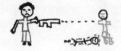

Hunted.

That's how I felt. What I was. I went home and checked the whole house...nothing. Then posted up in my bedroom, Little League bat across my knees, and waited for my brother to get home. Nathan came in about an hour later. I guess he had some club. Robotics, maybe? Either way, when I heard the door open, I sucked in a breath, afraid it might not be him. But then the cabinet opened, and the toaster clunked, and I could smell Pop-Tarts. Nathan's after-school snack ritual.

It felt good having someone else in the house. Comforting. Enough that I pulled my phone out and looked at the pictures again. Hector had taken three. I checked the first one, breathed a sigh of relief when I didn't see anything lurking on top of the gymnasium. Ditto the second. I put the phone aside, got up, and paced my room, working up the courage to look at that last picture.

*Just do it,* a voice that sounded like Hector whispered.

So I did.

And this time—this is going to sound crazy, I guess—I could see what I'd been looking at earlier by the picnic tables, but it wasn't the same thing. Before, I could see the Hurlyburly clear as day. Now it looked like a smudge. Sure, it was thick, but all the details I'd imagined, the nails grinding into brick, the skin flap, the slimy mucus, those must've been in my head. Like I said, this was just a smudge, an outline.

Something bothered me about it. I clicked *Edit,* then hit the back button.

The smudge disappeared.

I texted Hector. *You're a shithead.*

He replied with a bunch of question marks. I didn't respond.

Twenty minutes later, he called me. "Dude, what's up with you?"

"The picture? I know what you did."

"What I did?"

Footsteps clomped by in the hallway, Nathan heading for his own room. I lowered my voice.

"I know you photoshopped that thing into the picture. And it was just, like, a little squiggle. You were messing with me."

"I have no idea what you're talking about."

"You keep saying that, but—"

"I wouldn't do that. Remember, the Hurlyburly wants to divide us."

"What? How do you—"

He hung up.

Five minutes later, he texted me a screenshot from some knockoff Creepypasta site.

*The Hurlyburly will manipulate reality to separate you from your friends and family.*

"Sure it will." I snickered and went to see if there were any of Nathan's Pop-Tarts left.

I SLEPT GUILTLESSLY THAT NIGHT. CLOSED MY EYES, didn't need to count rhinos or zebras or tapirs, just drifted off. The Hurlyburly was a figment of my imagination, nothing more, nothing less. And Hector? Maybe it shouldn't have surprised me. His left eye was slightly smaller than the right, made him look like he was always about to wink, and that was his thing, wasn't it? Playing jokes, and worse—he was the one who put me up to stealing Mrs. Barclay's laser pointer for our idiotic Flat Earth experiments. Maybe he was, as my mom would have said, a *bad influence.* Which would've been okay if it was me and Hector against the world, which is what I *thought,* but now it was obvious it was Hector against me.

Thought we were friends. Then again, even that young, I got the sense that there were kids who couldn't be friends with anybody, not because they were dorks or whatever, but because they didn't have it in them, they were born missing some crucial piece. Hector hid it well, or maybe he didn't and I was just stupid.

I'm not stupid, though. I'm not.

At some point I woke up. Like full-on awake, heart hammering. I sat up in bed, thinking it must've been a dream. The sheets felt wet, and I checked to see if I peed myself like when I was eight, but I hadn't, thank God. Just sweat.

I wondered what woke me until I heard the tapping on my window.

*Tap, tap, tap-tap.*

My stomach clenched. The window was a few feet away, the blinds down, thank God. I stared at it, unable to wrench my eyes away.

*Tap.*

The blinds shook, just slightly.

*Tap. Tap-tap.*

Something was on the other side. Maybe a bird. Maybe a squirrel. Maybe Hector.

But all I could imagine was the Hurlyburly, standing in the ankle-high grass outside my window, a flap of skin hiding its face while it tapped one fat, sluglike finger against my window, over and over, pushing the nail back in the cuticle until sludgy black blood ran down its hand and dripped down the window glass and—

Dad started coughing, the sounds reverberating through the thin walls of our postwar ranch house, and the tapping stopped. And by the time I got the balls to look outside?

Nothing there.

HECTOR STOPPED SHOWING UP AT SCHOOL, WHICH WAS too bad because I really wanted to give him shit about the little trick he'd pulled. I wasn't sure if he was sick or skipping, since he didn't answer my texts.

*Maybe the Hurlyburly got him,* I remember thinking. *Maybe it climbed into his bed and ate him right up while he was sleeping.*

And even though I could picture the whole thing, it didn't make me shiver. It made me laugh. No cap. Something seemed kind of, *right,* I guess? Getting killed by the fake monster he created.

At first, it was a relief not having to deal with him because I was still pretty pissed about the way he messed with me. Or tried to, because I saw right through the whole thing. And that's what really bothered me. A guy like Stevie D, who puts on a basketball jersey and becomes someone else, I could see him doing something like this. Maybe not to me, but some other kid. But Hector? We were both scraping by near the bottom of the social ladder. We should've been partners in crime. We should've Hurlyburly'ed someone else, together.

I made it through the first three periods, but then, come lunchtime, I panicked. Where was I supposed to sit? The thought of walking up to a tableful of kids and asking to sit down made me want to throw up. Sitting by myself at a picnic table wasn't much better, I'd look like a loser, but hardly anybody came out to the courtyard anyway but Officer Presbitt.

I stopped by the cafeteria for a hot dog and a bag of chips, then shouldered my way outside. The day was overcast, the courtyard empty as usual. I grabbed our table. Dawned on me I hadn't done all of my history homework, so I pulled out the assigned reading and started on that while I ate my hot dog.

I never heard the door open, so when a voice asked, "Is anyone else sitting here?" like, two feet away from my ear, I yelped like a dog with its tail stepped on. Looked up to see a girl with short black hair backing away, hands up.

"Sorry, I didn't mean to—"

"No, no," I said, standing. "Just caught me by surprise, that's all." I gestured to the bench. "You want to sit?"

I blinked, surprised at myself—that was more words than I'd

said to anybody who wasn't Hector or a teacher in longer than I could remember.

The girl stopped backing away, looked me up and down. "If you're sure. I don't want to bother—"

"It's okay."

She sat, dropping her backpack on the table.

"No lunch?"

"I brought my own." She unzipped her backpack and removed a brown paper bag. "My moms are vegan."

"Oh." I didn't know any vegans.

"I'm not, but they want me to be, so they don't give me money for school lunch." She dumped out the contents of her lunch bag onto the table: a plastic-wrapped sandwich with lots of green sprouts sticking out, a Ziploc bag of carrots, a tub of rice. She held up the sandwich, grinning. "Only good part is they're *so* bad at it."

"How do you mean?"

She peeled the plastic back with a nail. "You know what Saran Wrap's made out of?"

I shrugged. "Plastic?"

"That's right. And plastic is made from petroleum. And petroleum is?"

I chewed my lower lip. This I didn't know. Was it a mineral or something? Not a plant, since people were always complaining about it ruining the environment. "Chemicals?"

She slapped the table. "Dead dinosaurs!"

I narrowed my eyes, leaning back and crossing my arms. "Guess I could never be vegan. Dinosaurs are all I eat."

She laughed. "That hot dog is probably made from plastic."

"Kinda tastes like it. You want a bite?"

She snatched the hot dog and took a bite from the end I hadn't. Closed her eyes, chewing, a blissful look falling over her face. She had a lot of freckles. "Mmmm." She took another bite, bigger, before setting the hot dog back down on my plate. There wasn't much left, but I didn't mind.

"I'm Wesley, by the way."

"Heather." She held out a hand. I wiped mine on my napkin, then shook. Her hand felt cold and clammy.

"So you new here?"

"Why do you say that?"

"I dunno, never seen you around before."

"Well, I've never seen you around either. Maybe you're new."

"I'm not." I tried to get back to my hot dog, but it was cold now. And tasted weird. My tongue tingled, and not in a good way like from Pop Rocks and Sprite. Meanwhile, Heather was tearing into her own lunch, wolfing down her sandwich like she hadn't eaten in days.

We more or less ate in silence, except for the exceptionally loud sounds of Heather's chewing. Or she ate, I mostly just picked at the splinters in the picnic table, trying to come up with something to say. This was uncharted territory for me. If you had told me I turned invisible over the previous summer, I would've believed you, because other than Hector, nobody ever talked to me. Yet here was this girl, out of the blue, with a bubbly personality and freckles all over her nose and two moms, which, in a suburban stronghold like Yorba Linda, marked her as at least a little exotic. I wondered where she came from, what made her want to sit with a guy like me.

I guess I could've asked, but that would've shattered the illusion. Maybe she'd suddenly turn into a flock of crows and fly away, like some old fairy tale. Some things you don't question because they can't stand up to it. They'll die.

The bell rang. Heather shoved the remnants of her lunch in her paper bag and slung her backpack over one shoulder.

"Nice eating with you. Maybe we can do this again?"

Surprised me, since I'd clammed up for most of the meal, but I nodded. "I'm out here most days."

She smiled and headed for the door, then turned back. "You want to take a quick selfie?"

"Huh?"

"To commemorate the occasion. New friends and all."

"Uh, okay?" I realized that didn't sound like a yes, so I added, "Sure."

She came back and sat next to me, so close our thighs were touching, leaned her head on my shoulder, and held up her phone. I could see the gymnasium roof at the top of the screen and tried not to think about Hector and his stupid Hurlyburly.

"Say hot dog. Um, no, dinosaur. Er, dead dinosaurs, that's it!"

"Dead dinosaurs."

She took the selfie, then sprang up, breezing across the courtyard. "I'll send you a copy," she called.

And was gone before I could remind her that she didn't have my number.

EXCEPT SHE DID.

I had just brushed my teeth and laid down when my phone buzzed. I was supposed to turn it off at exactly eight p.m. sharp —my dad was concerned about *blue light* and *screen time* but not enough to actually take it away from me—but technically, I couldn't because it was also my alarm. Thought about leaving it till the morning, especially since it was probably Hector, but I remembered what Heather said about texting me our photo (somehow) and picked up my phone.

One message from an unknown number. *Wanna see our pic?*

I started texting back a thumbs-up, but I overheard Stevie D saying emojis were lame while walking by their lunch table, and he would know, so I just replied, *Yah.*

Three dots. She was typing.

I sat there watching the dots. Seemed like she was writing a book. They disappeared for a minute, and I thought maybe she'd changed her mind, and then a link popped up, a bunch of random letters and numbers.

My dad always told me never to click random links, Nathan said the same, so I know he wasn't just being paranoid, but I had an iPhone and those don't get viruses, at least I think they don't, and part of me wondered why she didn't just send the picture. Maybe she'd already uploaded it to the cloud or something?

*You like it?*

I had to click the link. My finger hovered over the screen, apprehension filling my body even though I couldn't say where it was coming from. Now, I know what it was.

Primal instincts.

Fight-or-flight.

Couldn't stand up to my hormones.

I clicked the link. My web browser opened. The site loaded slowly, a black background, then the picture in the middle, chunkily unfolding top-down. A sliver of sky, the roof of the gym, the top of my head—my hair was really sticking up—and then my zit-covered face, and then—

I screamed and threw the phone across the room.

Footsteps pounded down the hallway. "Wesley?"

I was shaking. I couldn't breathe. My door opened and my dad was standing there, skinny form bathed in hallway light, and in that moment I was glad he was so thin, because that meant he couldn't be the thing on my phone.

"Wes? You okay?"

I swallowed, nodded. "Sorry. I, I saw a spider."

Dad's eyes narrowed behind his wire-rim glasses. "A spider?"

"Yeah. I was going to turn off the light, and it crawled across the nightstand."

"What kind of spider? You think it was a black widow?"

I shook my head. "Regular spider. Just surprised me."

"Hmm." He stared at me a moment longer, then muttered, "Keep it down in here."

Once he was gone, all the nervousness left me, and I felt really stupid. I padded across the floor and grabbed my phone from underneath the desk. Not cracked, thank goodness, or I'd have never lived that down. The website was still up with the picture of me, and not Heather, not like I'd thought, but a horrible, bloated pale monster with stringy hair and a rancid flap of skin hanging over its face, leaning against my shoulder.

There was only one explanation. Hector put her up to this.

Probably paid her to eat lunch with me and then photoshopped his pet monster into the frame.

*What an asshole.*

I texted him, *You're a dick.* Then turned off my phone and slid under the covers, staring at the ceiling until my eyelids grew heavy and I drifted off.

NEXT DAY, I SAT AT MY USUAL PICNIC TABLE PICKING AT my food—chicken nugget day— half-hoping Heather would come and half-hoping she wouldn't. Okay, more than half. I should've known it was too good to be true. I pictured myself jumping up on the table, shoving her weird vegan lunch in her face, yelling at her for the part she'd played in Hector's idiotic little game.

Luckily, she never showed.

What I needed to do was learn how to stop being so trusting. Whenever someone miraculously floated into my life, I glommed onto them, thinking they were just a loner like me, when in reality, they were predators—vultures, even—feasting on what little shreds of self-respect I still had. Heather, Hector, even Stevie D, faking like he was my friend all through elementary only to abandon me the second we walked through the doors of Bernardo Yorba Middle School.

More than them too. Practically the only person I'd ever met who hadn't acted like this was Nathan. Small consolation, seeing how he was so freaking *Nathan* all the time.

I wouldn't say I finished my lunch, but rather, I reached the end of it, then went to throw it away. The second I flipped up the trash can lid, a pale, skin-covered face stared up at me from amidst all the refuse.

"Gah!"

I dropped my tray, stumbling away until I smashed my lower back on the picnic table. My heart was hammering about a billion beats per minute. I stared at the trash can, frozen, waiting for the lid to swing up and a fat, sore-covered form to crawl out, cross the courtyard, sluglike fingers pulling back its skin flap to show me all its teeth like, *Show and tell, Mr. Franz, show and tell.*

"Mr. Franz!"

I turned. Officer Presbitt was standing just outside the door, scowling.

"Uh—"

"Trash goes *in* the trash can. Like I said the other day."

I nodded, my mouth suddenly dry. "Right." I stumbled over to my inverted tray and picked up the picked-over chicken nuggets. I was just seeing things, had to be. Hector was in my head. Besides, there was a cop right there with an actual gun on his hip. Nothing was going to happen.

I swallowed and pulled the lid off the trash can. Inside, nestled amongst crushed soda cans and torn-open ketchup packets, was a white trash bag. The "face" I'd seen, apparently.

*Fucking Hector.*

I grabbed my backpack.

Officer Presbitt held the door for me. "Seen a lot of food fights in my day, but not too many solo ones." He was smiling.

"I'm in training."

"Well, if we ever get a team, I'm sure you'll make varsity. Take it easy, Franz."

Wish I could've taken his advice.

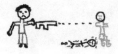

AFTER SCHOOL, HECTOR WAS WAITING FOR ME ON MY front porch.

I dumped my bike on the cracklegrass lawn, trying to summon up the best scowl my dad ever gave me. Probably I just looked like I smelled a fart.

"What're you doing here?"

Hector rose shakily, putting a hand on the railing. He looked like shit. Pale, or paler than usual, with deep bags under his eyes. Made him look old. Like, so old the clerk at the Save 'N Go might actually sell us beer. "We need to talk."

"Yeah? Talk about how you've been messing with me? How much did you pay Heather? I thought she was my friend. I thought *you* were." I'd been on a roll, saying a bunch of shit I couldn't imagine myself saying, until that last part came out like a whine and that was it for me asserting myself.

"Wes, I haven't been messing with you."

I rolled my eyes. "Bullshit. You made this whole Hurlyburly thing up. Well, guess what? I'm not two years old. You can't scare me."

"I need to show you something."

"What?"

Hector was wearing a baggy flannel shirt. He unbuttoned the

cuff, then rolled his sleeve up. His forearm was covered in bite marks.

"So?"

He let the sleeve fall back to his wrist. "So I woke up two nights ago and the Hurlyburly had my whole arm in its mouth. Biting me. I screamed and it disappeared. It's been following me, Wes. Everywhere."

I pushed past him to the front door. "You're really committed to the gag, aren't you? Even chewed up your own arm. I told you I'm not falling for it."

"Wes"—he grabbed my elbow—"this isn't me, I swear. Look, I'll prove it to you."

I shrugged him off but didn't go inside. "How?"

"Every time I take a picture, it's there. In the background. Watching me."

"Oh, like the picture you took of me? I saw what you did. Real slick, editing it on the sly like that. I'm not stupid, Hector."

"Take a picture of me right now. I guarantee you'll see it."

"I'm not—"

"If we were ever friends, just do this one thing, please? What's the harm? If there's nothing there, I'll fuck off forever and you'll never have to see me again."

I bit my lip, staring him down. Part of me wanted to slam the front door in his face. But he looked so earnest, so *real,* I felt like I owed it to him.

Like he said, "What's the harm?"

"Fine." I pulled out my phone. "Say cheese."

Hector didn't smile. I lined up the shot, him framed by the two houses across the street, and took a picture. Took a couple, just so he couldn't say, *Come on, one more, it'll be in this next one, I promise.*

"Happy?"

"Aren't you going to look?"

"Fine." I pulled up the pictures. First was just Hector, looking like a walking corpse. Ditto the second one. But the last one...

Across the street, the Stedmans' bushes. I zoomed in. "Jesus Christ."

A look of relief washed over Hector's face. All the tension sapped out of him at once; he lowered himself down to the steps, leaning against the railing, sobs wracking his body.

As for me? Completely frozen. I couldn't move, couldn't do anything. Not even think.

*It's real. It's fucking real.*

"Can we go inside?" Hector asked.

I shot a look across the street. Nothing there, now. "Is it going to follow us?"

Hector shrugged.

"I don't want it in my house."

"You think I want it in my head?"

And there, in that moment, he looked so small and pathetic, his eyes doe-wide, still watering and red-rimmed, and even though he was three months older than me, he seemed infinitely younger. He was my friend, wasn't he? Against all odds. I felt like shit for distrusting him, utter shit. Maybe I didn't have a bunch of friends because the other kids? They could tell just by looking at me that I didn't have what it takes to be one.

I took him by the elbow, pulled him up. We went inside. I left him on the couch, got us both Cokes, and threw some S'mores

Pop-Tarts in the toaster. Laid it all out on the coffee table but Hector wouldn't touch anything.

"What are we going to do?" I asked.

Hector shook his head slowly. "I wish I knew."

"Those internet forums, there's got to be a way to, to"—I searched my seventh grade vocabulary for the right words—"banish it."

"They don't say anything about that. Wes, I wish... I wish I'd never heard of it. And"—his eyes watered—"I *really* wish I'd never told you."

"Yeah. Well, *I* wish I'd believed you."

We sat quietly, Pop-Tarts cooling on the coffee table. "Look," I finally said, "I'm not going to let it get you. Or me." I went over to the counter and pulled a steak knife from the block. Tested its point with my finger. Sharp. Mostly because Dad didn't cook.

"You really think a knife's going to work?"

"We've got to try something."

The front door opened. My heart lurched, I gripped the knife tighter, but it was just Nathan. I palmed it, sliding it up my sleeve.

He threw his backpack on the couch and glanced at the coffee table. "Are those *my* Pop-Tarts?"

"Technically?"

Nathan shook his head and disappeared into his room.

I laid awake all night, hoping the Hurlyburly wouldn't get me. Hoping I wouldn't stab myself in the ear with the steak knife under my pillow. And wishing Hector and I had never gotten mixed up in whatever this was.

Every time I closed my eyes I could see it, lurking in the Stedmans' bushes. A fat, sluglike finger brushed its chin, the yellow nail slipping under the skin fold covering its face, peeling it up and away.

I guess I was asleep because I woke up in a cold sweat, my PJs so soaked I thought I'd started peeing myself again. Hadn't done *that* since Mom.

My phone told me it was almost six. No point in trying to go back to sleep. I texted Hector to see if he was okay. After a few minutes, he sent back a thumbs-up emoji.

I hoped that was really him. Not the Hurlyburly playing tricks again. Only good thing about school, I could see him in the flesh. Know it hadn't gotten him.

Except I had to wait until lunch, because we didn't have any of the same classes. The first couple of periods crawled by. I tried to pay attention, but Civil War battles and geometric equations ran together into an incomprehensible educational soup. When the bell rang, I couldn't grab my lunch tray—turkey sandwiches today—and get outside fast enough.

Hector wasn't at our usual spot.

But his bag was.

I set my tray down, looked around the courtyard. "Hector?"

Wind kicked a crumpled Doritos bag across the asphalt.

I turned in a slow circle, calling his name again. That's when I saw the gym door.

Open a few inches.

I unzipped my backpack and pulled out the steak knife, slipping it up the sleeve of my hoodie. If I got caught, I'd probably get expelled. But that was the least of my worries. If that thing got Hector?

I'd be all alone.

Hands shaking, I crossed the courtyard and toed open the door to the gym. The interior was dark, quiet.

"Hector!" I hissed.

"Wes!" a muffled yell came back.

Then something else I couldn't quite hear. But it sounded like "Help."

I screamed his name again and charged into the gym, tennis shoes slapping on the waxed floor. Where was he? The bleachers were all rolled up; he wasn't under those. Across the basketball court, two doors led to the boys' and girls' locker rooms.

A light was on in the boys' room.

I ran across the court faster than Mr. Fenwick had ever seen me hoof it in gym class. Hector's cries grew louder, and my heart hammered faster. I had no idea what I was doing. But I was doing *something,* which seemed like a pretty good change of pace from my usual nothing.

At the locker room door, I paused, put an ear to the wood. Hector wasn't yelling anymore, but I thought I heard a faint murmur. And something else.

Wet snuffling sounds that turned my stomach.

I drew my knife, took a deep breath, and whipped the door open.

Hector was lying on the tile by the bank of sinks, a grotesque, hulking shape straddling him. The stench of swamp rot and raw sewage filled the air. He screamed, and then I screamed, too, and the figure slowly turned its misshapen head, lank wet hair caressing its mottled back skin. The Hurlyburly stared at me with its blank face, then slowly lifted a finger, cruelly curving nail tucking under the flesh flap covering its features, and began to lift...

"No!" I cried, throwing myself across the locker room. I jabbed the knife into its shoulder, the blade sinking into its diseased flesh like soft cheese, then pulled back, stabbing it again and again and again. No blood spurted; it was like I was tearing holes in crepe paper. Thin, insubstantial.

Yielding.

*This* was what we'd been so afraid of?

I growled, kicked it in that horrible face flap. The Hurlyburly fell over, tried to crawl under the sink. But I wasn't letting it get away. I grabbed an ankle and yanked it back across the tile with a wet *schlumpf*. For something so big, I shouldn't have been able to pull it like that, but I was running on pure adrenaline. Nothing was going to stop me from ripping the thing to shreds.

I pounced on its back, driving it to the floor with my knees, peppering its flesh with stab wound after stab wound. The thing made a noise like it was crying, but I ignored it, just kept driving that knife home.

"Franz! Stop, put the knife down!"

I froze at the sound of the voice. Risked a glance over my shoulder. Officer Presbitt was standing in the doorway, service pistol aimed right at me.

*Shit.*

Or was he? Maybe this was some trick, some vision conjured by the Hurlyburly to save its own sick existence?

"I have to kill it!" I shouted back. "I can't—"

"Drop the knife, or I'll have to shoot. Come on, son, don't make me do that."

My hands shook, but I didn't drop the knife. I couldn't. The second I did, it would get us.

*Us?*

I glanced over at the floor next to me. Hector was gone. I couldn't understand it. He was just there a second ago. Nothing made sense.

Footsteps behind me, Officer Presbitt's pleading voice. "Son, just put the knife down, and we'll talk, okay? Whatever happened with you and Mr. DeLongo, we'll figure it out."

I heard every word he said, but it took me a second to process it. Mostly because nobody called him Mr. DeLongo.

He was always just Stevie D.

My stomach tightened, and something pulled my gaze down, down to the form between my legs slumped on the bathroom floor. No stringy hair, no greasy, weeping flesh. Just a kid, wearing jeans and a Kobe jersey. No longer Laker-yellow but Bulls-red.

"What the—"

The whole room swayed around me. I wasn't going to stab him again, I really wasn't, but I guess Officer Presbitt thought I was because the first shot hit me in the back, a half-inch from my spinal cord, the next in the shoulder, spinning me around. I hit my head on the bottom of the sink and sprawled on the floor.

Bleeding just like Stevie D.

Things got dark. My ears rang. I couldn't figure out why I was lying on the floor, and then I think I thought I was lying on the floor at home, or maybe Disneyland, down on the floor of one of those carriages that take you to Peter Pan, and just before I passed out a dark form loomed over me.

Not Presbitt.

With a fat sluglike finger, it peeled up the flesh flap covering its face, the skin tearing away, a sickening *skritch skritch skritch* filling my ringing ears, wet sticky mucus dripping straight in my mouth, and I finally saw what was underneath, and it was worse than anything I could've imagined.

FLESH WOUNDS.

For me, at least. Two weeks in the hospital, handcuffed to a bed with a mustached deputy sitting on a stool outside my door. Nathan came by a few times. Dad didn't, which was all right. I didn't want to see him.

Plus, with Mom a couple of years ago, the Franz family had surely had its fill of hospitals.

Eventually, they pronounced me fit enough to be transferred to jail, where I've been ever since. It's not so bad. Since I'm a minor charged as an adult, I get some perks. Privacy. Protection. And lots of visits from doctors.

The head kind, not the bullet hole kind.

In some ways, I'm lucky. Most kids in here, they're in for shooting somebody, but they did it for their gang so nobody really cares. Me, the media's all over the story: "The Hurlyburly Stabbing, a Creepypasta come to life." So I get shrinks, I get journalists. I get the chance to tell my side of the story.

If I can even figure out what the hell it is.

But I'll tell you this. I'm not stupid, and I'm not delusional. Jail's given me the chance to really look at the whole thing, every angle. And I'm pretty damn sure of one thing.

The Hurlyburly is real. It's not some bloated, faceless figure lurking at the edges of our photographs. It's inside of us, burrowed so deep it's not some separate entity, some externalized, puppeteering force. No, it's all tangled up in our DNA, just waiting for its moment. Trying to trick us into letting it pull that skin flap up and show us what it really is.

And if you can't guess what was under there for me, well, I'm not sure what to tell you.

# Joey Eats Anything
## Jeff Strand

"Ewww!" said Greg, one of the many bullies at Dogwater Elementary School. "Joey just dipped his French fry in his chocolate milk!"

Joey paused, mid-chew. What was wrong with making his fries taste better? He liked both French fries and chocolate milk equally, so why not combine the flavors?

"You'll eat anything, won't you?" asked Greg. "I bet you'll eat anything in the whole wide world!"

"I'm open to new experiences," Joey admitted.

"I bet you'd eat a booger!"

Joey nodded. "I sure would."

"Then let's see it."

Joey leaped up from his chair and lunged at Greg. He chomped down on Greg's nose to get at the boogers contained within...

JOEY'S PARENTS SAT ACROSS FROM THE PRINCIPAL. MR. Walterson couldn't stop fidgeting, so Ms. Walterson elbowed him in the ribs.

"Your son bit off a classmate's nose," said Principal Rebull.

Mr. Walterson cleared his throat. "From what we understand, the nose didn't come all the way off."

"The fact that a dangling flap remained does not excuse your son's misdeed. That poor boy is going to require reconstructive surgery."

"We should look at the bright side," said Ms. Walterson. "His new nose might be an improvement. I always wanted a nose job, but it would've been a frivolous act of vanity. He pretty much *has* to get one if he wants to keep breathing through it."

Principal Rebull groaned and rubbed his forehead. "The parents won't be pressing charges."

"Oh, good. That was neighborly of them."

"But Joey is being expelled."

Mr. Walterson leaned forward. "Are you serious? Expelled for what?"

"For the nose thing!"

"Oh, right."

"Nobody is saying that your son is a raging psychopath," said Principal Rebull. "But nobody is trying to make the opposite point either. If he was a dog, we'd recommend that he be put down, but since he's human, that option isn't available even if you were amenable."

"We're not amenable," said Ms. Walterson.

"Anyway, whether you choose to homeschool him or simply let him go feral is up to you. But he is no longer permitted within five hundred yards of this building."

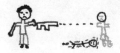

"SO," SAID MR. WALTERSON, SITTING ON THE EDGE OF Joey's bed. "Why did you try to bite Greg's nose off?"

"To get at his boogers."

"Excuse me?"

"He dared me to eat boogers."

"Oh. Okay. That's very much not the answer I was expecting. I assumed he was bullying you."

"He was."

"And you disfigured him for revenge?"

"No."

"Son, if you have rage issues, it's okay. I get a bit steamed myself on occasion. Did Greg ever make fun of you?"

"Yes."

"Ah! And so you wanted people to make fun of *him*. You tried to bite off his nose so that your classmates would point and laugh. Did you have a cruel nickname picked out? Nose-Free Greg?"

"No. I wanted to eat his boogers, and they were in his nose."

"That's very disturbing," said Mr. Walterson. "You're disturbing your own father. What exactly made those specific boogers so enticing that you felt the need to bite through carti-lage to get to them?"

"I told you. He dared me."

"If he dared you to gouge out your own eyeballs and eat them, would you do it?"

Joey shrugged.

"Son, dares are for running around naked in public. Kissing people you wouldn't otherwise kiss. Maybe—*maybe*—some light self-harm. Mutilation should be off-limits."

"Okay."

"The next time somebody dares you to do something, tell me about it first, and I'll let you know if it's a good dare or not. I have experience with these things. It's why I married your mother."

"Okay."

"Do you promise to only use your teeth for chewing food and smiling?"

"Yes."

Mr. Walterson sighed with relief. "Thank you, son."

HOMESCHOOLING IS CHALLENGING WHEN THE PARENTS are frightened of their own child. Though Mr. and Ms. Walterson began the process with the best of intentions, they gradually transitioned to a curriculum of choosing the most educational programs on television. The definition of "educational" expanded each day, until they finally decided that as long as he wasn't watching R-rated movies, they were doing their jobs as teachers.

Joey's social skills, never superb, began to deteriorate.

"I THINK WE SHOULD CONSIDER LOCKING HIM IN THE basement," said Mr. Walterson.

"What?" asked Ms. Walterson. "No! That's crazy talk!"

"I don't mean that we should chain him to the wall and toss down scraps of raw meat. I just mean that if we keep letting him roam around free, eventually somebody is going to have their neck torn open."

"He's only ten. Surely his victims could fend him off."

Mr. Walterson wiped a tear from his eye. "I don't like this any more than you do. But we have to accept that, through no fault of our own, our son poses a clear and present danger to our neighbors."

"No," said Ms. Walterson. "I refuse to accept that. Almost biting off somebody's nose does not mean he's going to graduate to ripping out throats."

"Darling..."

"How many dogs has he killed? Zero. How many cats has he killed? Zero."

"He ate a lizard raw. Bit it right in half. Stared into its eyes before he popped the top half into his mouth, probably to watch the life drain from them."

"So what? It's a lizard. When did we become emotionally

invested in the safety of lizards? Name one thing a lizard has done for you in the past ten years."

"It's not about caring whether a lizard lives or dies," said Mr. Walterson. "It's about our son murdering an innocent creature."

"How do we know it was so innocent? Maybe it gave him attitude."

Mr. Walterson sighed. "Darling, you need to get your head out of the sand. Joey has not thrived in this environment. When he's hungry, he just points to his open mouth. He communicates through snarls and grunts. He won't let us cut his fingernails. Sometimes his eyes roll up in the back of his head and he just stays that way for hours."

"I'll admit that the eye-roll thing is haunting," said Ms. Walterson. "And I'd be up for installing an invisible fence and making him wear a shock collar. But locking him in the basement is simply taking it too far. That's how local legends get started."

"Couldn't we just try it? For forty-eight hours? If the guilt becomes overpowering, we can let him out."

Ms. Walterson thought about it for a few minutes. "All right," she said.

JOEY PACED AROUND THE DARK BASEMENT, ALONE WITH his thoughts.

*Death. Blood. Pain. Death. Blood. Pain. Death. Bloody blood. Bleeding bloody blood.*

*Eat them all.*

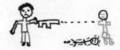

"Isn't this nice?" asked Ms. Walterson, as she and her husband enjoyed a candlelit dinner. "We don't have to worry that anybody is going to leap across the table at us and stab us with a fork. You were right all along."

"It *is* very pleasant," Mr. Walterson admitted. "I know the guidebooks tell you not to keep your children locked in the basement, but it's a very narrow-minded stance. If your child, through no fault of your own parenting, has become a monster, why not hide him away? Who does it harm besides the child?"

"Please don't call Joey a monster," said Ms. Walterson.

"I didn't mean a monster with horns or fur. I meant a human monster."

"I won't have you calling our son a monster! He's not sweet, or well-adjusted, or tame, but he's not a monster! Frankenstein is a monster!"

"No, Frankenstein's monster is a monster. And I'll be perfectly honest, I'd rather have Frankenstein's monster lurking in our basement than Joey!"

"How dare you?"

"He's *wrong*, darling! Our son is all wrong! I think he would cheerfully gnaw our faces off, given the chance, and show absolutely no remorse afterward! He's savage! He's an evil little fu—"

"Don't you dare use the F-word in relation to our son!"

"He's an evil little fudge. I've known this since he spilled out of your birth canal, with eyes that looked like they should be glowing red even though they weren't actually doing it. I've been uneasy around him for the entire decade that we've known him. Perhaps he's not a monster, but he's monstrous. I'll come right out and say it: I dislike him."

Ms. Walterson looked at the floor. "What do you think we should do about it?"

"Burn the house down and flee."

"But what will people think?"

"They'll think you left a lit cigarette unattended. Will they judge you for it? Yes, most likely. But they'll judge you less harshly than if your son goes on a killing spree, and trust me, there *will* be a killing spree if we don't burn down our home with him inside."

Ms. Walterson nodded. "Okay. I'll get our passports and my grandmother's pin cushion. You start the fire."

JOEY SNIFFED. HE SMELLED SOMETHING COOKING.

Actually, it smelled like the house itself was cooking.

*Fire. Death. Burning. Sizzling. Boiling blood. Boiling bloody blood blood.*

Joey raised his arms and waited for the flames to take him to Hell.

"Welcome back, young man," said the doctor. "Do you know what a coma is?"

Joey shook his head, which really hurt.

"It's when your mind can't cope with the horrors you've experienced and it just shuts down, leaving your body an empty shell without a soul. In your case, it's the third-degree burns that covered ninety-seven percent of your body that caused your mind to flee. But we put you through surgery after surgery after surgery, and we worked some miracles."

"I want to see my mom and dad."

"I'm sorry, young man, they aren't around. They're currently attending court-ordered classes on cigarette safety. But I'd like to show you your new face. Are you ready?"

"I guess."

"Now, you won't be impressed by the improvements unless you see where we began, so here's a photograph of how you looked when they pulled you out of the burning rubble."

The doctor held up a photograph. Joey screamed for six solid minutes.

"A reasonable reaction," said the doctor. "But take a look at yourself now."

He held up a mirror. Joey screamed for three solid minutes.

"See? You're only half as grotesque."

"I'm a freak!"

"Now, now, we don't use the word freak anymore. Although I suppose since you're using it to describe yourself, it's politically correct, in the same way that a Black person can say... Well, anyway, I don't think you appreciate the hard work we've done on your behalf." He held up the "before" picture again. "You could still look like that, so a little gratitude would be nice."

Joey wept.

JOEY SAT UP IN HIS HOSPITAL BED AS THE DOCTOR entered his room, looking exasperated. The doctor walked right up to his bed and held out his hand. "Spit it out."

"Spit what out?" asked Joey, his words muffled.

"You know what."

Joey spat the finger out into the doctor's palm.

"Let me explain something to you, young man. When you look the way you do, people automatically assume you're capable of heinous acts. You have to work extra hard to convince them your mind is not a cesspool of violence and depravity. So when you bite off your roommate's finger, you're playing right into their expectations."

"It was just his pinky."

"It doesn't matter. You can't do things like that. You've got an uphill road in getting adopted, and you're making it far worse if you're the kind of child who bites off fingers."

"Adopted?" asked Joey.

The doctor nodded. "Yes. Your parents had your relationship annulled, and you're a ward of the state now. I certainly won't be adopting you—I have three burned children of my own—so you need to stop being a scary psychopath. You've gone through four roommates already, and if you put your teeth on a fifth, we'll have no choice but to discharge you from the hospital."

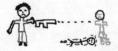

"AAAHHHH!!!" SHRIEKED JOEY'S NEW ROOMMATE. "HE bit off my ear!"

"No, I didn't," said Joey, spitting out the ear.

"That's it. I warned you, but you just had to keep testing the boundaries, didn't you?" scolded the doctor.

"I'm sorry."

"It's too late for apologies. Take your bottle of ointment and get out."

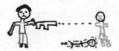

JOEY ATTACKED A NURSE ON THE WAY OUT, WHICH DIDN'T help his situation.

"What do I do?" he asked the doctor as they exited the hospital.

"I'll be honest, you don't have many options. You could walk into the ocean, but it's several states away, and you'll never hitch-hike that far without trying to bite a chunk out of the drivers who are kind enough to give you a ride. That leaves you with living in the sewer."

"But I don't want to live in the sewer!" said Joey. "That's where the turds go!"

"You should have thought about that before deciding to act like a turd yourself," said the doctor. He frowned. "I apologize for that. You've inflicted a lot of ghastly violence on people who entered the hospital in hopes of *improving* their health, but that's no reason to hit you with a zinger."

"Don't I have any other choices?"

"I'm sorry, but it's the ocean or the sewer for you. If I extend my hand politely, will you shake it or try to bite off one of my fingers?"

"Shake it."

"You licked your lips when you said that," said the doctor. "There'll be no goodbye handshake for you. Best of luck in the future, young man."

"It's not so bad being a sewer dweller," said their mayor. "People think of us as walking around all day smeared in feces, but that's not the case. A couple of the old-timers have even gotten used to the smell. Is the food great? No, not really. It's actually quite awful. Everything is awful down here. We live in a sewer. We're subhuman. We're creatures of the reeking darkness. But at least it's better than walking into the ocean."

"Thank you for taking me in," said Joey.

"No problem. It's too dark down here to really get a good look at your horrific visage. Now, to get back to the matter of food; do you see any restaurants down here?"

Joey looked around. "No."

"Correct. Even the most highly developed cities in the world don't have restaurants in their sewers. That means we have to scavenge for our own food. Sometimes we get lucky and somebody flushes a baby alligator down the toilet, but usually we have to drag a screaming tourist down to their death. Are you okay with that?"

"Yes, sir. Very much so."

"They often shriek and beg for mercy, sobbing about how they have families that depend on them. They've made sounds of misery that echo in my mind to this very day. Are you prepared to cope with that?"

"I sure am!"

"It's no small matter, taking a bite out of a human being while they're still alive. Have you ever accidentally pinched yourself, Joey?"

Joey nodded.

"And did it hurt?"

"Yes."

"Imagine that times a trillion! Just think about it! Teeth sinking into flesh! All those nerve endings! It's one of the most nightmarish things I can imagine, save for some events instigated by a Mr. Adolf Hitler. It will haunt you, Joey. Every time you close your eyes, you'll hear those shrieks."

"Why would I hear them when I close my eyes?" asked Joey. "Don't you mean when I close my ears?"

The sewer mayor smacked Joey upside the head. "We don't allow sassing down here. We have to do unspeakable things down here to survive, and I need to know that you aren't going to be a whiny little bitch about it."

"I'm not."

"The most important thing is that we do not try to devour our own kind. We will eat tourists galore, but you do not attack your fellow sewer dwellers. Ever. Under any circumstances. No matter how hungry you get. Do you understand?"

"Yes," said Joey.

"My appendix!" wailed one of Joey's fellow sewer dwellers. "He tore out my appendix!"

"Why would you do that?" asked the mayor. "We've got a nice succulent dying tourist right here. You just finished eating six ounces of his leg. The only reason you tore out Bartholomew's appendix was to cause him pain!"

"That's not true," said Joey, swallowing.

"It's very much true! You're evil! Even Jack the Ripper didn't munch on anybody's appendix! Get out! You're banned from the sewer! Permanently!"

Bartholomew gasped. "Permanently? Isn't that a bit extreme?"

"You're right," the mayor admitted. "Joey, you're officially banned from the sewer for the next ten years!"

"Fine!" shouted Joey as he grabbed a handful of Bartholomew's intestines. "But I'm taking these with me!"

"You most certainly are not! Put his guts down *now*!"

Joey licked the lower intestine. "It's mine. I called it."

"Begone, deviant! Begone!"

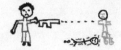

As he wandered the city streets, Joey wondered if he was, in fact, evil.

He didn't even like the taste of boogers or human flesh. He just liked causing pain.

Was it evil to make others suffer for his own enjoyment?

Maybe he could use his sadism to help humanity. Only bite body parts off of bad people.

He could be a superhero!

Joey heard screaming in the distance. He hurried over to the source and saw a woman in an alley being held at knifepoint by two muggers. This was his chance to turn his life around!

The muggers had departed with the woman's purse, and Joey crouched in the alley, gnawing on her face.

Okay, maybe he wasn't going to be a superhero.

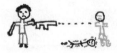

The man in the top hat and tuxedo got out of his limousine and smiled at Joey. "Well, hello there, little boy. I've never seen anybody quite so charred as you. Does it sting?"

"Constantly," said Joey.

"I have a Jacuzzi filled with ice water at home," said the man. "Does that sound like something you'd enjoy?"

"Are you a child molester?"

"Oh, no, no, goodness no, not in ages. But my wife and I are unable to conceive a child, thanks to my low sperm count and her frigidity, and we've thought about adopting but never quite got around to it. How old are you, if I may ask? The scarring makes it difficult to tell."

Joey decided to fib. "I'm nine."

"Open your mouth."

Joey did, and the man peered inside. "Nope, I can tell by your teeth that you're ten, going on eleven. You can close your mouth now. I was just about to have the adoption papers drawn up, but you had to go and start our father/son relationship off on a lie. Disappointing. My home has eighteen bathrooms and a bowling alley. Like I said, you can close your mouth now. I have butlers that I can humiliate and maids who will let me brush up against them for no reason at all. Why haven't you closed your mouth?"

Joey sunk his teeth into the rich man's chin.

THE OTHER PEOPLE IN THE HOLDING CELL GAPED IN horror as Joey chewed off Mad Dog Larry's tattoo.

Joey wiped the blood off his mouth. "If he didn't want me to eat his tattoo, he shouldn't have had 'Eat Me' tattooed on his back!"

"I didn't!" said Mad Dog Larry with a whimper. "It said 'Love is Strength.'"

"Sorry. I'm not a big reader."

One of the men pounded on the cell bars. "Let us out! We're trapped in here with a sociopath!"

"He's not a sociopath," said another man. "He clearly has emotions. Look at him! He's practically dancing around with glee over what he's done!"

"All right, all right, enough with the commotion," said the guard, walking into the holding cell area. "Joey Walterson, you've made bail."

"Who would bail out that maniac?" asked Mad Dog Larry. "My tattoo is in his tummy!"

GREG LOOKED WEIRD WITHOUT A NOSE.

"We kept trying," his mother told Joey. "But after thirteen surgeries we had to accept that it was never going to look quite right, so we asked the surgeon to just snip it off."

"It doesn't look so bad," said Joey.

"It makes his voice sound odd and unsettling, but we still love him."

"We've always felt bad about what happened," said Greg's father. "We can't help but feel that Greg's bullying, which led to you biting off most of his nose, is what set you off on the path that turned you into the abomination you are today. And we'd like to help you. Isn't that right, Greg?"

Greg shrugged.

"I said, isn't that *right*, Greg?"

"Yeah, I guess."

"You'll have to excuse him," Greg's mother said to Joey. "He's still a smidge bitter."

"Because he bit off my nose!"

"Could you please stop talking?" Joey asked. "Your strange voice is making me uncomfortable."

Greg stormed out of the room.

"Sorry about that," Joey said to Greg's parents.

"It's all right," said Greg's mother. "It's nothing he hasn't already heard from us."

"So why am I here?"

"We'd like to try to rehabilitate you," said Greg's father. "Some children are born evil. We had one of our own, but that's what bathtubs are for."

"You drowned your baby?" asked Joey.

"No. We just didn't help him swim. My point is that I don't think you were born evil, which means that with a lot of hard work we can make you stop being evil, or at least make you less evil. Perhaps you could trip people instead of taking bites out of them. Wouldn't that be nice?"

"Would my parents take me back?"

"I'm pretty sure that ship has sailed," said Greg's mother. "Do you know what a suicide pact is?"

Joey shook his head.

"When a mommy and a daddy love each other very much, but they no longer love themselves, sometimes they decide that the world is better off without them. But the mommy doesn't want the daddy getting over it and going off to live a fruitful life with a new mommy, so they agree to use teamwork. Do you know what carbon monoxide is?"

"We're getting sidetracked," said Greg's father. "Let's just say that the only way you're reuniting with your parents is in Hell or through a necromancer."

"Oh," said Joey.

"Anyway, I'm sure we can cure or tone down your evil," said Greg's mother, picking up a long metal stick. "What we're going to do is, every time you make a move to take a bite out of somebody, we're going to zap you with this cattle prod. Pretty soon you won't want to take a bite out of anybody. Isn't aversion therapy wonderful?"

THIS WAS GREAT.

Joey'd never had uninterrupted time with his prey before. Somebody always pulled him away from them. But the corpses of Greg's parents weren't going anywhere, offering him the opportunity to do whatever he wanted to them. It was glorious.

Greg had come back into the room a few hours ago, but he hadn't yet moved out of the fetal position, and his occasional whimpers actually made this more satisfying.

Joey's entire body was slick with blood. He briefly went upstairs to look in a full-length mirror and could barely tell that he was a burn victim. He wondered if it was practical to spend the rest of his life drenched in blood. Probably not.

The fun didn't stop until he broke one of his front teeth on a rib.

"Ow!" he shouted. "Gosh darn it!"

Greg sat up. "What happened?"

"Broke a tooth!"

"What's the matter, Joey? Scared of breaking a teeny tiny little tooth?"

"It hurt!"

"I dare you to keep biting my mom and dad's bones until *all* of your teeth are broken!"

"All right! I will!"

THAT HAD BEEN A MISTAKE. NO MATTER HOW MUCH blood Joey spat out, more kept pooling in his mouth.

His mouth hurt so much that he couldn't even eat Greg's lungs, though he could see them.

AS HE WALKED DOWN THE STREET, QUITE A FEW PEOPLE pointed and screamed.

Was he evil?

Greg had been kind of a dick, and Joey didn't appreciate the cattle prod, but the people at the hospital, and in the sewer, and in the jail cell had all been kind to him.

After running the numbers in his head, Joey decided that yes, he was indeed an evil little fudge.

This realization bummed him out.

A woman hurried over to him. "Little boy, do you...do you need help?"

"Yes," said Joey. "I need directions."

"Directions?"

"Which way to the ocean?"

# About the Authors

**Rebecca Rowland** is the American dark fiction author of two fiction collections, one novel, a handful of novellas, and too many short stories. She is the curator of seven horror anthologies, including the bestsellers *Unburied: A Collection of Queer Dark Fiction* and *American Cannibal*, and is the 2023 winner of the Godless 666 Award for Best Novelette. Her speculative fiction, critical essays, and book reviews regularly appear in a variety of online and print venues. The former acquisitions and anthology editor at AM Ink Publishing, Rebecca manages the small, independent publishing house Maenad Press. In her spare time, she pets her cat, eats cheese, and drinks vodka, though not necessarily in that order.

Find her at RowlandBooks.com or on Instagram @Rebecca_Rowland_books.

**John Durgin** is a proud, active Horror Writers Association member and lifelong horror fan who decided to chase his childhood dream of becoming a horror author. Growing up in New Hampshire, he discovered Stephen King much younger than most probably should have—reading *IT* before he reached high school—and knew from that moment on he wanted to write horror. In 2021, he started submitting short stories in hopes of getting noticed in the horror community and launching a career. He had his first story accepted in the summer of 2021 in the *Books of Horror Community Anthology Vol. 3 part 2*, and an alternate version of the story in *Beach Bodies: A Beach Vacation Horror Anthology* from DarkLit Press. His debut novel, *The Cursed Among Us* released on June 3, 2022, to stellar reviews. Next up, his sophomore novel, *Inside The Devil's Nest*, was released in January of 2023, followed by his debut collection, *Sleeping In The Fire*, in June of 2023. In 2024, he is set to have two novels and a novella released through DarkLit Press and Crystal Lake Publishing.

Find out more about John at www.johndurginauthor.com.

**Jeremy Megargee** has always loved dark fiction. He cut his teeth on R.L. Stine's Goosebumps series as a child, and a fascination with Stephen King, Jack London, Algernon Blackwood, and many others followed later in life. Jeremy weaves his tales of personal horror from Martinsburg, West Virginia, with his cat, Lazarus, acting as his muse/familiar. He is a member of the West Virginia chapter of the Horror Writers Association, and you can often find him peddling his dark words in various mountain hollers deep within the Appalachians.

He can be found on Facebook, Instagram, and Twitter.

**Megan Stockton** is an indie author who lives in rural Tennessee with her husband and two children. She has had a love for all things horror and macabre since she was a child and has been writing for fun most of her life.

She enjoys delivering her readers horror and horror-adjacent works that are character-driven and immersive. Find out more about Megan at www.meganstocktonbooks.com.

**Bridgett Nelson** is a registered nurse turned horror author. Her first collection, *A Bouquet of Viscera*, is a two-time Splatterpunk Award winner, recognized both for the collection itself and its standout story, "Jinx." Her two latest collections, *What the Fuck Was That?* and *Sweet, Sour, & Spicy* are available now!

Her work has appeared in multiple anthologies, including *Deathrealm: Spirits, October Screams: A Halloween Anthology, Y'all Ain't Right, American Cannibal, A Woman Unbecoming, The Never Dead*, and *Razor Blade in the Fun-Size Candy: A Horror Comedy Anthology*.

Bridgett is working on her first original novel and has been contracted by Encyclopocalypse Publications to write a novelization of the cult classic film *Deadgirl*.

She is an active member of the Horror Writers Association and the co-chair of HWA: West Virginia.

To learn more, visit her website at www.bridgettnelson.com.

**Candace Nola** is a multiple award-winning author, editor, and publisher. She writes poetry, horror, dark fantasy, and extreme horror content. Books include *Breach, Beyond the Breach, Hank Flynn, Bishop, Earth vs The Lava Spiders, The Unicorn Killer, Unmasked, The Vet*, and *Desperate Wishes*.

Her short stories can be found in *Baker's Dozen, Second-Hand Creeps, American Cannibal, Just A Girl: A Badass Women of Horror Anthology, The Horror Collection: The Lost Edition*, and

*Exactly the Wrong Things*, with many more coming throughout 2024.

She is the creator of Uncomfortably Dark, which focuses primarily on promoting indie horror authors and small presses with weekly book reviews, interviews, and special features. Uncomfortably Dark Horror stands behind its mission to "bring you the best in horror, one uncomfortably dark page at a time."

Find her on Twitter, Instagram, TikTok, Facebook, and the website UncomfortablyDark.com. Sign up for her Patreon for exclusive content, free stories, and more.

**LP Hernandez** is an author of horror and speculative fiction. His stories have been featured in anthologies from *Dark Matter Magazine*, Cemetery Gates Media, and Cemetery Dance Publications, among others. He is a regular contributor to The NoSleep Podcast and has released two short story collections. His novella, *Stargazers*, was published under the My Dark Library banner with Cemetery Gates Media. When not writing, LP serves as a medical administrator in the US Air Force. He is a husband, father, and dedicated metalhead.

Find out more about LP at www.lphernandez.com.

**Lisa Vasquez** - Leading Stitched Smile Publications, Lisa's visionary approach transformed the publishing house into a sanctuary for emerging horror writers.

As the former editor in chief of *House of Stitched* magazine, Lisa Vasquez (also known as The Unsaintly Queen) spotlighted the unsung heroes of the horror industry, showcasing behind-the-scenes contributors. Retired from *House of Stitched*, her editorial legacy reflects a deep commitment to revealing the intricacies of dark fiction.

In her mentoring role, Lisa guided aspiring writers through the labyrinthine paths of horror, sharing wisdom and nurturing talents. Beyond literature, Lisa's artistic talents shine in multi-media artistry, utilizing acrylic, charcoal, watercolor, and her current fascination with black light paint.

The Unsaintly Queen can be found within the shadows of her lair by visiting www.unsaintly.com.

**Kristopher Rufty** lives in North Carolina with his three children and pets. He's written over twenty novels, including *All Will Die*, *The Devoured and the Dead*, *Desolation*, *The Lurkers*, and *Pillow-face*. When he's not spending time with his family or writing, he's obsessing over gardening and growing food.

His short story "Darla's Problem" was included in the Splat-terpunk Publications anthology, *Splatterpunk Fighting Back*, which won the Splatterpunk Award for Best Anthology. *The Devoured and the Dead* was nominated as Best Novel for the 2022 Splatterpunk Awards. He can be found on Facebook, Insta-gram, and Twitter.

Find out more about Kristopher at www.kristopherrufty.com.

**Rayne Havok** lives in the Arizona desert. Free to leave her house whenever she wants, she chooses not to risk death by sweltering sun demons. Instead, she stays safely indoors with a computer and all the words she knows, slapping them together in any which way she chooses in the moment.

**Brian Asman** is a writer, actor, and director from San Diego, California. He's the author of *Good Dogs and Man* and *Fuck this House (And Other Disasters)*, both forthcoming from Blackstone Publishing. His other books include *I'm Not Even Supposed to Be Here Today* from Eraserhead Press, *Our Black Hearts Beat as One*, *Neo Arcana*, *Nunchuck City*, *Jailbroke*, and *Return of the Living Elves*. He's recently published short stories in *American Cannibal*, *Pulp Modern*, *Kelp Journal*, and comics in *Tales of Horrorgasm*.

A film he co-wrote and produced, *A Haunting in Ravenwood*, is available now on DVD and VOD. His short *Reel Trouble* won Best Short Film at Gen Con 2022 and Best Horror Short at The Indie Gathering International Film Festival.

Brian holds an MFA from University of California, Riverside-Palm Desert. He's represented by Dunham Literary, Inc.

Check out his website www.brianasmanbooks.com or find him on social media @thebrianasman.

**Jeff Strand** is the Bram Stoker Award–winning author of over fifty books, including *Pressure*, *Autumn Bleeds Into Winter*, and *Clowns Vs. Spiders*. Several of his books are in development as movies—a slow, maddening process.

You can visit his Gleefully Macabre website at www.jeffstrand.com.

# More from Sinister Smile Press

## ANTHOLOGIES

If I Die Before I Wake:
The Better Off Dead Series
Volumes 1-9

A Pile of Bodies, A Pile of Heads
Let the Bodies Hit the Floor Series
Volumes 1 & 2

Screaming in the Night:
Sinister Supernatural Stories
Volume 1

Institutionalized:
Tales of Demented and Deranged

Just a Girl

Evil Little Fucks

## COLLECTIONS

Lethal Lords and Ladies of the Night
Volumes 1 & 2
Scott Harper

Strange Frequencies
Richard Clive

Dark Days
Steven Pajak

Everything Went to Shit
R.E. Sargent

Shadows of the Damned
James Watts

## NOVELS

Devil's Gulch:
A Collaborative Horror Experience

By Mike Duke
The Book of Smarba

By Steven Pajak
Project Hindsight
Wolves Among Sheep
Nowere to Run

By R.E. Sargent
The Karen Carter Trilogy
Fury: The Awakening
Fury: Unleashed
Relative Terror

By James Watts
Them
Beasts of Sorrow

By EV Knight
Partum

Visit our website for
full list of publications
www.sinistersmilepress.com

Made in the USA
Monee, IL
28 November 2024

c93e271f-7971-4af4-a9c3-4e394c267548R01